Bright Montana Sky

DEBRA HOLLAND

Chapter One

Chicago
June 1894

Constance Taylor stood at the half-opened front window of her aunt's home, watching the house across the street. Partly hidden by the curtains, she waited for the carriage carrying her beloved home from his studies at the university. Outside, she heard the sounds of life—a dog barking, a child shrieking with laughter, and a crow cawing harshly.

For the last half hour, she'd been on the alert—too early really, for Marcus to travel from the train station in downtown Chicago. But she could no longer contain her impatience.

She hadn't seen Marcus since the Christmas holidays, when he'd kissed her under the mistletoe ball. He'd called her sweet Constance and hinted of marriage after completing his engineering studies at the university. With a blush and a brilliant smile, she let him know his suit would be most welcome.

Once Marcus had returned to school, he sent her a note mentioning how glad he'd been to see her and that he looked forward to spending more time together in the summer. After that correspondence, she hadn't heard from him. But Marcus was so busy with his studies, he also rarely sent letters to his family.

The months dragged by. Her Aunt Hannah sickened, growing weaker as the weather grew warmer, until she quietly died a month ago, leaving Constance alone.

A wave of grief made her tighten her grip on a fold of the crimped silk skirt of her crepe mourning gown, the dress her aunt insisted Constance make in the month before she passed away. As she sat next to her dying aunt's bedside, a lump of sorrow clogging her throat so she could barely speak, Constance had hand-sewn the tiny tucks in the bodice.

"You must present an elegant appearance at the funeral, my dear." Then Aunt Hannah had repeated one of her favorite maxims. "The sophisticated style of your clothing is the best advertisement for our dressmaking business."

Her aunt's advice always proved right, even if black wasn't a good color on Constance, tending to overwhelm her fairness. But Marcus knew how she looked and loved her anyway. Aunt Hannah had made Constance promise to wear black only until right before Marcus arrived home, then to move to half-mourning. Purples and grays better suited her complexion, but she wasn't quite ready to make the change.

The pain of her aunt's death remained too sharp. Aunt Hannah had been a mother to her and deserved more than the token three weeks of black that showed respect for the passing of an aunt. Still, she hoped Marcus wouldn't insist on her waiting out a suitable mourning period before they wed. She was more than ready to transition away from pain and into her new life as Mrs. Marcus Miller.

Around her, the big, old house seemed to echo with emptiness. Constance leaned closer to the glass and angled her head to see down the street, hoping to glimpse the Millers' carriage. But to no avail. She took a breath, inhaling the scent of the red roses on the bushes growing underneath the window, and urged patience.

Dusk deepened, and one-by-one, the downstairs windows of the Queen Anne house opposite illuminated with electric lights, casting a welcoming amber glow into the yard. A face appeared at the drawing room window, and Constance wondered if the woman was Marcus's sister, Victoria, or his mother, for they looked much alike.

After the New Year's party, Constance confided in Victoria about the kiss and the almost-proposal from her older brother. Her best friend was nearly as excited as Constance about the fact they'd soon be sisters. The two formulated wedding plans and dreamed of how their lives would be intertwining.

Nothing much would change, for Marcus would move across the street into Constance's house, and the two friends could see each other as much as ever—or at least until Victoria married. But that wouldn't be for a while. Currently, no suitors were in sight. Men shied away from her friend's high spirits and dramatic mannerisms. Not that Victoria minded. She was holding out for an Italian count and, for the last year, had badgered her parents to allow an extended visit to her maternal second cousins in Italy.

Today, the Millers had invited Constance to await Marcus's arrival with them. Mr. and Mrs. Miller had high hopes for matrimony between their son and Constance and often gave her broad hints about being part of their family.

Constance chose to remain by herself. Marcus couldn't greet her with a kiss if he was in front of his family, and she couldn't wait to feel his strong arms around her. She had no doubt he'd hurry over as soon as he'd spent some time with his family— probably after supper. But she couldn't help wishing he'd visit her first.

Finally, Constance heard the clip-clop of horses' hooves and the rattling of wheels over bricks before she spotted the carriage. Again, she leaned forward to make sure it was the Miller vehicle, not some other that had business on this quiet street on the outskirts of the city.

At the sight of the familiar carriage, she couldn't help but clap her hands, and then she lifted her pressed hands to cover her trembling mouth, straining for her first glimpse of him. The carriage door opened on the other side of the street, so she wouldn't see Marcus until he moved up the walkway. Her body shook in anticipation.

Constance couldn't stand the suspense any longer. She wanted to throw herself into his arms. Casting away her resolve to remain at home, she picked up the black straw hat on a nearby table and used a hatpin to anchor it to her hair. She tugged on black gloves and buttoned them, then grabbed up her skirts and rushed to the door.

Pulse racing, Constance flung it open. She ran across the porch and down the steps like a hoyden.

She was halfway down the brick walkway when she realized that presenting such exuberance to her future husband might make her appear gawkish instead of a grown-up twenty. She wouldn't want him to think she was too young to wed.

Dropping her skirt, Constance slowed to a gliding swan stroll across the street. She'd drawn abreast of the back of the carriage when Marcus's voice stopped her.

"Here is my home, my dear Mrs. Miller. What do you think?"

Mrs. Miller? Constance froze, confused about what she just heard. She inched forward and peered around the carriage.

Marcus had his back to her.

A tall woman stood next to him, her hand crooked through his arm.

"Are you sure, Marcus?" The woman tilted her head to look up at him. "Your parents won't be upset that we married without telling them?"

Married? She leaned a hand on the back of the carriage for support. *Impossible!*

"Never." He waved toward the house and turned to look at the woman. "I've promised you a million times, dearest. They'll adore you almost as much as I do."

Constance gazed at his familiar profile, so dear to her. She pressed a hand against her chest, feeling the knock of her heart so strongly she thought the sound would give away her presence.

But with some sort of morbid fascination, she couldn't make herself pull back.

Time seemed to stretch. She couldn't absorb what she'd heard, only taking in the details of the woman's exquisitely cut, gray traveling coat, far more elegant than the shapeless over-garment usually worn by female train travelers to protect their clothing from the dust and soot.

Leaning, Marcus dropped a tender kiss on the woman's lips. "Welcome home, my darling Mrs. Miller."

No, Marcus! Constance stepped back, almost tripping on her hem. Her stomach coiled in horror and heartbreak. Her eyes stung. She lifted the skirt off the street and crept away, treading lightly so as not to make any noise. She made another short shuffle, before her composure broke and she turned and hurried back to her house.

"Don't run. Don't run," she chided aloud, forcing herself to keep to a reasonable, although fast, pace. "The Millers must be watching and might notice."

Feeling like a marionette with her limbs jerked by strings, Constance somehow reached the house, passing through the double doors with their transom stained-glass windows and into the parlor.

She sank onto the edge of the settee, back straight, knees and feet together, hands clasped tightly in her lap, as if the stiff ladylike position could keep her from crumpling to the floor to lie among the wreckage of her dreams. The knot in her stomach grew and squeezed into her lungs, already constricted by her tight corset, making it hard to breathe.

For a long time, she stared unseeing at the flowered wallpaper, her emotions numb. Over and over, she thought, *I was supposed to be Mrs. Marcus Miller!*

Nausea pressed into her stomach. Her skin felt flushed and clammy, although her body grew chilled. The first hint the numbness might melt into torrential pain made her mind change tracks.

I can't stay here and live across the street from them!

Horrified, she realized the new Mr. and Mrs. Miller would expect a social call from her, by tomorrow at the latest. *I can't do it! I just can't.*

Although her body had turned into ice, her mind scrabbled for escape from her circumstances. *Where can I go?* She couldn't put a coherent thought together. An idea shimmered into her chaotic thoughts. *My father in Sweetwater Springs!* Although Constance had little desire to live in a small Montana town, she grasped the thought of sanctuary with both hands.

A knock sounded on the front door. Before she could escape to another room, it opened and Victoria poked her head in. Upon seeing Constance, she thrust herself inside, slamming the door behind her. "I'm so mad at him! I don't care what that woman thinks of me for disappearing right after her arrival. Horrid cat! Stealing my brother away from you."

Victoria was a pretty, plump version of Marcus, with the same auburn hair and pale blue eyes, startling against her olive skin. The sight of Victoria, even though she dearly loved her friend, was a reminder of everything Constance had lost. *Now, we'll never be sisters.* She couldn't even move her mouth to say a word.

Victoria paused, surveying Constance, and her expression crumpled. "No, no, don't look like that, dearest. I can't bear to see your eyes so empty." She rushed across the room, knelt down on the floor, and put her soft arms around Constance's waist.

Constance held herself stiffly, not daring to lean into Victoria's lavender-scented warmth, for if she did, her composure would slip, and she'd weep for days.

"Come back to me, dearest friend, from where you've gone away," Victoria begged, squeezing tight. "Oh, I could just beat my brother over the head with my parasol."

And I'll join her. That image of her laying into Marcus freed some of the constriction in Constance's throat. Among the ashes of her dreams, faint embers of anger smoldered, melting her frozen paralysis.

She fisted her hands, realized she still wore her gloves, and relaxed her fingers. In a deliberate manner, she unfastened the four buttons on each glove and yanked them off. "What's done is done, Vicky."

Constance tossed the gloves at an empty wing chair, and then reached up and yanked the hatpins from her hat, stabbing them into the cushioned arm of the settee. The hat followed the gloves to the seat of the wingchair. "But even if we beat him bloody, the fact that your brother has married will not change." She turned her head so as not to see her friend's troubled expression.

"What will you do? You can't stay here where you'll see them every day. I'll move in with you," Victoria babbled, rocking back and flinging an arm in the direction of the staircase. "No, that won't do. Those two will still be across the street. We'll run away together."

Constance couldn't see Victoria living in Sweetwater Springs.

Her friend gave a little bounce on her knees. "I know! How about we visit Europe? Maybe even meet and marry Italian noblemen. Surely now, I can coax my parents into letting me go."

I don't want an Italian nobleman. I just want Marcus. The saying that a heart could break must be true because hers had shattered. She could almost hear the tinkling of the glass shards as they sprinkled on the floor. She imagined them as blood-red splinters, splaying across the Oriental rug and obscuring the pattern.

"Ever so handsome, those Italian fellows."

Hearing Victoria's impetuous suggestions crystallized Constance's resolve. She eased out of Victoria's embrace. But not wanting to hurt her, she pulled her friend up from her knees and onto the settee.

"I'll go to my father in Montana."

"Your father!" Victoria gaped, wide-eyed. "The *same* father who abandoned you when you were small? Sent you away after your mother died. You'd go to *him*?"

"He didn't abandon me," Constance lied and arranged a fold of her full skirt.

Victoria narrowed her eyes. "I was there, remember? You just had your sixth birthday a few days after your arrival. You cried every day for months. You'd lost both your mother *and* your father."

Constance gave her a faint smile. Even that much movement hurt her face. "But I found Aunt Hannah and you and your family." *Marcus, too.* The boy had been her friend for many years before he kissed her and changed everything.

"You *should* be crying now. I'd be weeping all over the house. Your stillness worries me."

"What good would tears do?" *Crying hadn't brought back my mother or my father.*

Victoria frowned. "I know. You're Sense—" She tapped her chest "—and I'm Sensibility," she said. "But a bout of tears is very...." Her friend paused, her forehead scrunching, obviously searching for words. "*Refreshing.* In a *bad* way, I mean. You feel better after the flow of tears is over." Her voice softened. "*I'd* feel better if you cried. At least I could cry, too, and try to comfort you. I'd not feel so helpless."

Constance wanted nothing more than to weep copious tears. But even as she tried to reach for some, nothing would come. Instead, she had dry, burning eyes and a lump like an unrisen loaf of bread in her stomach.

Her efforts must have shown on her face, for tears welled up in Victoria's eyes and rolled down her cheeks. "You can't leave Chicago, Constance. What would I do without you?"

"How can I stay?" The bleakness of the question settled between them. She saw the painful truth on Victoria's face.

"I hate him for doing this to you. Mama and Papa are beside themselves, although they greeted Gladene politely enough. Marcus didn't even notice, but I'm sure *she* felt their coolness."

Constance swallowed down the bitterness that wanted to spill out into angry, nasty words and keep Victoria on her side against the woman. But as hurt and embarrassed as she was, Constance wouldn't want to cause a rift in the family she loved. "If

Gladene—" how she disliked even saying the name "—is to be your sister-in-law, then you must be cordial." She prayed Victoria wouldn't see what the words cost her.

"Never!" Victoria shook her head so violently a curl of hair escaped a pin and tumbled down her cheek. "After she has caused you such pain?"

"The new Mrs. Marcus Miller probably doesn't know of my existence. And—" Constance gripped Victoria's wrist. "I don't want to see them. I don't want to pay a courtesy call and pretend everything is well. In private, please explain my decision to your parents. They'll understand."

"I will." She bobbed her head. "And to Marcus. I'll kick him first, though."

"No!" Her chest heated. "Don't say a word to him."

"Marcus must know he's done wrong by leading you—all of us—to believe his intentions were serious." Victoria leaned forward, setting the stray curl swaying. "Therefore, the cretin will avoid you. Though it's possible he might come over alone to explain and apologize."

Constance started to speak.

Victoria held up an imperious hand. "I doubt the latter. My brother was never one to admit wrongdoing. I'm just mentioning the scenario as a possibility."

"Do you think…looking back at that New Year's party…he imbibed too much and later had no idea what he'd said and done? I remember smelling alcohol on his breath."

The sweet encounter that meant so much to me, that I've based my future life on, held no meaning for him. How humiliating!

"The whole family believed his intentions, Constance," Victoria reminded her. "But Marcus probably convinced himself you knew he was only flirting. In that case, he'll expect you to pay a visit, and if you don't, he'll probably seek you out because he'll have no idea of your feelings and the expectations he raised." She clutched Constance's forearm, her eyes wide. "Marcus will bring that bride of his to show her off, probably thinking that as such a close friend of the family—of his—you'll be pleased."

Oh, Dear Lord. Sighing, Constance closed her eyes and sank back against the settee.

"However, if I hint of your disappointed expectations due to his despicable behavior at the party, he'll avoid you like the plague. And he certainly won't bring his bride anywhere in your vicinity."

Victoria having that conversation with Marcus is far better than facing the newlyweds myself. "Do it."

Victoria's expression crumpled. In a rapid change from wise counselor to upset friend, she let out a low wail and collapsed against the back of the settee until their shoulders touched. "I don't want you to go to Montana. I'll never see you again."

"I don't want to go either. But I must." That her father was a virtual stranger—known only through twice-yearly letters, a man she hadn't seen since she was small and barely remembered— didn't matter.

Now he represented a refuge and provided somewhere for her to flee. *Ironic that after losing the love and stability I anticipated with the Miller family, I'm going to the father who gave me away. Can I rely on him? I'll have to take the risk.*

As soon as Victoria left, Constance would begin packing and hope her father would take her in.

The next day, Constance sat at the secretary in the parlor, a cooling cup of peppermint tea nearby, writing a letter to her father. Last night, she'd dashed off a note to inform him of her impending arrival. The letter had gone out in the morning mail. But she figured a more complete accounting should follow.

A knock sounded on the door—three taps, then another three—the signal she and Victoria always used. She let out a sigh, for the first time ever not wanting to open the door to her best friend. Constance didn't want to hear the latest news of Marcus and his bride. But she knew how persistent Victoria could be. Might as well allow her inside, or she'd just go around to the kitchen where Mrs. Walsh, the cook/housekeeper, would let her into the house.

To prolong the task, Constance looked down at her half-finished letter, picked up the teacup, and sipped the sweet tea. Her stomach was still knotted, and she hadn't been able to eat breakfast.

This time, the tapping came from the nearby window. Knowing Victoria could see her through the glass, Constance glanced over.

Victoria scrunched a face and gestured wildly for Constance to let her in.

With a sigh, Constance stood and smoothed the skirt of the same outfit she'd worn yesterday, feeling the dark color symbolized her state of mind. She'd donned the dress because she assumed either Marcus would bring his wife to call upon her, or she'd be summoned across the street to meet the new bride. Either way, she wanted to look her best, *not* like a woman Marcus had rejected.

That thought stung. *Don't cry. Don't cry. No red eyes and nose allowed.* She couldn't do anything about the shadows under her eyes from an almost-sleepless night.

She reached the door and, after another sigh, opened it. Stepping back, she let her friend into the house.

Victoria practically bounced into the room. "I have the *best* news."

Constance stared at her friend, her mind blank, as if she couldn't absorb the meaning of the sentence. *How can she have any good news?*

For a brief traitorous moment, Constance deluded herself. *Yesterday must have been a mistake. Marcus hasn't really married another woman.*

Eyes alight, Victoria seized Constance's hands. "As I thought, Mama and Papa are *not* pleased with Marcus's choice of wife."

Victoria's statement dispelled Constance's hopeful delusion. *He is indeed married.*

Wickedly, she had a momentary sense of satisfaction that Mr. and Mrs. Miller disapproved of his match. She had thought to be the treasured daughter-in-law, welcomed into the family and given all the love her lonely heart desired. Now, displaced by the interloper, Constance would never be part of the Miller family. "Why not?" she forced herself to ask.

"They are mostly displeased with *him*. For marrying in secrecy and haste to someone we don't know." Victoria released Constance's hands and ticked off the reasons on her fingers. "We don't know her family. Gladene seems fine enough but *reserved*, and she did *not* make a good first impression. Although, who would, being sprung on a new husband's family like that, poor girl?" She gave a dramatic shudder and waved the hand holding up four fingers. "Like me, my folks really had their hearts set on *you* as a daughter-in-law."

Constance bit her lip, holding back the pain panging through her heart.

"They're quite concerned about how Marcus's marriage will affect *you*. Mama wants you to come see them later when Marcus and Gladene are out paying calls."

Constance wasn't sure she had the fortitude to step into that house and face the woman she loved and who would now *not* be her mother-in-law. "What's your news?"

"You know how I've been trying to talk them into a trip to Europe to visit Grandmama's family in Italy? Well—" she clapped her hands together "—they have *finally* consented."

Constance's heart dropped at the thought of losing her best friend's support, but she didn't want to put a damper on her friend's excitement. "How wonderful." She forced brightness into her tone. Hopefully Victoria couldn't hear the false note in her voice. "But I thought your parents objected to you traveling alone.

Surely, they wouldn't accompany you right when Marcus returns home with a bride? Such an action would be terribly rude."

"Not at all. This is the best part." Victoria grabbed Constance's hand again and tugged her to the settee. "*You* are coming with me!"

Constance had received a small inheritance from her aunt but not enough to squander on a prolonged trip to Europe. The bulk of her aunt's legacy was the house and the dressmaking business, which only brought in money if she were here to do the work. Gallivanting around Europe would not only mean lack of income, but also the loss of the clientele carefully built up through the years.

She sank down on the cushions beside Victoria. "Although, I wish I could—" Constance said with sincere regret, "I can't afford to pay for the trip, much less lose the business. Now that I'm not marrying your brother, I have to provide for myself."

"You're going to Sweetwater Springs," Victoria pointed out logically. "You already intended to give up your dressmaking business."

Constance tried to smile. "I'm glad for you, really, I am. I know how much you've longed for this trip. I'm sure you'll have no problem finding a respectable female to travel with."

Victoria gave a small bounce on the cushions of the settee and squeezed Constance's hand. "The next part of my good news is that my parents are paying for *your* trip."

"No," Constance protested, curling a hand into the crepe fabric of her skirt.

"They'd set aside a sum of money for Marcus, intending to give it to him when he married. He will not be receiving it now," Victoria said with a malicious smile. "Guess who will?"

Constance pulled away from Victoria's grasp to cover her suddenly hot cheeks with her cold hands. "I couldn't possibly accept such a generous gift."

"The money would have been yours anyway," Victoria said matter-of-factly. "If you don't accept, Papa will become all stern with you and insist you travel with me. You know how he can be. Do you really want Papa striding over here and giving you a lecture on *what's best for you?* Believe me, it will probably be a strong one—sounding like a scolding, even, given that he can't unleash on Marcus the way he wants to. All that ire is bottled up inside."

Constance couldn't help but smile at the picture her friend painted.

"Although…" Victoria tapped her chin with one plump finger. "Perhaps that circumstance would be best. You'd do Mama and me a favor by uncorking Papa, especially since you wouldn't *really* be in trouble. Then you'll give in, anyway. Therefore, you'll still come to Europe with me." She gave Constance a triumphant smirk. "*Yes*, it's best you first stand your ground, or at least pretend to." She popped to her feet. "I'll go home and inform Papa."

"You wretch!" Constance grabbed Victoria's arm and pulled her back down to the settee. "You are such a master manipulator!" She narrowed her eyes. "I'll bet *you* put the idea into his head about using Marcus's money for my trip."

"Me?" Victoria gave her a look of limpid innocence.

"I'm on to your tricks, Victoria Mary Miller." Constance shook her finger at Victoria's nose. "But I feel sorry for your future husband."

"I intend to find him in Italy. Handsome, rich, titled," Victoria said smugly. "With your help, of course."

Constance rolled her eyes. "Of course," she said, giving in. "I guess Sweetwater Springs will have to wait a while before I descend on that town and wreak havoc on my father's peaceful life."

Chapter Two

London, East End
May 1896

His hands slick with blood, Dr. Angus Cameron held the miniature body of the baby boy, born prematurely. In the flicker of the two candles—one he'd brought along and the other belonging to the two young prostitutes who shared the single room—he could see the stillborn infant was pale, flaccid, and *perfect*. In that moment, with an overwhelming feeling of pain and powerlessness, Angus felt his heart break with an almost-audible snap that sent him back in time to his childhood when his was five years old and his baby brother was born.

Angus was so excited about no longer being the baby of the family, and his parents prayed for a daughter after seven sons. On that long ago night of his brother's birth, he crept past the midwife to his mother's bedside, where she held the babe with a sorrowful look on her face.

He leaned close to examine his brother. He'd seen babies before, of course, but never one so tiny. Angus reached out and gingerly touched the back of the baby's hand, the pale skin softer than anything he'd felt before. "How long before he grows up and can play with me?"

Mama reached out and brushed a finger across Angus's cheek. Her smile trembled, and her eyes filled with tears. "Our Aden is playing in heaven."

The girl on the bed stirred, bringing Angus back to the

present. He inhaled the nauseating smells of unwashed flesh, blood, vaginal discharge, urine, stale sweat, dirty clothes, and feces permeating the air of the dank room of the tenement.

In my time in London, I haven't changed anything.

I'm done here.

I need to leave to get out of this filthy city. He thought of his brother Fergus's letters, of their earlier plan for Angus to join his practice in Sweetwater Springs, Montana. He glanced over at the young mother. *But first, I need to save her.*

If I can.

The girl, barely seventeen, lay on a bed—a heap of rags, really—piled on top of a broken bedstead. In another life, Maeve would have been an Irish beauty—with long-lashed blue eyes, auburn hair, and delicate features. But suffering from obvious malnutrition, her body was gaunt, her skin pale, lips bloodless, and eyes dull. "Me babe," she whispered in the cockney accent of the East End, raising one skeletal hand toward him in entreaty.

Angus didn't tell Maeve the sad truth about her son, for he knew in spite of his best efforts, she'd probably soon walk the pathway of death after her infant. Instead, he leaned over and gently set the tiny body into the crook of her arm. "A bonnie laddie." He forced the words out, his brogue thickening from sorrow. With a jerk of his head, he ordered Betsy, the other prostitute who'd sat quietly in the corner, toward the bed. "Prop up her shoulders a bit, lass."

From the gush of blood between the mother's legs, Angus could tell the placenta was separating from the uterus. With no live baby to suckle at the breast and cause the uterus to contract, he couldn't stop the hemorrhaging. *But I have to try.*

He strode to the cracked enamel washbasin, where the water fetched from the common pump in the courtyard and boiled on the small stove had gone cool. He grabbed the bar of soap he'd brought with him, thrust his hands into the water, and scrubbed away the blood. After he dried his hands on a clean towel, also brought with him, he returned to the bed.

The dying mother gazed upon her child. "Me sweet Charlie." Her bloodless lips turned up in a faint smile. "'e's beautiful."

"He is indeed, lass. Now, you're still bleeding." Angus told her. "I'll do what I can to stop the flow." He held up a hand. "I'll need to go inside ye."

Maeve stared at her son.

He motioned Betsy away from the bed, manipulated one hand into Maeve's vagina, and placed the other on her belly, massaging the uterus internally and externally.

But to no avail. Minute by minute life drained from the mother. Her eyes glazed.

He withdrew his hand, wiping the blood on the towel, and then used the cloth to clean Maeve in a last gesture of respect. He bowed his head. *Lord, into Thy hands I commend her spirit.*

Heavy with sadness, Angus stood, his leg and back muscles stiff and aching from the awkward position. He walked to the washbasin, emptied the pinkish water into the slop pail, and poured in the last of the clean water.

The small coal fire had gone out, and the room was turning chilly. Once again, he took up the soap and harshly scrubbed his hands, as if he could metaphorically wash away his responsibilities as well as the sheer exhaustion and futility of trying to affect the abject conditions of the East End slums.

A frisson of energy moved through his exhausted body. *I need to flee to the new world, to a new life, to clean air and blue skies, and to wide open spaces. Perhaps there, I can make a difference.*

As he hurriedly packed up his big leather bag, Angus gave terse instructions to Betsy about the bodies.

A shocked sound made him stop and look into her face. In the dim light, she appeared almost as wan and hollow as the deceased mother. Angus fished a couple of coins from his pocket and pressed them into her hand. "Buy some food," he ordered, knowing the futility of the gesture. "Also, a small sponge you can soak in vinegar. Before you lie with a man, tie a string around it, and insert the sponge inside yourself." He jerked his head toward the bodies on the bed. "Using it will help prevent pregnancy and keep you from ending up like her."

"Thank ye," she said in a low voice.

Angus grabbed up his bag and strode out of the room, closing the door firmly behind him.

In an exhausted daze, Angus leaned against the corner of the hackney. He'd been lucky tonight, locating one so close to the East End tenement. Usually, he either had to head in the direction of the nearby brothels or leave the slum entirely to find transportation.

A dirty, yellow fog had fallen, muffling the sights and sounds, but not the smells of this part of London—the reek from the factories, the stench of overcrowded, poverty-stricken humans, and the odor of rotting trash and horse droppings. The chill air had grown colder. Even in his frock coat, with his hands in his pockets—for he'd forgotten his gloves—Angus shivered.

Normally, he'd have returned to his lodgings to bathe and change before calling upon Sir Henry Vail—one of the well-known doctors who sponsored the medical clinic for the poor of East End. Even though the man was a physician, he'd married into a wealthy family and lived in a mansion on Mayfair. For Angus to show up uninvited in the clothes he'd worn to make his rounds wouldn't do. Yet he was too tired and heartsick to care about his appearance and even dozed a bit on the way.

Angus didn't awaken until the hackney stopped. He thrust open the carriage door and stepped out, carrying his heavy leather doctor's bag, only to see all the lights of the mansion ablaze and shiny carriages dislodging people dressed in expensive evening clothes. He groaned, remembering tonight was the coming-out ball for Anastasia Elizabeth Margaret Vail, Sir Henry's only daughter.

Anastasia Vail had taken an unaccountable romantic liking to Angus—feelings he didn't return or encourage and, he suspected, not approved of by her parents. Although Sir Henry had sponsored him and stated pride in Angus's work, a poor doctor from a middle-class background—even if his father had a lucrative practice with the wealthy of Edinburgh—wasn't the husband he'd choose for his daughter.

Before Angus could order the driver to take him back to his lodgings, the hackney pulled away, leaving him stranded. He stared blankly at the retreating carriage, debating about chasing after the vehicle. Before he could decide, another coach pulled up—this one glossy black with a crest on the side panels.

A couple, wearing well-cut coats over their evening clothes, climbed down.

Angus recognized one of the other doctors Sir Henry had taken under his wing, although unlike him, Max Prine was also a member of the aristocracy—a younger son of a younger son of an earl—and had an income from his family. Well, to be sure, so did Angus. But fifty pounds a year was a far cry from the five thousand he knew Max received.

"Angus, old chap." With a quizzical lift of an eyebrow, Max surveyed him. "Looks as though you've been put through the wringer," he said, not unkindly.

"A confinement that went...." Angus glanced at the brunette beauty on Max's arm and shook his head, not wanting to put the truth into words.

"That happens." Max grasped Angus's arm. "Either take my carriage, old man, and go home, or—" he jerked his head in the direction of the mansion "—get inside and warm up. Looks like you need some food, too. Surely, a room can be found away from all the hubbub."

"Thanks for the offer." Angus didn't know which to choose. The pull to sever his life in London was strong. Even though he had an invitation to the ball, he could hardly barge into the house tonight and tender his resignation to Sir Henry.

The woman pulled on Max's other arm. "Darling, I haven't met your friend." Although she held her head in a haughty tilt, her gaze was soft with obvious compassion.

"Venetia, my dear. This is Dr. Angus Cameron. You've heard me talk about his dedication to the poor." He smiled at Angus. "My beautiful fiancée, Lady Venetia Fenton-Boyce."

Lady Venetia gifted Angus with a cool smile. "Your work is admirable, Dr. Cameron. Although, I agree with Max that you...." She hesitated and eyed Angus's rumpled, blood-splotched clothing, obviously searching for a polite way to phrase her suggestion. "Need to take care of yourself."

Angus nodded. "I'll go around to the servants' entrance, make my way to the kitchen, grab a bite, and find a quiet spot to eat. Then I'll return to my lodgings."

Lady Venetia chuckled. "The kitchen will be the center of the hubbub, not quiet at all."

"I'll tuck myself into a corner."

Max frowned. "Nonsense, old fellow. No need to go to the servants' entrance, wherever that is." He tugged on Angus's arm before extending his elbow to his betrothed. "Come on in through the front. Once inside, instead of going to the ballroom, head toward the kitchen."

Angus had no desire to enter the house, but he could hardly cause a scene by pulling away from Max. With an internal sigh, he allowed himself to be towed up the steps.

Once inside the spacious entry, lit by gas lamps, and fragrant with the scents of flowers and perfume, they divested themselves of their coats and handed them to the waiting servants.

Self-conscious about his lack of evening attire, Angus separated himself from Max and Lady Venetia. He hugged the wall next to the door and moved behind a round table with a towering arrangement of flowers, wishing to stay out of sight. He'd been a guest at the Vail's mansion enough to know the general direction of the kitchen—although, of course, he'd never been in there—and waited to catch the attention of a servant to ask for directions.

His brief nap had somewhat refreshed him but hadn't budged Angus from his decision. He needed to shake off the filth and despair of this city and head to America. First, though, he'd have to go home to Edinburgh to say goodbye to his family, whom he'd probably never see again. The sober thought gave him a pang.

A flurry of arrivals distracted him. A group of debutantes exchanged airy kisses.

The women's fashions made Angus grit his teeth. Despite the information available about the dangers of tightly corseting the female form, these women persisted in imprisoning their bodies to achieve a fashionable wasp-waisted figure. In addition, several wore shades of purple or green—both colors often made from poisonous dyes.

These women are throwing away their health for temporary beauty and fashion.

He held in a growl, remembering Maeve's skeletal limbs and the dirty ragged clothes she'd worn when he'd first seen her at the clinic. Although they were about the same age, the difference in the women's circumstances—from the wealth and elegance to the abject poverty—was so incredibly strong. *Incredibly wrong.*

Sickened, he turned away and changed his mind about staying. Angus wasn't sure he could contain the anger boiling up in him. He'd better head back to his lodgings before he exploded.

Yes, indeed, I need to escape to the peace of Montana.

Chapter Three

Sweetwater Springs, Montana
June 1896

Standing on the platform of the train station of the frontier town of Sweetwater Springs, Constance kept a weather eye on the porter offloading the six trunks and eight crates she'd brought, containing two sewing machines—hers and her aunt's—as well as patterns, fabric, thread, and notions collected during her three-year sojourn abroad. In addition, she had everything from the dressmaking business that she'd stored in the attic in her house in Chicago while in Europe.

The train had arrived late, near dusk, and Constance was so weary she could barely keep her shoulders back and head held high. All she wanted was a bath and a bed, in that order. A cup of tea and some food would be a bonus. The large reticule and the leather satchel she carried, showing wear from accompanying her on the last two years of her journey, grew ever heavier.

Over her forest green traveling dress, Constance wore the same sooty duster that had seen plenty of use on the continent. Since she was here to stay in Sweetwater Springs and wasn't planning on any more traveling, she intended to burn the offensive garment as soon as possible. *I'd better like living here.*

A chill wind swirled around her. Shivering, she looked away

from her belongings being unloaded and looked around.

From the brown railroad station with cheerful yellow trim came an older man, small and bent. He scurried over, his weathered countenance alight with interest.

For a panicky moment, Constance wondered if this man was her father. But he didn't look anything like the few memories she had of Mack Taylor, nor the old photograph she possessed. Plus, her father didn't know she was coming. *Wanting to surprise Papa might have been a mistake.*

"Hello, hello." The man directed an unexpectedly warm smile her way. "Welcome to Sweetwater Springs, Miss. I'm Jack Waite, the stationmaster. May I direct you somewhere?"

"Thank you, Mr. Waite, I'm Constance Taylor, my father—"

"Daughter of Mack Taylor, who owns the livery stable," he interrupted with a congenial grin. "You've been living in Italy for the last few years."

"My goodness," she said, astonished by his knowledge of her doings.

"I'm also the postmaster," Mr. Waite explained. "I keep track of everyone's mail." He wrinkled his brow. "Mack didn't tell me you were arriving and ask for me to keep watch for you." He glanced around, as if looking for her father to make an appearance.

"Papa doesn't know. I thought I'd surprise him."

His grin crinkled the lines on his face. "I can't imagine a better surprise. Mack'll be over the moon."

"I hope so," she said fervently.

"For the last several years, Mack's talked about you coming here."

Guilt squeezed her chest, but she didn't let her reaction show.

"Your father sometimes shared your letters—the ones where you'd describe where you were staying. Why, hearing your words was like having a history or language or a geography lesson. In fact, Mrs. Gordon—she's the schoolteacher—bought a map of Europe and put pins in every place where you stayed."

Constance chuckled, amused rather than offended by the notion of the townsfolk following her travels.

"But on the other hand," Mr. Waite continued without seeming to take a breath. "Plenty speculated that you'd find a man in Italy and stay there."

Really? Suddenly the gossip about her was no longer amusing. She'd taken a long time to recover from what she'd considered a betrayal by Marcus. At age twenty-three, she was no longer the sheltered, naive girl she'd been.

Unlike Victoria, who'd indeed married an Italian count, Constance planned to remain unwed and concentrate all her efforts on her dressmaking business. After all, Aunt Hannah had provided an excellent example of a woman remaining a spinster and providing for herself, independent of a husband.

"The livery is right over there." Mr. Waite pointed to a large building of weathered gray clapboard. "You just leave your luggage here, Miss Taylor. I'll watch over everything. Mack'll probably send Pepe for your trunks."

From her father's letters, Constance knew Pepe Sanchez was his stable hand.

Mr. Waite glanced over at her many trunks and crates, and his eyes widened. "Send over Pepe with a *wagon*...for several loads."

Constance chuckled. "I'm sure Pepe will manage, and I can leave everything in your capable hands."

Mr. Waite straightened as much as his bent frame allowed. "That you can, Miss Taylor. All will be right and tight." He waved a gnarled hand toward the livery. "Now, you just mosey along and give your pa the best shock of his life."

Buoyed by the idea of her father's surprise at her appearance, Constance thanked Mr. Waite and walked across the platform and down the steps to the road, paved with big bricks of rough-cut brownish-pink stone. To her left, the four-story building nearest the train station was as imposing as any she'd seen on her travels. *The Livingston Hotel,* a sign out front stated. The livery was across the street and down a ways, but still in view of the hotel. She wondered how the owner liked looking at her father's weathered, clapboard building, which looked more like a barn than a combination home and place of business.

A wide-open space between the train tracks and the livery held several unhitched wagons. Her father had once written that he lived in rooms next to the stable, but she'd assumed he'd meant a house. But no home was in sight. *Perhaps it's on the other side, out of view.*

Constance hesitated in front of the building, not sure if she should walk along the side or enter the partially opened barn doors.

A man with shoulder-length white hair limped out of the big barn. He was dressed in faded denim, a material that seemed popular for men's trousers in the West.

From her memories and the single photograph she possessed of her father, Constance immediately recognized him. Shocked by how much he'd aged, she faltered and stopped. Mack Taylor wasn't the big, strong man she'd remembered, but one who looked frail and shrunken.

Her father saw Constance standing there and squinted in her direction, his brows drawing together. Then he grabbed his chest and stepped back like he'd been struck. "Melanie?" His voice quavered. He extended his other hand in her direction before shaking his head as in disbelief. His knees bent, as if he were about to collapse.

He thinks I'm Mama. Hundreds of times, Constance had fantasized about their reunion—always a joyful experience. She'd imagined a much-younger version of her father in varying states of shock, surprise, and joy. Sometimes, he gave her a big hug. In other daydreams, he'd taken her hand and looked lovingly into her face. Each time, she'd beamed and laughed, and sometimes even cried.

Never had she imagined the fear that stabbed through her. "It's me, Papa. Constance." Gasping, she dropped her bags,

25

grabbed up her skirts, and raced toward him, afraid he'd keel over before she could reach his side. *Have I given him a heart attack?*

"Connie? That you, girl?"

She grasped his arm and held on, wondering what she'd do if he toppled over. "Papa, I've come to live in Sweetwater Springs."

His breath wheezed in his chest. "Connie?" As if he hadn't heard or understood, he repeated the question and peered into her face. His green eyes had a yellowish tinge and white whiskers stubbled his chin. He reached out a shaky hand to touch her arm. "Is it really you? My little girl?"

"Not so little anymore, Papa." Guilt stabbed her. "I never dreamed seeing me would be such a shock to your system, else I'd have given you warning."

"You're all grown up. I knew that, of course, but still…." He stared at her in wonderment. "You look just like your dear mother. Just as beautiful." His eyes teared. "I wasn't sure I'd ever see you again, Connie girl. Feared I'd go to my grave…."

Remorse made her vision misty. She blinked back the tears. Over his shoulder she saw a stocky Mexican man about her age stride from the barn.

A big, brown dog trotted behind him—some kind of hound with floppy ears and a black muzzle.

The man saw them and slowed, a worried expression on his round, brown face.

She smiled and waved him over.

The dog loped ahead to her father.

"Rex," Papa said, placing a hand on the hound's head.

Pepe hastened to her father's side.

"You must be Pepe Sanchez. I'm Constance Taylor. I've just given my father quite a shock."

The man grinned. "Ah, Señorita Taylor! That's the best kind of shock." He took her father's other arm. "Yesterday, Señor Mack, he took a big kick to his leg."

Her father grimaced. "Ain't able to dodge quick no more."

Pepe made a sweeping motion with his arm. "Knocked him

over. He hit his head and landed on his hip. He lay on the cold ground for a long time before I found him."

"Did you see a doctor?" Constance asked, already suspecting the answer.

"No need. I'm stiff and bruised is all."

"And stubborn," Pepe added, sounding more like a friend than an employee.

Her father waved a hand in obvious irritation. "Stop your fussing now, Pepe. I'll be fine. Been using horse liniment, and you know how good that works."

"On horses." Pepe met Constance's gaze, sending her a silent message.

Papa definitely isn't fine.

"Well, *I'm* not fine," Constance said, truthfully. "I'm so tired I'm about to fall over. The air's cold, and night is falling. I'm chilled to the bone." She gave an exaggerated shiver. "Why don't we go inside?"

Pepe's smile split his face. "I came to tell you that my wife Lucia is about to set supper on the table. I hope you're hungry, Señorita Taylor. There's plenty of food."

"More than hungry." Her stomach gurgled. "Starving."

Pepe glanced behind her toward the train station and raised his eyebrows in a question.

"My belongings are still at the depot. Mr. Waite is watching over them. I've brought ten trunks and crates."

Her father's eyes widened, and he lifted his hand from the dog's head. "Mercy me, daughter. What all in tarnation did you bring?"

"I'll get them later," Pepe said. "Don't you worry."

Released, Rex moved to Constance and stuck his nose in her crotch.

She evaded him, petting the hound's silky head. "Hello, Rex."

"Behave." Pepe bent to wrap his arms around the dog.

Constance laughed and took her father's arm, turning him in

27

the direction of the barn and giving him a gentle tug to limp forward. "I'm here to stay, Papa. I've sold Aunt Hannah's house and stored most of the contents in my neighbor's attic for now."

He halted and gave her a searching look. "You sure 'bout that, Connie girl? No more traipsing around the world?"

"For the last few years, I've had more than my share of traipsing. I'm looking forward to settling down in one spot."

A familiar smile lit up his face.

For a moment, he looked more like the father she recalled, and love tugged at her.

"Well, then, won't be a problem to get you hitched. Plenty of fellows in this place will fall over their tongues as soon as they see you." He waved a hand down the street. "I'll have a line of suitors. Wait and see, Connie girl. You just wait and see. But don't be in no hurry, hear? I want you around for a while."

"I go by Constance, Papa, not Connie." In spite of her best efforts, an edge slipped into her voice. "I'm not here to marry, but to start my own dressmaking business."

"No reason you can't do both," he said in a logical tone. "At least until the young 'uns come along."

Constance rolled her eyes but didn't let him see. *Now isn't the time to get into my lack of matrimonial aspirations. We'll have plenty of opportunities to talk about my plans.* "Where's your home, Papa?"

He pointed his chin to the left of the barn. "Tacked on the end there."

Tacked didn't sound very promising.

They walked through a black-painted door at the side of the building and into a small office. Her father kept on going past a small table that, from the open ledger and inkwell in the shape of a horseshoe, served as a desk. They moved through another door and into a combination kitchen, dining, living room, where she inhaled the savory smell of simmering meat, baking, and kerosene from the lamp on the table and one hanging on a hook in the kitchen ceiling.

A young woman with beautiful brown skin stood at the stove

stirring a pot. She was slight with glossy black hair pulled back in a simple bun, and a round-necked white embroidered blouse. She turned when they entered, revealing her pregnant belly. Her cheekbones were rose-tinted from the heat and her large, long-lashed eyes widened when she saw Constance.

Pepe gestured to the woman. "My wife, Lucia."

She gave Constance a shy smile.

"Hello, Mrs. Sanchez. Whatever you're cooking smells wonderful."

"Beef stew. Not the best meal for a guest." She spoke with a soft Spanish accent, perhaps Mexican. "I didn't even make a dessert because we are out of sugar, and Señor Mack didn't have time to go to the mercantile."

"Shopping at the mercantile is never a good experience for Pepe or Lucia," her father explained with a grimace. "The Cobbs who own the place are not fond of anyone who doesn't have lily white skin, so I get stuck with that chore."

"No, Señor Mack," Pepe corrected, flashing his wide grin. "The Cobbs are not fond of *anyone*."

How horrible to only have one store in town and be forced to put up with such rude behavior.

Her father let out a cackle. "Right you are, son. But even less so, if you have brown skin, or, heaven forbid, red or black."

Constance noted the use of the word *son*, not sure how she felt about her father using such an intimate term. *Does he really see Pepe in the light of a son?*

Well, I wasn't here. We have no other family. Papa's probably been lonely. So, it's good he and Pepe are close. Or so her logical mind thought. Her heart wasn't so sure.

Her father shrugged. "The Cobbs own the only store in town, so what can you do?"

"I keep telling you, Señor Mack, to sell more than just horse feed." Pepe winked at Constance. "Give them some competition."

"The Cobbs sound quite unpleasant," Constance commented,

wondering what the couple would think about her opening a dressmaking business and, from their point of view, *stealing* customers away from them.

"Takes all kinds to make up a town," her father commented. "Most folks around here are good people, and that's what really matters."

Lucia gave the men a fond smile before lowering her eyes and turning back to her cooking.

Constance glanced around, and her stomach sank. Although the room was scrupulously clean, it seemed about the same size as her parlor at home. The kitchen area held a black stove, a square table with three place settings and four chairs, a counter with a dry sink, several cupboards, and a pie safe.

In the rest of the space were a small, chesterfield settee that looked vaguely familiar with worn deep-buttoned leather upholstery next to a sturdy end table, as well as a narrow bookshelf crammed with books and ledgers. A brick fireplace was positioned on the right wall, which she supposed was shared with the barn. A carved wooden horse with a flying mane and tail and three framed photographs rested on the mantle.

Curious at what held a place of honor, she moved closer to examine the images. The first was a family grouping. Her mother was seated, holding a young Constance, with her father standing, his hand on her mother's shoulder. From the clothing and the background, she could tell that this photograph was taken at the same time as the one she had of her father.

Remembering those happy years before her mother's death made a lump rise in her throat. With her mother's passing, Constance had essentially lost both parents, for she'd never seen her father again. In spite of their letters, Papa was basically a stranger.

Striving to hide the emotions welling up inside, she kept her back to the men and examined the other photographs. The second one was of her mother, and the third was the one taken on the day Constance graduated from Miss Elsom's Academy for

Girls. She'd worn a white dress that she'd fashioned entirely on her own.

She smiled, seeing the rows of pleated tucks on the bodice, painstakingly made by winding the fabric through the tines of a fork. Her gown had been just as elegant as those of the richest girls in her class, and Constance remembered basking in some of the envious glances tossed her way.

Turning from the mantle, she continued her perusal. She nodded in the direction of an open door.

"My room," her father said.

Constance glanced around, not seeing another door. "No spare room?" She dreaded his answer.

He gave her a sheepish look. "If I'd known you were coming, I could have bought you a bed."

And put it where? Constance didn't voice the sarcastic thought out loud. *This is what I get for arriving without warning.*

Her father waved toward the doorway. "You can take the bedroom. I'll make up a pallet and put it on the floor in the corner." He gestured to a space near the fireplace. "Too bad, the settee isn't long enough."

Constance directed a pointed look at his injured hip. "You are *not* sleeping on the floor."

Pepe nodded. "You are injured, remember, Señor Mack? Too bad we rented out my old room in the barn." He walked toward the front door. "I'll go get your things, Señorita Taylor. He glanced around. "I can bring a trunk in here, but the rest, we'll have to store in the tack room. Whatever doesn't fit, I'll put in an empty stall."

"Perhaps, I'll stay at the hotel," Constance said, not liking the idea of her clothes and fabric in a barn.

Hurt flashed in her father's eyes.

Feeling guilty, she hastily said, "Never mind the hotel. I'll take the pallet, Papa. But, please tell me there's a place I can bathe?" She glanced around again, hoping for a bathroom to miraculously appear. Then she studied the kitchen, noting the sink didn't even have a pump. *No indoor plumbing whatsoever.* She held in a groan.

Her father rubbed his chin, the stubble making a rasping sound. "There's a bathhouse in town. But mostly we use a washtub."

A washtub wasn't her first choice. She'd prefer a tub with hot and cold running water. But she'd used plenty of washtubs on her travels.

Lucia turned from the stove. "After supper, you and I can take the washtub to our house, Señorita Taylor. There you can bathe in privacy while the men stay here."

"Thank you, Mrs. Sanchez." Constance tried to make her tone and expression grateful rather than resigned. "I appreciate you accommodating me."

"Call me Lucia, please. Not Mrs. Sanchez. Señor Mack, he is family."

"Then you must call me *Constance*." She empathized her name with a glance at her father, hoping he'd stop calling her Connie.

He stared at the photographs on the mantel and didn't seem to notice her hint.

"While you are bathing, I'll make up your pallet." Lucia frowned and fluttered her hands. "I have clean sheets. They are not the best, but I've mended each tear. The good ones are on Señor Mack's bed."

"I'm sure I'll manage," Constance said lightly. "As long as they are clean and not damp, I'll be fine. Somewhere in one of my trunks, I have bedding. In Europe, I traveled with my own sheets because you never knew how clean the ones at the inns were." With dread making her stomach tense, she avoided looking at the corner where her pallet would go. *This place was little better than camping.*

Why did I think coming to live here was such a great idea?

The next morning, well after she should have risen and gotten ready for the day, Constance stepped out of the office space and into the outdoors. She moved slowly, stiff from sleeping on the pallet, and squinted into the bright sunshine, wishing she had a dress in the color of the vivid blue sky.

As she walked to the street, she pondered how she could procure fabric of the same hue. After all, she could hardly write to the warehouse in Chicago and say she wanted something in Montana sky blue. *Maybe I could experiment with indigo dye.* She'd never done so before, but in France, she'd toured an establishment that had been making dye for generations.

She stepped into the barn but didn't go far inside, not wanting to risk collecting dust smudges on her finery—an outfit of fashionable green-and-yellow stripes, colors she knew brought out the grass green of her eyes. She'd made the basque a few inches longer than her normal bodice to give herself a more elegant silhouette.

Wrinkling her nose at the earthy smell of hay and horses and manure, she hoped the odor wasn't seeping into the clothes and fabric in her trunks and crates.

The light in the barn was dim, and she had to let her eyes adjust before she scanned the row of stalls and saw Pepe in one, grooming a black horse. "I'm going for a walk," she called to him.

He waved in response.

At the sound of her voice, Rex peeked around the stall door.

"Stay!" Pepe must have grabbed the dog, for the hound didn't approach Constance.

With a swing of her beaded reticule, she turned and stepped out of the wide doors of the barn, just as a young blonde woman, her eyes bright with tears and her expression twisted in obvious anger, barreled toward her. Constance stopped abruptly to keep from a collision.

The woman jerked back only inches from Constance. Tears spilled from her soft blue eyes. "I'm so sorry," she gasped, wiping the wetness with her fingertips and stepping back, obviously fighting for composure. She was painfully thin, and her navy-blue dress hung loosely on her frame. Shadows under her eyes gave her a haunted look, and her translucent skin made a scattering of freckles across her nose stand out.

Constance grasped both of the woman's arms to steady her. "It's my fault, too. I wasn't looking, either." She released the woman, opened the clasp of her reticule, and handed over a lace-edged handkerchief with an embroidered violet in each corner.

The woman waved in negation. "Oh, no, that's too pretty. I have one with me." From inside the cuff of her sleeve, she withdrew a serviceable handkerchief, which looked wrinkled and damp. She dabbed at her eyes and blew her nose, finally tucking the handkerchief back into her sleeve and looking up. "Are you a guest at the hotel?"

Constance glanced at the elegant hotel across the street and thought of her hard pallet and poor night's sleep. "I wish I were," she said in a wry tone. "And if conditions here become worse—" she tilted her head in the direction of the livery "—perhaps, I *will* move over there."

The woman furrowed her brow and gave Constance a puzzled glance, but the corners of her mouth flickered.

I'll coax a smile from her yet. "I'm Constance Taylor." She flicked a hand at the livery. "Mack Taylor's long-lost daughter. You must call me Constance, for I can tell we're going to be friends." *Please. I need a friend, and so, I sense, do you.* After going almost her whole life with seeing Victoria on a daily basis, her best friend's absence made Constance feel as though a part of her was missing.

With widening eyes, the young woman nodded.

"I just arrived in Sweetwater Springs yesterday. I don't know who was more surprised—my father when I descended upon him unannounced, or myself when I saw the small space he lived in, and therefore, I'd have to *share*."

Hopefully, I don't drive her off with my babbling. But even that thought didn't stop the words from tumbling out of Constance's mouth.

The woman's expression lightened, as if Constance's prattling was taking her mind off her cares. So, she rattled on. "Can you believe I was so tired I missed church today? Between traveling, and then sleeping on a pallet on the floor, I was so exhausted that I moved into my father's bed when he got up, and I finally slept deeply."

The woman gave Constance a sympathetic glance. "I can imagine."

"And the rooms have no place for my trunks, so they're stored in the barn. I'm sure my clothing will end up smelling like manure."

That comment finally brought a smile to the woman's face. "The situation might not be that bad," she said in a teasing tone. "Your clothes might only end up smelling like *horses*, and since most people here like horses...."

Constance chuckled, enjoying the woman's sense of humor. "*Eau de perfume* of equine," she said with an exaggerated French accent. "I knew I'd like you."

The woman's smile widened.

"Please, tell me your name."

"I'm Felicity Woodbury."

"Felicity.... May I be informal at short acquaintance and call you by your pretty given name?"

"I'd like that."

"You're lucky that it can't be shortened into any kind of nickname. I can't abide when people call me Connie. I have yet to break my father of that dreadful habit. Although, I only corrected him once last night and once this morning." She rolled her eyes.

Without waiting for an answer, Constance linked her arm through Felicity's. "I'm in *desperate* need of a friend, and from the looks of things, so are you. Pepe, my father's stable man, said a sweetshop is around here somewhere. Let's go get some hot chocolate and become acquainted. That is—" she paused and frowned "—unless the place isn't open on a Sunday."

"Oh, Sugarplum Dreams is open. A common custom in this town is for the businesses to open for an hour or so before and after church, so those who come far distances can shop. Sometimes, people who live on prairie homesteads or distant ranches only make it to town a few times a year for a Sunday service. Mrs. Ritter usually opens Sugarplum Dreams after the church service for several hours. People buy treats to take home for Sunday dinner or candy for the children to eat on the long walk or ride home." She fell silent, her expression troubled.

"You're looking downcast. Is it something I said?"

Felicity grimaced. "Oh, no. I'm sad all the time now. You see, I lost my Johnny five days ago. He was a logger and was killed in an accident. We were to be married soon."

"My dear Felicity," Constance exclaimed, remembering how deeply she'd mourned Marcus—not even a real relationship—and pitying the poor woman. She squeezed her arm. "I'm so sorry." She put all of her sincerity into her tone. "You're definitely in need of a new friend and hot chocolate, in that order, to give your hurting heart a little ease from sorrow."

The hopeful look in the young woman's eyes made Constance determined to help her. She clapped her hands together. "Oh, Felicity, isn't it a wonderful coincidence that we happened to run into each other?"

"I almost knocked you flat," Felicity corrected and waved a hand between them.

Constance laughed. "Fortuitous that we met and neither of us ended up in the mud."

Felicity made a sweeping gesture to indicate her simple dress. "You should know…I'm a maid at the hotel," she said in a self-deprecating tone. "This is my uniform."

"Another working girl," Constance said gaily, not caring an iota for Felicity's social status. She was just grateful to make a friend. "I'm a seamstress, and I intend to open my own dressmaking shop. Papa says no such business exists in Sweetwater Springs."

"Your father's right."

Constance gave a little tug to their joined arms. "Lead on, Felicity."

The two, or rather Constance chattered all the way to the sweetshop, which turned out to be about a block away from the livery. A hand carved sign—*Sugarplum Dreams*—hung over the door. On the left side of the building the wood looked new, clearly a recent expansion, in contrast to the faded clapboard of the rest of the store.

Constance stepped inside, inhaling the sweet scent of chocolate and sugar. Couples occupied most of the tables. A family of six sat crammed around a middle table, leaving the last one free. The large glass display case was filled with all kinds of pastries and candy.

Constance gave Felicity a happy smile and directed her to sit while she ordered hot chocolate, paid for the two drinks, and carried the pretty ivy-patterned cups and saucers to the table.

While she waited, Felicity stared out the window, her shoulders slumping.

Her sad expression made Constance's heart ache, and she wondered what she could do to help the young woman cope with her obvious grief. She eyed the shapeless uniform. *I'll start with making Felicity a proper mourning gown. I'll have to be clever about convincing her, for I doubt she can afford my usual rates, and she strikes me as someone who won't take charity.*

Constance breezed back to the table and set down the cups and saucers. "Hot chocolate and whipped cream. What could be better? At least—" she added hastily, remembering Johnny's death "—the perfect beverage when one is in need of consolation." She scooted a cup in front of Felicity and sat across from her.

They both took several sips, savoring the drinks, and Constance coaxed Felicity to talk.

Soon Felicity shared about Johnny and her distress about already being courted by other men when her beloved was still warm in his grave. *Stupid, annoying men. Well, that's one way to weed out those who'd make bad husbands—too focused on their own wants and desires to pay attention to the needs of a wife.* At least the situation gave Constance an opening to suggest she make Felicity a mourning gown, and she did a lot of fast-talking to make her new friend give in.

She overcame Felicity's resistance by insisting, truthfully, that she needed someone to model one of her outfits as an advertisement. In addition, if Felicity bought the fabric from the mercantile, Constance could give her a deep discount. She had no idea which of her boxes and trunks held the black crepe or wool bombazine fabric suitable for mourning.

Felicity stared out the window, her brow wrinkling. Then with an exclamation, she rose. "Just a minute. I see someone I must speak with. I'll be right back." She almost flew out the door.

Curious, Constance leaned to the side and craned her neck to see out the window, to where her friend spoke with a big, handsome man who looked Scandinavian. From his smile at Felicity, she deduced he might have feelings for her yet wasn't one of the importuning suitors.

Well, well. Constance sat back in her chair, thinking. She'd need to know the character of the man, but perhaps he might be just what Felicity needed to help her through her grieving. Sipping her cocoa, she began to formulate some ideas.

Only in Sweetwater Springs for a day, and I've started meddling in other people's business—in a good way, of course.

After Felicity returned to the hotel escorted by Lars Aagaard—who turned out to be a logging friend of Johnny's—Constance finished her chocolate and stared out the window, watching people walk, ride, or drive by on their way home to Sunday dinner.

An unexpected pang of loneliness went through her, and she glanced around the shop looking for company. The other three tables were now empty, and the proprietress, who'd worked behind the glass counter of pastries and candy, had disappeared into the kitchen.

Constance looked back out the window, but watching the townsfolk had lost its appeal. She didn't have Sunday dinner waiting for her at the livery because Pepe and Lucia spent the day with her family. Her father had long-standing plans with one of his cronies, who lived too far away to send word to about Constance's arrival. "You won't like it there, daughter," was all Papa said, so she hadn't pressed to go along.

The proprietress of the sweetshop, a woman about Constance's age with a round face, green eyes, and dark hair, came out of the kitchen and moved from behind the counter. She wore an apron over a greenish-gray work dress and carried an ivy-patterned porcelain pot and a cup and saucer. Bustling over to Constance's table, she said, "I don't usually do this—offer free seconds—but there's a lull in business, you're new in town, and I'd like to chat—at least until more customers come." She raised the pot and tilted her head in askance. "Would you like more cocoa?"

Constance smiled and gestured toward her cup. "The chocolate is delicious. I'd appreciate some more, *and* I'd love some company."

"I'm Julia Ritter." The woman set the cup and saucer on the table and poured hot chocolate into Constance's cup before filling her own and taking a seat. "My husband Sam and I own Sugarplum Dreams. We live upstairs."

"I'm Constance Taylor."

"I know. Mack's daughter. Word has already spread. The gossip in our small town flies around fast."

Constance shook her head. "I guess it's not unlike how gossip goes around a neighborhood in a city." She sipped her chocolate. "I'm quite impressed with your shop, Mrs. Ritter."

The woman's smile showed pride. "This place is a labor of love."

Constance felt immediate kinship with the woman. "I can't claim to have your talents with sweets, but I do understand the satisfaction that comes from being in charge of your own business."

Mrs. Ritter raised her eyebrows.

"I'm a seamstress, and in Chicago, my aunt and I had a dressmaking business."

"I'm from Chicago, too." Her brow wrinkled. "I thought you were living in Italy."

"Before going to Europe and settling in Italy, I should say."

Mrs. Ritter clasped her hands to her chest in a praying gesture. "Please tell me you're going to open up a shop here." She lowered a hand to her still-flat stomach. "I'll soon need clothes to fit my growing stomach."

"I'm going to open a shop here," Constance echoed with a chuckle. "Just as soon as I can find somewhere to rent, preferably with living quarters." She took a sip of her hot chocolate. "Congratulations on the baby."

Mrs. Ritter's expression glowed. "Sam and I are thrilled."

"I'd be delighted to make you a maternity dress."

"Do you, uh…" Mrs. Ritter hesitated and then plunged ahead. "If I'm to help you, I'll need to ask an indelicate question. How are you situated financially? Are you on a tight budget?"

"Well, I don't want to be extravagant, but I can afford to rent a nice place."

Mrs. Ritter's eyes sparkled. "The reason I'm asking is that Ant Gordon, owner of *The Sweetwater Springs Herald*, has an office building with shop space available as well as living quarters above. The rent will be more expensive because the building is newly constructed. It's the one that has the same Sioux quartzite façade as the hotel."

"Sounds perfect." Constance wrinkled her nose. "I suppose I'll have to wait until tomorrow to meet with Mr. Gordon." She leaned forward. "What sort of landlord do you think he'd be?"

"Fine, I'm sure. He's a good man." Mrs. Ritter stretched her hand toward the ceiling. "A *big* man. Married to the schoolteacher, which means he holds a progressive opinion of females having occupations."

"The schoolteacher is married? How unusual. In a good way, I mean."

"In a very good way." Mrs. Ritter nodded decisively. "Why should a woman have to give up teaching just because she's married? Men can be married *and* have children and still be teachers."

"We think the same," she said in relief. Before moving here Constance had doubts about finding many progressive thinkers in Sweetwater Springs, much less friendly *businesswomen* of a similar age and outlook. "I hope we can be friends." *Two friends in one day!*

Mrs. Ritter chuckled. "If we're to be friends, you must call me Julia. My best friend, Lily Dunn, is the reason I came to this town. She married a rancher and just had a baby." Julia touched her stomach again. "Our children will be close in age, a miracle for both of us, really. Neither of us thought we'd be married or have children." She radiated happiness.

Constance felt an unexpected stab of envy, which surprised her given her resolve not to think of marriage.

"Their ranch is several hours away, and I usually only get to see Lily on Sundays when the weather is good. And Sundays, as you saw are quite busy. Sometimes, I'm lucky and she drives to town on other days, although less so now that she has Adeline."

Just then the door opened, and a family entered, the three children rushing over to the glass case to stare at the sweets.

"Speaking of busy," Julia said in a low voice.

"I understand." Constance waved her away. "I'm so glad we had a chance to talk."

41

"Come back and visit. Mornings after the rush are good, once the children are in school." With a smile, Julia picked up the chocolate pot and hurried behind the counter.

Constance opened her reticule and took out a small notebook with a battered cover. The journal had traveled to Europe with her, and she'd filled the pages with her experiences, thoughts, and hopes for the future, as well as sketches of architecture and gowns she'd seen or designed. Fittingly, only a few blank pages were left, and today, she could recount her journey to Sweetwater Springs and then start a fresh journal about her new life.

Constance pulled out a pencil and began to write out everything she wanted in an office. As her list grew, so did her sense of trepidation. *I'm about to invest a lot of my savings in this venture. Will this small town have enough customers to support my business?*

Chapter Four

The next day, Constance dressed with care, wanting to look like a prosperous businesswoman in order to persuade Mr. Gordon to rent to her. She'd designed the sage green outfit and several others when she'd returned from Italy, incorporating the latest trends. As she'd sewn the bodice and skirt, she'd imagined a decorative sign on the wall of her new shop—*Fashions in the Latest European Style.*

She placed her hands on her waist, feeling the hardness of the stays under her fingers. Sixteen inches. Not quite as small as a lady's form should be at the coveted span of fourteen. But at least her waist remained under the dreaded twenty-one inches.

Her father had already left for the barn, so she could get ready in the privacy of his room. The evening before, Lucia had insisted on ironing the creases out the outfit, as well as the petticoats that were worn underneath. So far, the young woman remained quiet around Constance, either through shyness or uncertain command of the English language. Hopefully, her reticence would change as she became comfortable.

Constance peered into the age-spotted shaving mirror that hung on the wall above the washbasin. As far as she could tell from looking back and forth in the six inches of glass, she looked presentable. But after she met with Mr. Gordon and returned here, she resolved to unpack some of her belongings, such as the big mirror that belonged over her dressing table.

Her bangs frizzed over her forehead, and the sides of her hair were pulled up in combs and combined with the rest into a French twist. Perched on top was a hat of her own creation—a modified low bowler, saved from looking mannish by the addition of netting wrapped over a ribbon wound around the brim and tied with a bow. The ends trailed over the back and down her neck. Decorative hatpins with green glass beads anchored the hat to her hair.

She glanced out the side window. The day was fine but, she surmised, cold. She decided to wear her velvet half-cloak in an appealing shade of emerald. After one final check in the mirror, Constance left.

Once outside, she walked down the street, holding up her skirt a few inches, so the fringed hem wouldn't trail over the dirt. She carefully avoided the many manure piles, but still, she could feel muck collecting on the bottom of her kidskin boots.

In only a few minutes she arrived at the office building, which looked to be three-stories tall. The smooth façade was made of stone in a pinkish-brown color. Sioux quartzite, she recalled Julia saying—an unusual and attractive material. The shop on the corner had a big plate glass window and, when she slowed to glance inside, appeared empty.

Constance wanted to lean closer and peer through the glass but thought that would look brazen, and she didn't want to chance Mr. Gordon seeing her poking around. Instead, she walked down the wide, dirt alley on the side between the office building and the mercantile and saw several smaller, sashed windows that would let in light and air.

Back in the front, Constance opened one of the large, carved doors that led into a broad hallway and went inside. The hall was lined with paneling, punctuated by four doors leading to shops or offices. Her footsteps echoed on the polished, wooden floors.

The first door on the left had a sign: *Sweetwater Springs Herald*. Her heart beating hard, she turned the knob and entered, inhaling the smell of newspaper and ink. She glanced around.

No one manned the desk near the entrance. A leather bench in front of the window provided seating. Framed newspaper articles protected by glass lined the walls.

Constance followed the sound of tapping and walked across the room to stop in the open doorway of an office, lined with deep shelves that held books, magazines, and newspapers.

A dark-haired man with an interesting, angular face sat at a huge desk, which looked higher than normal. Several piles of paper were stacked near the front corners. He typed away on a typewriter and glanced at notes for reference. Cuff-protectors kept the sleeves of his shirt clean. The jacket of his suit hung on a nearby coatrack.

The sound of her footsteps must have alerted him to her presence, for he looked up.

"Mr. Gordon?"

He rose, becoming the tallest man she'd ever seen, with broad shoulders and a trim waist.

Clothing him must be a challenge.

He pulled off his cuff protectors, reached for his jacket, and shrugged it on. "Forgive me. I hadn't expected a visit from a lady this early."

Constance admired his well-tailored suit and wondered where he'd had the garment made.

Mr. Gordon waved for her to come in with hands that looked the size of dinner plates. He gave her a shrewd look, one eyebrow pulling up into an upside down V, followed by a charming, crooked smile. "Miss Constance Taylor, I presume."

She dipped her chin and chuckled. "Small towns."

He shot her a look of mock offense. "I'd prefer to say it's because of my brilliant deductive reasoning. In spite of the fact that Mack tells everyone you look like your mother, I can see the resemblance to him. And, of course, yesterday I heard about your arrival. My wife and I intended to welcome you after church, but we were caught up in several conversations and never saw you."

"That's because I wasn't there. I was so exhausted from the journey, and there wasn't a comfortable bed...."

"I understand the rigors of travel." He waved for her to take a seat in one of the wooden chairs in front of the desk. "I also intended to interview you for the paper but thought I'd have to seek you out."

"Actually, I'm here to see about renting your retail space. In Chicago, I ran a dressmaking business with my aunt. I intend to open one here."

He sat back in his chair, a big smile on his face. "My wife will be delighted to hear this. She's an indifferent seamstress, and, being the schoolteacher, has little opportunity to make her own clothes. A couple of times, we've traveled to Crenshaw to patronize a dress shop there, or she orders from catalogues. I predict she'll be one of your first customers."

She hoped he wasn't just being polite—that Mrs. Gordon really would commission some outfits. "I look forward to meeting her."

He gave Constance a wistful glance at odds with his angular features. "I don't suppose you'll tailor men's clothing?"

She ran an assessing eye over his apparel. "Perhaps shirts."

"If so, you might just keep me out of trouble with my wife. She says I'm too hard on my shirts and scolds when I get ink on one. I'm supposed to wear an apron when typesetting or picking up freshly printed pages, but I often forget."

The comical face Mr. Gordon made told her the scoldings he'd received couldn't be too severe.

His expression became more serious. "Tell me what you had in mind."

She gestured in the direction of the corner shop. "I noticed you had an empty space across from this office that looked perfect. Is there another room attached that I can use for dressing rooms, storage, and as a workroom? I'd also like to live here, if possible."

He steepled his hands together. "I believe I have just what

you're looking for—two attached rooms on the first floor—one with the front office. Living spaces of several different sizes are located on the third floor. Two single rooms. A one-bedroom space and a two-bedroom space. The floor has two shared bathrooms with a toilet and bathtub. One for women and one for men."

The more he spoke, the more hopeful Constance became, her stomach bubbling with excitement. She clenched her hands on her reticule to keep them still.

Mr. Gordon frowned and tapped the desk. "Would you be comfortable living here alone? At this time, no one else resides in the building. When I have more tenants, it's possible that they all will be male."

She hesitated. Being by herself at night in this big building might be scary at first, but she didn't let her doubts show. "I've never lived alone, but I've traveled extensively by myself."

He nodded. "Would you like to see the space?"

"Please." She rose.

He stood and waved for her to go ahead through the doorway.

At the empty desk in the front office, Mr. Gordon stopped to open a drawer and fish out a ring of keys. Then he led her out of the office, across the hall, and to the opposite door.

The large, carved door matched the one to the newspaper office. He reached up a long arm to tap the lintel. "You'll notice that these doors are higher than usual. I didn't want to stoop in my own building."

"I imagine not. Low doorways must be very tedious for a man of your height."

He grimaced and rubbed his forehead. "Painful, too."

"You wouldn't fare well in Europe. Many of the doors in old buildings are tiny."

"Oh, I know," he said in a wry tone. "I was the foreign correspondent for a New York newspaper, which meant I lived in various parts of Europe, returning home only for short periods of time."

She looked at him with interest, wondering how he'd ended up in a small town in Montana. *If I live and work in this building, no doubt I'll have time to get to know him and his wife and hear their stories.*

Mr. Gordon inserted the key and twisted to open the lock. Then he turned the knob and pushed open the door, stepping back to allow her to precede him into the space. "This room and the one in back are the same size. They each take up half the building from front to back. The two rooms are designed to make one suite or two separate places of business. Both have doors that exit to the hallway, and, if separation is desired, the connecting door can be locked with a key that only I retain."

The big plate glass window in the front and two smaller ones that opened on the side let in plenty of light that shone on polished wooden floors. Two brass electric chandeliers hung from medallions on the ceiling. The wall was paneled to chair-rail height, with white painted plaster extending to the molding on the ceilings. A radiator between the side windows would provide heat on cold days.

Constance glanced around, imagining outfitting the room—the Persian rug she'd lay over the dark floor, the oil paintings she'd bought in Italy that would go on the walls once she had them painted a pale shade of pink that flattered all complexions, the plaster of Paris statue also bought in Italy of a curvy, nude woman that she'd thought would be perfect as a dress mannequin to display a gown in the latest style. She would fashion the brocade from France into curtains and for a nearby bench with matching cushions. A counter would showcase hats. She'd place a rack near the door to hang ready-made shirtwaists and skirts. Here against an interior wall, she'd install a wardrobe that, when opened, would display intimate apparel—corsets, camisoles, drawers, and nightgowns.

Mr. Gordon remained silent, apparently giving her time for her imaginary decorating.

Constance tilted her head toward the door in the back of the room. "May I?"

He made a *go ahead* gesture. "The light switch is on the wall to the right."

The second room, with only the two windows on the side and two in the back, held less light than the front. She flipped on the switch. This room, too, had two chandeliers with electric light, with each bulb shedding an orangy glow. *Not quite as good to work in as the other room, but perhaps, if I put the main sewing machine and a comfortable chair under the windows, I won't strain my eyes.* She gestured from the front room to this one. "I believe these two will work just fine."

Mr. Gordon flashed his appealing, crooked grin. "You haven't even asked me about a price. But before we discuss terms, why don't you inspect the living quarters on the third floor? I'll give a discount if you take both the shop and living space."

They returned to the front room, entered the hall, and went right to reach the stairway in the back.

Mr. Gordon led the way, flicking on the light switches as he went. Instead of chandeliers, the illumination came from plain glass globes. "The second floor is divided into smaller rooms for offices and shops."

On the landing of the third floor, he pointed to the left. "The single bedrooms."

She shook her head. "I want something larger. Why don't you show me the two-bedroom space?"

"Probably the best choice given your occupation. I imagine you'll probably be working at home, and the bigger space has the most light. But first, the ladies' bathroom, which will be for tenants and their customers."

He led the way to the right and stopped at the second-to-last door, took out a key to unlock it, pushed open the door, and stepped aside for her to move past him.

From her home in Chicago, Constance was used to indoor plumbing, which her aunt had added to their house. But on her travels, such facilities had been rare. One of Victoria's stipulations to her husband-to-be before she married was that Count Armodo would add indoor plumbing to his villa.

The room was bigger than she'd expected, with a pedestal sink, toilet, and tub, and the floor was paved with white, hexagonal tiles. Large metal hooks with porcelain knobs on the ends were screwed into molding along the length of the wall. A cabinet ran from the floor to the ceiling. Constance opened the door to see empty shelves.

"My wife thought the female tenants would like to store towels and toiletries here instead of carrying them to and fro." He gestured toward the hooks. "Hang towels and such. I've hired two of the maids from the hotel to come and clean once a week. They alternate days off every other week but wanted to earn extra money. The other days, keeping the space neat will be up to you and the other tenants."

"This is perfect." *Is it selfish to hope that there aren't more female tenants so I don't have to share? Well, maybe one woman,* she amended. *I'd like to have a friend living so close.*

Mr. Gordon stepped back out of the bathroom and tilted his head toward the left where the hall ended in a doorway. He waved in that direction, and then selected a key from the ring and extended the batch. "I'll let you do the honors."

Eagerly, Constance unlocked the door and went inside to a combination living, dining, and kitchen area that was far more spacious than she'd expected, in fact bigger than her father's quarters. A stove, counter and cupboards, and, best of all, an indoor sink had been tucked into the kitchen. On the other side stood a white radiator. The floors, paneling, and electric light fixtures were the same as downstairs.

"There's hot and cold water," Mr. Gordon said from his place near the door. "Radiators in each of the bedrooms."

This is more like what I was used to in Chicago. Constance smiled. "Luxury, indeed."

He grimaced. "We live in a log house on the outskirts of town, with an outdoor privy. Not even a pump in the kitchen.

Sometimes, I'm tempted to move in here, although my wife and nephew—and all our animals—love the cabin, so I wouldn't dare suggest leaving."

She laughed. "What if you built a new house on your property?"

"Just between you and me…I intend to do so. But I'll have to wait until this—" he made a circling motion with his hand to indicate the building "—is rented out."

Constance crossed the room to peer into the first bedroom in the front corner. Although it didn't have a plate glass window, the two in the front and on the side allowed plenty of light. She walked over to look at the street, wondering if this room would be too noisy and she should sleep in the back. *That's a detail I can decide later.*

Excitement and trepidation rushed through her. "I'll take both—the two-room shop and this suite." As Constance made the commitment, she was fully aware she risked her whole life savings. Mannishly, she held out a hand to seal the bargain.

Mr. Gordon smiled and reached out to shake.

Her hand almost disappeared in his large grasp.

Now, I'll have to ensure my dressmaking business succeeds.

Feeling light, as if freed of a burden, Constance walked home. If she weren't a grown-up lady, she would have sashayed down the street, swinging her reticule and singing a happy, albeit off-key, song. But as a staid businesswoman and a newcomer, whom everyone looked curiously at already, she held herself to a sedate stroll, smiling and nodding to passersby.

When she reached the livery, she stopped to look inside the barn to see if her father was there. A glance around showed her the cavernous space was empty of humans, and she continued on to the side of the building and into the office space.

Her father sat at the table, bent over a piece of paper, sketching lines on it. He looked up and grinned. "There you are, Connie girl." He stood and walked around the table, waving the paper. "I have something to show you." He jerked his head toward the inner rooms. "Follow me."

He led her toward the bedroom, moving as fast as his limping gait would allow. Once inside, he stopped at the corner of his bed. He held up the paper and tapped the drawing, then laid a palm on the side wall. "If we partition off this space and make a hallway, we can add a bedroom for you at the back. Bigger than this one, what with you having all those female clothes and such." He lowered his arm.

The way her father beamed at her with such openness and love made her heart sink. Constance reached to take his hand. "Papa, I've just rented a shop in Mr. Gordon's building for my dressmaking business."

"Eh?" With a sheepish expression, he glanced around the room. "Guess that's good. Ain't room to do it here."

"I'll have plenty of space."

"Sure you got the money for that, Connie girl?"

"I sold the house, remember?"

"Still…." His brow creased.

She inhaled as deep a breath as her corset would allow, which wasn't much. "There's more, Papa. I've also taken a suite of rooms to live in—in the same building."

The expression of hurt on his face made her throat tight.

"Why?"

Feeling a chill in her chest, Constance guided him toward the side of the bed. She perched on the edge and tugged for him to sit next to her. "I suppose I should have informed you in more detail about my plans so my news didn't come as such a shock."

"You can't do that, Connie. Live all alone. Ain't right for a young lady to do so."

"Papa," she said in a gentle tone. "I've been on my own for a long time. I'm used to taking care of myself."

His eyes sad, he swallowed audibly. "Guess that's my fault, not keeping you with me when your ma died."

Now wasn't the time Constance would have chosen to have this conversation, but she supposed it was inevitable considering the topic. "I wouldn't say *fault*. I'm proud of my independence." Constance took a deep breath, deciding to be honest. "I'll tell you of my thoughts, if you'd like."

"Go ahead."

As gently as she could, Constance said, "I would have been a totally different woman if I'd have stayed with you. I'm not passing judgment on *that* Constance." She pulled a wry smile. "*Connie*, probably. I will say that Mama's death was devastating, but even worse...."

"Sending you away?"

She nodded, pausing just a second, knowing this was a talk that would cause pain. "Aunt Hannah was a stranger. Yes, I grew to love her, but she wasn't the papa I adored—the one who, who...."

"Say what you need to, child. I can take it."

"All right." Constance took a breath. "You *abandoned* me. You broke my heart. That *choice* was even worse than Mama passing away. She couldn't help dying."

He shifted, "Well now—"

Constance held up a hand to stop him. "I understand that you felt you were doing what was best. You certainly told me so enough times. Now, I can look back and agree with your decision."

He let out a slow sigh as if relieved. "You agree?"

"But, Papa...." She took another breath and decided to give him the blunt truth. "That choice—living with Aunt Hannah—made me into the woman I am today. One who *loves* you but isn't *close* to you. One who's used to—" she released his hand and extended both arms "—different surroundings. One who owns her business instead of relying on a husband's income."

His eyes held grief. The lines seemed to deepen on his face.

Seeing him hurting, made her heart ache. Constance glanced in the direction of the barn and back to him, grasping for a little levity. "One who knows *dresses* and not *horses.*"

The last comparison made him smile, although the sadness lingered in his eyes. He squeezed her hand. "I'm darn proud of you, Connie girl."

His words warmed her. "Thank you, Papa."

"Still don't like it, though."

She laughed. "I doubt any father likes his daughter leaving home."

"Do you suppose…?" He hesitated, swallowing audibly again. "That you can come to forgive me? Eventually…we can be close?"

Constance thought a moment, wondering if she could give him the truth or a polite fiction, and decided to continue as she'd begun. "I'm not purposely *withholding* forgiveness." She smiled. "But I promise to work on it."

"Thank you." He leaned to press a kiss to her forehead.

Her eyes grew misty. "As for closeness…I think we've just made a good start."

"Well, then…it's time for you to get back on a horse." Her father let out a cackle, patted her knee, rose, and tottered from the bedroom. "I'll pick you out a good one."

Openmouthed, she stared after him. *I don't even have a riding habit.*

Chapter Five

A week after he'd given notice to Sir Henry Vail, Angus relaxed in the parlor with his parents in the family home in Edinburgh. Outside, a thunderstorm pounded rain against the windows. For once, the house was quiet, with none of his brothers or their wives or offspring buzzing around.

This substantial manor wasn't the home Angus had grown up in. Three years ago, as his brothers acquired wives and children, his parents had bought a larger place to accommodate their rapidly expanding family.

Two brothers lived at home with their spouses and babies. The rest were in and out, and various grandchildren often spent one or more nights. Since Angus had arrived, the place was even fuller to overflowing, for his family wanted to spend as much time with him as possible before, as one of his sisters-in-law said dramatically, *losing you forever*.

Angus sat across from his parents, ensconced in their comfortable chairs on one side of the fireplace, a small table between them. Light from a three-globed lamp cast a fine glow on the tableau. The room was big enough to accommodate several settees and wing chairs so all the adults in the family could find seating.

Peat burned in the fireplace. After the coal fires of London, the smoke smelled of Scotland and of home. His father preferred using peat to coal, mostly because he disapproved of mining conditions and wanted to support the men who plied the ancient tradition of cutting the peat from bogs.

Children weren't allowed in the formal parlor. They stayed in the capacious attic nursery, but it wasn't unusual for one or more to sneak down and hide until caught and banished.

His mother knitted, her gaze on her handwork. She'd put on some weight in the year he'd been away, making her pleasantly plump, and the majority of her auburn hair had grayed. She was always making stockings for her husband, sons, and grandchildren and had determined to send him to America with ten pairs for himself as well as ones for his oldest brother Fergus and his baby nephew Craig in Sweetwater Springs. In addition, she was sending scarves, caps, and mittens. At the rate she was going, Angus might not have room in his trunk for his other clothes.

His father was a thin man with a growing potbelly. His gray muttonchop whiskers filled out his narrow face.

Now, he settled his hands on his belly. "I'm not sure if ye know this, but we've sent each of yer brothers into the world with five hundred pounds. We didn't gift ye with the funds when ye graduated and went to London, because I had a feeling ye'd give away all the money to yer indigent clients. I certainly would have done so in yer place."

Angus gave his father a wry smile. "There's nae doubt about that." The majority of the annual fifty pounds from his parents, as well as his small salary, had found its way into needy hands, usually in the form of medicine or money for food.

"We knew ye'd eventually be joining your brother in Montana and wanted ye to have the money to invest in a home and the practice." He leaned forward and handed over a small brown pouch, probably crocheted by his grandmother who loved to make the little bags. "We wish ye all the best, my boy."

Angus took the pouch. "Thank ye. Such a gift is very generous."

His mother let out a sob and then pressed her lips together into a determined line.

He knew she hated the idea of him going to America. But, to her credit, she hadn't tried to talk him out of emigrating, although royal battles occurred between his parents and oldest brother before Fergus left. He supposed his parents were resigned, given that he'd openly spoken of this plan for the last four years.

His mother took several sharp breaths through flaring nostrils before speaking. "We have a surprise for ye. A photographer will be here this afternoon. We want a photograph of the whole family. We didn't do that before Fergus left, and I've always regretted that omission."

His father nodded. "Ye'll have one for yerself, of course, and ye can take one to Fergus."

Angus couldn't imagine some of his younger nieces and nephews standing still for the time needed for a photograph to be taken. They seemed to be a wiggly bunch, although he'd seen them act decorous enough in church. "That will be a fine remembrance, and a gift that I'm sure will bring Fergus great pleasure."

His mother pointed her needles his way. "You tell Fergus that in return I want a photograph of him with his wife Alice and the baby." She sniffed. "Craig is over a year old now. Bad enough I'll never set eyes on my grandson, but at least I want to know what that baby looks like." She gave a decisive nod, although her eyes were wet, and she clicked away on her knitting.

His father reached over and patted her arm, a rare gesture of affection from a reserved man, who, nevertheless, deeply loved his family. He returned his attention to Angus. "When ye marry and have a child, we'll want a photograph from ye."

He couldn't imagine himself with a wife, much less a baby. As he had in London, Angus would have more than enough responsibility with his patients. But he could hardly say so to a man who was a physician and the patriarch of a huge brood. "I see no problem with making that promise," he said carefully. "Provided a photographer can be found in a small town in the wilds of America."

His father fingered the unlit pipe resting on a rack on the side table. "I'll send along my latest medical journals. Who knows what sort of ancient medicine yer brother practices?"

Angus held in a laugh and raised an eyebrow. "Considering Fergus attended Edinburgh University's medical college—" he stated the obvious "—the *same* one as ye did *forty* years ago, ye have no call to use the word *ancient*."

His father harrumphed. "I've kept up to date with the latest research."

Remembering all the discussions they'd had when Angus attended medical school at Edinburgh University, he directed a warm smile at his father. His insight and additions to the lectures of his professors had been invaluable and had enabled Angus to graduate at the top of his class, thus earning him Sir Henry Vail's attention. Referring again to his elder brother, he said, "I know for a fact that the letters ye and Fergus exchange are far more about medicine than his life in Sweetwater Springs."

"Thank goodness for Alice's correspondence," his mother interjected. "Else, I'd barely know anything about yer brother and his family." She lowered the knitting to her lap and shook her finger at him. "Since ye don't have a wife, I expect yer letters to be *newsy*. Medical information and questions are fine, provided you tell us about yer life. I don't want to worry about my youngest son, my baby."

Angus refrained from rolling his eyes. "After reaching the quarter of a century mark, I'm hardly a babe. With sixteen grandchildren, I think it's safe to say ye have plenty of other wee bairns to keep your attention."

She just shook her head. "Grandchildren, special as they are, are not the same as one's own."

No matter how old or experienced, I'll always be the baby in my family's eyes. Hopefully, Fergus would see him as a man and a doctor instead of his baby brother.

But what if he doesn't?

What if I leave everything here only to be viewed as less competent because of my place in the family?

Angus shook his head, stopping the thought. The feelings of futility caused by his work in London must be influencing other aspects of his life. He couldn't, *wouldn't*, allow that.

Good, bad, or some combination of the two, the future will be what I make of it!

As the train approached Sweetwater Springs, Angus turned his thoughts toward his future—something he'd deliberately avoided on the voyage. Instead, he'd decided to also make the crossing into a symbolic journey. More than movement from one country to the other, the trip was also the leaving behind of the old— hopefully, a form of mental purging and healing. Therefore, on the ship, he'd spent long hours at the rail, or if the weather was cold, in a deck chair wrapped in a blanket, staring out at the vast ocean and allowing his mind to drift.

Once he'd reached America, Angus had been astounded by the vigor of the young country. He'd spent the westward train trip observing with a scientist's eye his fellow travelers and the inhabitants of the cities and towns the train stopped in, as well as the folk he spotted from the window. The optimism and energy he sensed in most of the people felt so different from the downtrodden hopelessness of the East End slums.

Americans—whether new to the country, or with roots going back generations—seemed to believe in the endless possibilities of a better future for themselves and their families and were willing to take risks to make their dreams happen. He needed more observation to be sure, but he hypothesized that the lack of a class system—at least one as entrenched as in Great Britain— might have much to do with the differences. The other aspect was the vastness of the country and the availability of free land.

He overheard plenty of conversations between travelers going west to claim acreage.

In spite of his attempts to purge himself of the poison that had seeped into his system from the time in London, Angus still felt as heavy and dour as when he'd left Scotland and wondered if his outlook would ever change…if it was even possible to change.

The portly conductor entered the swaying train car and paused by his seat. "Your stop, Dr. Cameron."

Yesterday, Angus had given the man some horehound cough drops when he'd heard the hoarseness in his voice.

The conductor smiled and held up a finger. "Right about now." He brought his hand down as if cuing an orchestra.

As if so directed, the train slowed, brakes hissing.

Eyes twinkling, the man smiled and nodded. "Your cough drops helped tremendously, sir. You have my thanks."

Before Angus could respond, the man continued on, raising his voice and calling out, "Sweetwater Springs!"

Angus gathered his doctor's bag, which he'd stuffed to the gills with instruments and medicine. His new leather satchel, a going-away gift from his five other brothers, held medicinal herbs and the *carragheen* moss requested by Fergus, as well as the gift of the photograph of his family and his dirty linen, rolled into any available space. A trunk with bottles of medicine carefully wrapped in his clothing and other possessions and a crate with his books, medical journals, and instruments rode in the baggage car.

The train jerked to a stop. Peering through the window, Angus saw a group of people waiting on the platform.

A dark-haired woman in a flowered straw hat waved at someone in the car ahead of him. Angus noted with approval her neat blue dress—simple lines, few frills, with the more natural waist that came from a loose corset or maybe none at all. From what he'd seen in the small towns where the train had stopped, the majority of the women in the American West dressed sensibly. He thought back to the debutantes at Anastasia Vail's ball. *I'm glad to be done with silly females parading about in unhealthy clothing.*

He took his gaze from the woman to sweep the rest of the people and recognized Fergus right away. His brother had written that he wouldn't wear a hat so his red hair would be a recognizable beacon.

Fergus spied him, grinned, and vigorously waved. Apparently casting aside professional dignity, he ran a few steps to the exit.

Shocked and invigorated by his brother's antics, Angus stood, grabbed his doctor's bag and satchel, and hurried up the aisle. In his haste, he almost leapt down the steps to the wooden platform.

His grin still evident, Fergus extended his arms wide. "*Bràthair,*" he said warmly. "There ye are at last!"

Is he going to hug me? Their undemonstrative family didn't embrace. Not even when Angus had left home had his parents or siblings hugged him in farewell. *At least, he called me brother and not little brother.*

Fergus threw his arms around Angus's shoulders and slapped his back, beaming like a madman all the while. His brother's teeth were more crooked than Angus's, but he hadn't lost any in the intervening years.

Angus stood stiffly, grateful his hands were full with his baggage and he was unable to respond in kind. Once past the age of eight or so, he'd never hugged any adult in his life.

Fergus didn't seem to notice his reticence. Stepping back and studying Angus's face, he clapped him on his shoulder, obvious emotion in his blue eyes. "Welcome, brother."

A wave of something Angus couldn't name blurred his vision. He cleared his throat. "Good to be here."

"Took your time about it." Fergus waved to the street. "Alice is home with the baby, who's napping. She wanted to be here, but Craig wouldn't cooperate."

"Young bairns do tend to be that way." Uncomfortable with standing so close, he stepped back.

"Aye. But he's our greatest blessing." Fergus's smile held

wonder. "Our miracle after a long time o' waiting."

Fergus had married Alice, another immigrant from Scotland, whom he'd met in America, almost twelve years ago. Craig was their first baby, or the first Angus knew of. Alice could have miscarried one or more fetuses or had a stillborn child. His mind flashed back on Maeve's infant, and then to his own baby brother, and he fervently hoped Fergus and Alice hadn't experienced such pain.

His brother ran a hand through his auburn hair, making it stand on end. Lines around his eyes and mouth and some gray sprinkled in his sideburns bespoke his age. Fergus had on the black frock coat typical of doctors, although not as new as the one Angus wore under his duster. Fergus's pockets bulged as if they contained more than just a handkerchief and some money, as Angus's did.

Angus glanced down the platform. His trunk and crate had already been unloaded.

Fergus followed his gaze. "Those both yours? I have the surrey, and I can take the crate in the back seat, but not both. I'll send Naom Krutsky, my hired man, back for your trunk."

Angus glanced around, seeing the platform was empty of people. "Are there no porters?"

"Nae," his brother said in a cheerful tone. "But you're traveling light."

"Light? I'd hardly call a trunk and a crate containing all my worldly possessions *light.*"

Fergus laughed. "Our last newcomer, Miss Constance Taylor of Chicago, arrived with a total of ten trunks and crates."

Angus couldn't imagine traveling with so many unnecessary possessions. *One of those fashionable women,* he presumed, *with too many frivolous articles of apparel, probably unhealthy ones, to boot. Here I just thought I was done with them.*

They walked over to the luggage. Fergus extended a hand for the satchel.

Angus gave him the satchel and leaned to pick up the handle

on one end of the crate that he'd fashioned by nailing a leather strap on the short side. Fergus took the other. Together, they carried the crate to a black surrey parked near the steps to the street and heaved it into the back seat.

Fergus set the satchel on the floor next to his battered doctor's bag. He touched the worn leather. "I don't drive anywhere without this. Never know when I'll need the tools of our trade." He straightened and patted the wood of the crate. "We don't need to tie this down. The house is just down the street, and we'll go at a slow pace."

Angus deposited his own bag on the floor next to the satchel. His looked far newer than Fergus's, although the leather had already garnered a few scratches.

His brother motioned Angus to walk with him to the horse. *A Morgan*, Angus had written when he'd first bought the gelding. An American breed that his brother had taken half a page to describe.

At the Morgan's head, Fergus said, "This is Cookie. He's as strong and true as a doctor's horse should be. Many a night, in any weather, he's seen me home, with me almost asleep at the reins." He patted the tight arch of the gelding's neck and frowned. "We'll need a second horse and equipage for you. When we have a chance, we'll drive out to see what horses Nick Sanders has available. He usually has a good selection of well-trained horses." He climbed into the surrey.

"I did the same in London—shadowed the other doctors for a few weeks." *What a shock that experience was.* Angus went around to the other side and settled on the worn leather cushions of the seat.

As Fergus drove down the street, keeping the horse to a walk, he made a running commentary of the buildings and the people they passed, and his accent sounded more American than Scottish. "Our town banker, Caleb Livingston, built that hotel," he said about a large, four-story building with a polished stone façade. "There's a restaurant inside that Alice likes to frequent."

Angus glanced at his brother surprised he'd spend money when they could eat more frugally at home.

Fergus caught the look. "Until recently, we had no household help. What with acting as my nurse, all the housekeeping, the garden, and now the baby, Alice has her hands more than full. When she was pregnant, I didn't want her to work so hard and risk the baby, so we came here often. Now, we have the Krutskys. Hildie cooks and cleans. Noem sees to the garden, the horse, and any repairs needed about the place."

Angus made a noncommittal sound.

His brother nodded to the right at a brick building with a big glass window. "The mercantile. The Cobbs are the proprietors. Not a very pleasant couple but respectful to Alice and me. You being a doctor, they'll be polite and, at times, even obsequious."

Angus made a note to visit the mercantile as seldom as possible. He had no patience for people who toadied to those with a higher rank, wealth, or profession.

"Yon's a right chancer," Fergus said, frowning at a skinny man dismounting from a horse tied up in front of a green painted building with *Hardy's Saloon* on the sign.

"How so?"

"Cornelius Edson still owes me for the two times I treated him for a toothache. I'm told the Cobbs refused him credit at the mercantile because he hasn't paid them for months, and even Hardy's doesn't serve him ana'more with out cold cash. The next time Cornelius comes to me, I won't pull the tooth until he at least makes a partial payment, and so I told him. Be warned. That *sleekit* might try finagling his way with you because he knows I'm on to him."

"What if he has a serious injury or illness?"

Fergus shrugged. "Then we treat him and count it as a service to the Good Lord." He nodded to a stocky man with bushy, rust-colored hair, carrying what looked like a wooden bread bin under one arm. "There's Phineas O'Reilly, a carpenter and cabinet maker. He also builds coffins and unfortunately has more business that I'd like him to have."

Angus could understand that feeling.

"Mr. O'Reilly had pneumonia this winter, and I feared I'd lose him. But he has a strong constitution and pulled through. Still has a lingering cough, though."

Angus felt excitement rise. *Here's my first opportunity to be of service and show my brother I have skills to bring to his practice.* "I have a syrup that might aid him, horehound and honey, with some drops of oregano oil and eucalyptus oil from Australia added." He gave an anxious thought to the precious bottles of the eucalyptus oil he'd brought with him. *An export from Australia to Great Brittan is expensive enough. But to Montana? Probably prohibitive.*

"How did you come up with that concoction? Horehound syrup and honey is familiar, of course. But the rest?"

"A lecture at the university. Our instructor challenged us to list herbs and such that may help common ailments. Among the students was an Italian chap who suggested oregano oil—nasty stuff—and a fellow from Australia who contributed eucalyptus oil, also nasty."

"Ah, if only a way could be found to combine the healing knowledge that's known throughout the world."

They passed a white, clapboard church with a bell in the steeple. Fergus tipped his head in that direction. "I believe I wrote you when Reverend Joshua Norton joined his father as a minister. They seem to have a good working relationship, and I hope we can do as well as they do."

Perhaps, he's as anxious about our partnership as I am. "There are some similarities to the profession," Angus said wryly. "Being summoned for emergency situations at all hours is one."

"Dealing with peoples' emotional needs, which sometimes impacts their physical condition, is another."

The two exchanged smiles of understanding, and hope rose in Angus that they could make this a true partnership.

"Having two Reverend Nortons can be confusing, and I

expect two Dr. Camerons will be likewise. To distinguish between the two ministers, we have the elder Reverend Norton, and the younger is addressed as Reverend Joshua. I suspect that will work the same for us. I'm Dr. Cameron or Doc, and you'll be Dr. Angus or Doc Angus." He raised his brows and, with an apparent anxious expression, waited for Angus's reaction.

"As long as I'm Dr. *something*, either name will be fine."

Fergus shook his head, an expression of mock mournfulness on his face. "Sorry to disappoint ye, laddie," he drawled in a heavy brogue. "I doubt ana' one will be calling ye Dr. *Something*."

Angus chuckled. "Aye."

Fergus pointed with his chin to a couple in shabby clothes walking by. The man held a baby, and the woman carried a basket and clutched the hand of a blonde girl who looked about three. One slightly older walked on her older side. "The Swensens. She recently had her first boy after seven girls. That baby is healthy and so spoiled from all the attention of his parents and sisters. The family is as poor as church mice yet rich in love."

A fashionably dressed woman carrying a parasol strolled in their direction. She wore a green outfit that was probably full of toxic vapors and a matching straw sailor hat tilted forward over her face. The blonde was so tightly corseted she looked as if she could easily be cut in two. As she grew closer, he could see the beauty had emerald eyes and was about his age or a few years younger. She sent a polite smile toward his brother, and then a flirtatious one in Angus's direction.

"There's the newcomer I told you about," Fergus commented. "Miss Taylor is about to open a dressmaking shop."

In that moment, what calmness Angus had acquired on the sea journey vanished as if the state of mind had never existed. His chest clenched as if he was the one wearing a corset around his upper body.

That woman is perpetuating all that is unhealthy in female apparel. Angus crossed his arms over his chest and scowled at Miss Taylor.

She stumbled and lost her smile.

Fergus pulled up the surrey next to the woman. "Miss Taylor. I want you to meet my brother, Dr. Angus Cameron. Dr. Angus, this is Miss Taylor. She's come from Chicago to live with her father who owns the livery."

A woman so beautiful doesn't need outrageous fashions. She does just as well without them. Angus sent a pointed glance of disapproval at her tiny waist, which he had no doubt he could span with his hands. "Miss Taylor." He begrudged the introduction. The woman stirred his temper and, too *loused* from his journey, he couldn't find enough patience to overcome his annoyance and act with politeness.

Fergus glanced over at him and frowned. "You'll have to forget Angus's surly manners." His brogue thickened. "He's newly come from Scotland, and right *nahcred*. I'm sure ye remember well the feeling."

She gave Fergus a puzzled glance. "*Nahcred?*"

"Tired," Angus said in a clipped tone. He glared at Fergus. "Alice is awaitin' us. We'd best be off." He nodded goodbye to the woman but couldn't muster up a smile.

With a lift of her chin and flick of her head, Miss Taylor huffed off.

"Good day, Miss Taylor," Fergus called after her and flicked the reins, and Cookie started up.

Once out of earshot, Angus couldn't contain his ire. He jerked a thumb in the woman's direction. "Doesn't that fashion bother you?" He burst out. "Surely, Alice doesn't wear such tight corsets?"

"She did when I first met her," Fergus said in a matter-of-fact tone. "Alice took pride that I could span her waist with my hands. We didn't have a discussion on the evils of corsets until after we were married and she was about to order a new gown."

"How did she react?"

"Annoyed at first because she thought I was being difficult and husbandly." He grinned. "Which I was, to be sure. But she's a sensible woman, my wife. Once Alice understood how a corset compresses the bones of the waist and causes damage to the internal organs, she accepted my point of view. She still wears a corset but tied very loosely."

Angus jerked his thumb in the direction behind them. "Have ye spoken to Miss Taylor? If that's how she dresses, then I can only imagine the apparel she'll encourage other women to wear. She's dangerous."

Fergus pressed his lips together, as if holding in a smile. Then he took a breath. "As I said, Miss Taylor is recently come to Sweetwater Springs. I've only been introduced to her after church, although Alice intends to patronize her shop as soon as it opens, which I believe is in a few days." He glanced away to nod at a man riding by.

Angus waited impatiently, feeling a sharp need to make his brother understand his concern.

"As for changing her mind...." Fergus slanted Angus an amused glance. "Harder to do, now that you've been rude to her."

Knowing he was in the wrong, Angus remained quiet, his hands fisting on his lap.

"I'd decided to wait and leave that discussion in the hands of my brother." Fergus's brogue thickened again. "I assumed, she'd be more open to hearing the information from a man close to her age, just come from Europe, and thus more knowledgeable about the latest fashions than an old fuddy-duddy like me."

Fergus and Angus had fifteen years between them. But he was hardly *old*. "I don't know anything about the latest fashions."

"Ye kent more than me." The brogue was back.

Angus rolled his eyes and then stopped before he could be caught acting like a younger brother.

Fergus raised one eyebrow. "Shall we consider Miss Taylor your first case in America?" he asked in a challenging tone. "Of course, ye'll have to make up for your rude start."

"That woman's not ill. In fact, she appears quite...." *Beautiful.* "Healthy."

"If she does na' change her ways, she may soon become ill."

"True." He didn't like the thought of Miss Taylor making herself sick because of wearing her silly outfits and decided he'd would do all in his power to prevent her continuing down that path. *Fergus has a valid point. I'd be the better presenter of this information.*

He'd meet with Miss Taylor, logically lay out all the facts, and give her one of the pamphlets he'd brought from the Rational Dress Society. *Surely, Miss Taylor will see the wisdom of taking my advice?*

The tightness in his chest eased. *No doubt, she'll even thank me.* He let out a long, slow breath, feeling the sharpness of his anger soften.

Angus whiled away the rest of the drive with thoughts of the ways Miss Taylor might express appreciation for saving her life. Just as his imagination had worked up to her placing a hand on his shoulder and stretching up to kiss him, Fergus pulled the horse to a stop.

Abruptly recalled to reality, Angus felt heat rise in his neck at the improper direction his thoughts had taken him—to a woman he'd barely met. Pushing aside thoughts of Constance Taylor, he glanced at the Camerons' two-story house surrounded by a white picket fence covered in rose bushes. A lilac bloomed in one corner. A breeze wafted the fragrance in their direction—a welcome change from the manure smell of the street.

"The office is around back." Fergus tied off the reins. "I've recently added a stable with living quarters above so the Krutskys can live there. I wrote that information to our parents, but I don't think I included it in any of my correspondence to you."

Angus chuckled. "Far easier for the family in Scotland. We just had to write to you. You and Alice have far more people to correspond with."

Fergus laughed. "I mostly didn't bother with the boys. I knew our parents would share the news."

Angus couldn't imagine calling his older brothers "boys." He threw Fergus a sideways glance. He'd been young when his eldest brother had left for America, but from what he remembered, Fergus's personality was more staid. *Has he changed, or am I remembering him wrong?* He thought of the embrace at the train station. *He's changed. Been Americanized.*

Angus couldn't help wondering if a transformation would happen to him and what form those changes would take.

Fergus turned the horse into a wide dirt drive along the left side of the house and reined in near the front of the stables. The area had enough space for several vehicles, as well as a hitching rail near a horse trough with a pump. He set the brake and tied off the reins before stepping down.

A heavyset man with a belly came out of the stables and walked toward them.

Angus moved around the front of the horse to his brother's side.

"Ah, Noem. Here's my brother, Dr. Angus Cameron, come to join us."

The man pushed dark curly hair out of his eyes and bowed his head. "Welcome, Doctor."

Fergus gestured toward the house. "I'll take you in through the office entrance. I'm sure you'd like to see everything. But first, you must meet Alice."

"Of course."

They walked up a brick pathway. Fergus opened one of the white double doors with *Doctor's Office* painted in black and ushered Angus inside.

Compared to the bright outdoors, the interior was dim, but he could make out a wide hallway with cushioned benches running along each side.

"The waiting area." Fergus waved to a doorway on the right. "My office." He walked so quickly Angus only had time to glimpse two high, narrow beds. On the left was the kitchen, where a plump woman with dark hair stood at the sink washing dishes. Not Alice, apparently, because Fergus didn't stop.

They emerged into a parlor, where the woman who must be his sister-in-law sat in a comfortable rocking chair, her son in her arms.

Craig stood on her lap, bouncing. He reached for her hair.

With a laugh, she moved her head to evade him.

Alice was just as Fergus had described in his letters. Her curly hair was pulled back into a haphazard bun; wisps escaped the pins.

She looked up as they entered and gave Angus a warm smile. She rose, shifting the baby to one arm, before moving around a green velvet settee to meet them. "Angus, my dear. I feel as though I already know you." She placed a hand on his shoulder and gave him a kiss. "I can tell you two are brothers.

Angus wondered if he was supposed to kiss her back. As with hugs, their family didn't exchange kisses, and he wondered if Alice was the source of Fergus's demonstrative nature. Like his brother, her accent sounded slight, although he suspected it would come and go in the same way.

His brother took the boy from his wife and placed him into Angus's arms. "Uncle Angus, meet wee Craig Isaac Cameron."

The bairn stared up at him with the blue eyes of all the Cameron brothers and most of their offspring. His wispy hair shaded somewhere between Alice's sandy color and Fergus's auburn.

Angus smiled at his nephew—number ten in the batch of male offspring among his brothers—and held him in the air.

The boy gurgled a smile.

"Aw, he's a wee *brammer*, so he is. A bonnie laddie."

Alice beamed at his praise.

"Yer Craig has much the look of his cousins." A sad thought whispered through Angus's mind. *I'll never see my nieces and nephews again.* Now, he felt the loss ever more keenly. He lowered the boy and brought him close for a hug.

Angus glanced up to see the same pain in Fergus's eyes. He could only suspect how difficult it must be for his brother and

Alice, knowing their families back home would never see their miracle child.

Craig's face screwed up in the prelude to crying.

Wise in the way of babies, Angus hastily handed the boy back to his mother.

Alice jiggled him. "There, there, sweet laddie," she soothed.

The baby settled.

"Ah! I've a gift for you from our parents." Angus walked over to his satchel, opened it, took out the package, and handed the parcel to his brother.

Fergus unwrapped the brown paper to expose the family photograph in a silver frame. His mother had ordered a large size so everyone's face would clearly show. As he studied the photograph, his eyes grew damp.

Watching him made Angus's throat tighten again. *I never expected this reunion to be so fraught with emotions.*

Alice moved to stand at her husband's shoulder.

Fergus held up the photograph so she could see.

Smiling, she glanced at the portrait and then looked up at Angus. "Next to yourself, you couldn't have brought a more welcome gift. Can you recognize everyone, Fergus?"

Fergus tilted his head, keeping his gaze on the photograph. "I didn't think so at first, but now I see everyone is arranged in family groupings, so I believe I can figure out who's who."

"Mama's doing." Angus stepped to Fergus's other side. "She wrote the names on the back, as well as everyone's ages."

"That's helpful. But let me guess." Fergus's eyebrows scrunched together, and he held out the photograph so both Angus and Alice could see. Then he tapped each face and said a name.

To Angus's surprise, his brother got everyone right. Better than Angus had when he'd returned home from London to see the wee ones in reality. Too many redheaded, blue-eyed bairns—most with similar features. Of course, having them positioned in family groupings helped Fergus guess.

"Just so ye know, Mama is set on having a photograph of baby Craig with ye both. I'm charged with telling ye so."

Alice smiled. "I'd love to have one, too."

"The next time a photographer comes to town," Fergus promised.

Craig made a fussing sound.

Alice rocked him. "Someone's hungry. I'll go feed the baby and leave you two to talk. Dinner will be ready in about half an hour. After, I'm sure you'd like a bath," she said to Angus.

"Not just like, *need*. I've been making do with only washbasins for far too long."

She laughed and pointed with her chin to a hallway on the other side of the room. "You'll find the bathroom there. Fresh towels are already laid out. Your bedroom is upstairs. The one on the right of the landing."

He nodded. "Thank you."

Fergus sank into a brown wingchair. "You're looking good, Angus. Mama's last letter had you thin and drawn." He hesitated. "And heartsick."

Angus dropped into a neighboring wingchair. "I dinna' change anything," he said his tone gruff with remembered pain.

Fergus raised an eyebrow. "You mean you didn't change the social conditions of the East End, laddie. But I have na' doubt you impacted lives."

Remembering his concerns about Fergus taking him seriously, Angus pushed to his feet. "Don't call me *laddie*." The reprimand came out more sharply than he'd intended, and he softened his tone, "I'm sorry." He paced to a window and looked at the street with unseeing eyes, before walking back to lower himself into the chair. "It's just that I'm a *doctor*, not a *lad*."

Instead of looking offended, his brother grinned. "Just yesterday, I called old man Macalister—who must be ninety, if he's a day—a *lad*. It's more about sentiment, Angus, as well you know, rather than age."

Angus ran a hand through his hair, feeling sheepish. "Aye."

"And well I know you're a doctor, lad. As frustrated as I've been by you delaying in joining me when I could have used your help, I've been full of pride in your work."

Fergus might as well have shot a cannonball at him, for the impact of his words felt just as powerful and might have knocked Angus off his feet if he'd been standing. In their family, indeed with most of the families he knew, compliments were as scarce as hens' teeth. Even his father had never spoken of his pride in Angus.

"I do na' think I could have done what ye did," Fergus said in a gentle voice, fisting his hand and tapping his chest with his knuckles. "Labor in such hopeless conditions. Doing so would have torn my heart out."

Angus had to face away from his brother and swallow a sudden lump clogging his throat. He took several calming breaths to regain his composure, turned back to Fergus, and cleared his throat. "Thank you."

Angus knew he should say more. He certainly *felt* more. But he didn't have words for his emotions or an ease in conversing about his inner thoughts and feelings. He leaned his head back against the chair, suddenly exhausted and feeling all at sea. *Ironic, really*. When he'd actually been at sea, he'd felt emotionally on solid ground. And now…. *All this change is just too much.*

I need focus. Work.

Well, Fergus has given me an assignment—educating Miss Constance Taylor.

Chapter Six

Constance walked on past the buggy, fuming. She'd recognized Dr. Cameron and knew the other man must be his brother, also a doctor, and newly come to town. Unlike her, the man had sent an announcement of his arrival several weeks in advance. The whole town was abuzz with anticipation of meeting him and speculating what he'd be like or, in the case of the unmarried ladies, *looked* like.

As was I. Even if she wasn't interested in matrimony, still, a doctor, hopefully a *handsome* doctor, held potential for flirtation, an art she'd mastered in Italy, where all the men, no matter their age, seemed imbued with charm and an appreciation for females—especially blondes. After all, a lady liked to enjoy a gentleman's company on a stroll, at dinner, or a ball.

Because of the scowl Dr. Angus Cameron directed her way *for no reason*, Constance took the man in immediate dislike. *No possibilities of flirtation there.* She couldn't help feeling disappointed, given that she hadn't yet seen any options for flirtatious banter in Sweetwater Springs, even though there were available men aplenty.

Well, Papa assures me there are still many suitors I haven't met. Her father hadn't given up his insistence that she'd want to marry and seemed to encourage any half-personable man—at least in his eyes—to, as he put it, *come a courtin'.* Thus, Constance was

75

constantly fending off advances from men she wouldn't dream of seeing socially.

Lately, she had serious thoughts about acquiring a faux fiancé, if a potential candidate presented himself, to keep all the rest of them away. She'd actually toyed with the idea of Angus Cameron being a possibility. His brother and sister-in-law were kind people, and she thought he'd be as well. A man of medicine had certainly been educated in the classics, too. But he'd been extremely rude.

Never! In fact, I'll not even talk to the man, much less flirt with him.

Constance lifted her chin to a haughty degree. *His loss.*

At a clipped pace, her heels tapping sharply on the Sioux quartzite bricks, she turned into the path leading to the door of the hotel, where she planned to take tea with Felicity. The two friends had fallen into a routine of meeting every few days on Felicity's break, although only for the half hour allowed her. Better a short visit than not seeing her friend at all—unless the day was like today, when Constance had so much to discuss.

As she approached the double doors, she slowed to catch her breath, wishing her corset gave her room to breathe. It wouldn't do to enter the lobby flushed faced and panting.

Since her arrival Constance had worn her corset as tight as possible in order to present a fashionable appearance—so important for her business. Truth be told, she preferred the practical clothing she'd worn while traveling—so less restrictive. Even in Chicago, she'd worn looser tea dresses when at home, which was where she'd spent most of her time. *I was spoiled with living and working in a big house and having a beautiful, lush garden.*

Perhaps when the business is secure, I can dress more comfortably.

With another inhale, Constance opened one of the doors and entered. When she was inside the elegant lobby, she could pretend she wasn't living in a pokey town with dirty streets and far too many horses. Not that Chicago didn't have horses. But practically living among the creatures made it seem like Sweetwater Springs had more.

So far, she'd managed to evade her father's attempts to get her to ride. In fact, she avoided the barn altogether, truthfully claiming she didn't have a riding habit or the time to make one. Constance had refused the offer of a pair of his pants so she could ride astride like he claimed she had as a child. *As if I'd make such a spectacle of myself.*

Once inside the lobby, she nodded at the young clerk behind the counter and made her way to the restaurant in the back-left portion of the first floor. The paneling was more ornate than in Mr. Gordon's building and the coffered ceilings and electric chandeliers looked quite striking. As she wove around the wingchairs of blue velvet or damask and the marble-topped tables, her footsteps were soft on the Persian carpet.

The restaurant had round tables covered with white cloths and little vases of flowers. Felicity was already sitting at one with a china teapot in front of her and a plate of macaroons. "Look," her friend said, gesturing to the tea. "I finished making up the rooms a few minutes early, and Mrs. Geary allowed me the extra time, so I ordered for us."

"Wonderful. More time to ourselves." Constance took a seat, set her reticule on one of the extra chairs, pulled off her gloves, and studied Felicity's face. Her friend wasn't quite as thin as when they'd first met, but her eyes remained shadowed and her skin pale. She laid a hand over Felicity's. "How are you, dearest?"

"Oh no." Felicity wagged a finger. "In all our conversations, you've listened to *my* problems. Something's bothering you. I can tell just by the way you strode into the room with a full head of steam. Tell me what's on your mind."

"We only have half an hour," Constance said in a wry tone. "So, I'll just pick one topic." She bit her lip. As much as she wanted to complain about the new doctor, she had a more important concern on her mind. "Felicity, I haven't even opened the shop, and I've already been inundated with orders. I'll have more work than I can handle."

Felicity clapped her hands. "That's a *wonderful,* although challenging, problem to have."

Constance sighed and sat back, although, ladylike, she didn't allow her spine to touch her chair. "I suppose that's a better way of considering the situation."

"I'm claiming partial credit," Felicity said in a teasing tone. "I wear the mourning gown you made me when I leave the hotel. I received several compliments and directed all the ladies your way."

"Well, then, it's only fair to complain to you—" Constance put on a mock-solemn expression "—when you are contributing to the cause of my current dilemma."

"You need an assistant."

"At the rate orders are coming in, I need a staff the size of the one in this hotel. But I'll settle for one woman, because I suspect business will calm down as soon as all those ordering new outfits have them. But, in the meantime, where will I find an experienced helper?"

"You'll have to do what Mr. Livingston did here." Felicity gestured to indicate the hotel. "He imported many of us from Boston, where we worked at a hotel owned by his relatives. Surely, you know someone in Chicago who could move here to work for you? Or someone who knows someone?"

"You're right." Constance took a sip of her tea. "And my suite has the extra bedroom, so there's a place where she can stay." She wrinkled her nose. "But I hate taking a chance on a stranger. What if I don't like her but still have to live *and* work with her? I won't have the freedom to dismiss the woman if she's uprooted her life to come out here."

Felicity chuckled.

Just hearing the sound made Constance feel better. In her grief over the death of her betrothed, Felicity rarely laughed. "What?"

"If you don't like the woman, all you have to do is play matchmaker. Out here, the remedy is easy. With a little encouragement, some man's bound to quickly scoop her up and take her off your hands."

Constance laughed, thinking of her suitors. "Some won't need any encouragement whatsoever."

Felicity, having experienced her own share of unwanted suitors, raised her eyes heavenwards. "We can send ours in her direction."

"Perfect. You've set my mind at ease." Constance frowned. "What if I like her, and she leaves to get married? I'll be right back where I started. Worse, if I took on extra orders. Maybe even behind because I took time to train her."

"Constance," Felicity chided. "You make *clothing.* That doesn't have to be done in the shop. If your assistant marries, she can still do sewing from her home." She picked up a macaroon and nibbled on one end.

Grateful to have such a wise friend, Constance gave Felicity a mischievous smile. She also reached for a macaroon. "I'll just have to see that she doesn't marry a widower with children or she'll never have time to make anything for me."

Felicity rolled her eyes, and they both laughed.

The half hour ended all too quickly. The two exchanged goodbyes, and Felicity returned to work.

Constance lingered over her tea, her thoughts returning to the rudeness displayed by the new doctor. Now that some time had passed, she could make allowances. She remembered how exhausted and out of place she'd felt on her arrival. The man was tired and probably cranky.

She smiled, doubting the doctor would appreciate being labeled with a word usually used to describe a child in need of a nap. Soothed by her thoughts, she took one final sip, rose, and left the restaurant.

As she walked through the lobby, Constance couldn't help glancing around with a sigh. *How much nicer it would be to stay here rather than at my father's.*

Only a few more days, she promised herself. As soon as she'd rented the suite, Constance had telegraphed the Millers, asking them to ship the crates holding her furniture and other possessions. When the containers arrived, she was moving into her new home.

Can't come soon enough.

After a fine roast beef dinner and a bath in the porcelain tub with hot and cold running water flowing from a faucet—a luxury Angus had never before experienced—he dressed in the spare room that would be his from now on. While he'd bathed, Mrs. Krutsky had ironed some of his clean clothing, polished his boots, and brushed his frock coat. She'd also collected his dirty shirts and linen to launder on washday.

He cast a longing eye at the iron bed, covered with a fluffy down featherbed, and wanted nothing so much as to crawl beneath the covers and sleep. But Angus knew if he slept now he'd be awake far too long tonight. Best become accustomed to a regular schedule—or at least as regular a schedule as a doctor could manage, what with being apt to awaken for births, sudden illnesses, and nighttime accidents. With a tired sigh, he left the room and went downstairs to the parlor.

Alice sat in the nearest brown chair, darning a stocking. She looked up, her eyes widening. "Angus, I thought you'd be taking a kip."

"I'm loused, aye, but thought it best to stretch my legs. Too many days of sitting."

She nodded. "Of course, you're exhausted. Now's a good time for a walk, though. We have no patients, and Fergus is in the office reading one of the medical journals you brought. But, as you know, that situation can change in a moment, and then, all of a sudden, we'll be inundated with patients, probably all bleeding." She smiled, looking not in the least perturbed by the idea.

"Hopefully, I'll have a chance to get acclimated before that happens."

"Since Craig's asleep, I'm trying to catch up on the mending. The way your brother goes through his stockings." She tisked and shook her head. "I'm grateful for the ones you brought from your mother, but these ones still need darning."

Angus gestured toward the office. "I'll just let the doctor know I'll be out of the house." He strode from the room, down the hall, and into the office.

Earlier, his brother had briefly shown him the space, familiar also from his letters. Now, he inhaled the scent of herbs and glanced around again, taking a more in-depth look.

Two raised beds stood in the middle of the room, with a high table between them. Gleaming surgical instruments were neatly laid out on a tray. The beds were covered with cotton sheets over oilcloth that protected the mattresses. A cabinet held medical books, journals, and rows of jars and bottles of medicine. A desk stood in the back, behind which his brother sat reading. Fergus was in his shirtsleeves, his frock coat hung on a hook on the wall within grabbing distance.

His brother looked up and raised his eyebrows at Angus's frock coat. "Going out?"

"I thought tae gaun a roamin."

"Aye, a walk might benefit you." Fergus tapped the page of the journal. "I thank you for bringing these. I subscribe to the American ones, of course. But it's good to see what research is happening elsewhere."

"I read them on the journey. For the first time, I feel caught up on my professional reading. In London, I had so little free time, and when I did, I was too tired to do much beyond sleep." Angus hesitated, and then decided to admit the truth. "Although sometimes, try as I might, sleep eluded me."

The tilt of Fergus's head, showing he was listening, made Angus open up. "Sometimes, the sheer horror of my patients' existence—living conditions not even good enough for an animal—would not leave my mind at peace." He lifted his hands, palms up. "There was so little I could do. My efforts were simply a drop in the bucket."

"Being a physician means experiencing a great deal of powerlessness," Fergus said in a matter-of-fact tone and motioned for Angus to take a seat in the chair next to the desk. He glanced around. "We'll need another desk and comfortable chair in here. I wasn't sure if you'd bring any furniture with you—a fancy Hepplewhite or Sheraton desk that you might have acquired in London—so I didn't order anything."

Angus took a seat. "Sir Henry has a desk like that. Too fancy for my taste." He laid a palm on the smooth wood of the desktop. "A workable one like yours will suit me fine. You mentioned the man we passed on the street—the one who had pneumonia—is a cabinetmaker. Should I commission one from him?"

"Have you the funds?"

"Our parents sent me forth with five hundred pounds, which I exchanged for dollars in New York."

Fergus grinned. "Well, then, laddie, I think 'tis a fine desk ye'll be a buyin' yerself."

"Do ye do that a lot?" Angus demanded. "Break into a brogue so thick ye can walk on it? Or is it just with your *little* brother?"

"Well, laddie," Fergus continued, not seeming in the least deterred. "Ye'll find the tongue of our homeland comes in right handy when ye need it."

"I doubt you're going around speaking Gaelic," Angus said in a dry tone, making his accent as upper-class English as he could manage.

"Ach, Angus, ye need to find yerself a sense of humor. I do recall ye had one once." Fergus's expression turned serious. "You could fill the room with that belly laugh of yours." His accent lightened. "Made everyone around you break into chuckles. Quite a gift you had. I hope to hear that laugh again."

The very idea made Angus uncomfortable. "A doctor should be serious, sober-minded even." He'd certainly been told that enough when he was in medical school.

"Sometimes, aye." Fergus leaned forward. "But life is difficult enough, and our profession harder still. You need to take your laughter where you can find it. And I've found, a wee bit of teasin' helps make a patient relax and is good for the doctor as well."

Angus could see the benefit of gentle humor to relax a patient. Implementing Fergus's advice, though…. *I seem to have lost my sense of humor in London's slums.*

"I'm glad you're here, *bráthair*. I've been in sore need of you."

A sudden stab of concern made him study Fergus for any signs of ill health.

Fergus raised a hand in a negating gesture. "It's the folks of Sweetwater Springs I'm concerned about. Yes, the town itself is small, but we actually have a great many people scattered around on ranches and farms. I can drive almost a whole day to reach a distant patient. The next closest doctor is a two-day ride away." He waved, to indicate a direction. "That's why I have a Morgan—a good American breed. Sometimes, I toss a saddle in the back of the surrey, because I know I canna' drive all the way—the path is too narrow or steep."

Angus hissed out a breath. "And if ye're half a day's drive in that direction—" he pointed "—and there's an accident somewhere else, perhaps half a day's drive in the opposite direction? Before I arrived in this vast land, I had no idea of the lengthy distances. I can see more clearly now why ye need help."

"I didn't want to pressure you. You needed to keep your mind on your studies. Then when you had that opportunity in London…." He lifted his hand palm up in a *what can I do* motion. "You had to follow your own path."

"I thought ye were making room for me in yer practice because ye were my brother, and the need in the East End was so great…."

"You saved people in London. I know you did."

Angus saw a haunted look in his brother's eyes that he recognized in his own gaze when he looked in the mirror. "Ye've lost patients here when riding out to others."

Fergus gave a slow nod, as if reluctant to burden Angus with the truth. "Ones I knew and cared about, who would have lived if I'd been at their bedside."

Guilt speared Angus. "I did na' ken people were dying because I wasn't here."

Fergus raised his shoulders, as if trying to shrug off his obvious pain. "We are not God to decide who lives or who dies. The ones you saved were just as important in the sight of the Lord as the people here."

"But that's just it," Angus burst out, scooting forward in his chair. "Did I save them, the few I actually could? Or did I just prolong their lives of suffering?"

"Of course you did. Any care you gave would matter."

"Far too many died who would have survived if they had decent living conditions—regular meals, fresh water, a warm, clean shelter, and even *sunlight*." Angus shook his head in remembered despair. "The cases of rickets I saw…." He threw up his hands and stared at his brother. "I'll ask ye, *bráthair*. Percentage wise, would I have saved more here than I did there?"

"Who can say?" Fergus asked with a tired sigh. "When it comes right down to it, laddie, we just do the best we can. The rest abides in the Lord's hands."

In spite of his brother's hedging, Angus knew the truth. He shoved to his feet. Without another word, he strode from the room, guilt and anger snarling at his heels.

Chapter Seven

After meeting with Felicity, Constance didn't want to return to the cramped livery space. Nor could she go to her shop or the suite because Pepe was painting today. She decided to head toward Sugarplum Dreams and hope Julia might have time to talk. She figured her friend would have more knowledge about what woman in town might be available for hire than Felicity who'd only lived in Sweetwater Springs for the last six months or so.

When Constance entered, Julia, standing behind the counter in a snowy apron over a blue workdress, smiled a greeting. "Just in time before school lets out, and I have young customers flocking in. She lifted the chocolate pot in a silent question.

Constance shook her head. "I just had tea with Felicity." She moved to the end of the counter so if customers came in she wouldn't be in their way.

"How is Felicity?"

"Grieving."

"Of course, poor girl. She will be for a while."

Julia gestured toward the counter. "Any pastries?"

"I might take some home with me. Lucia is still lamenting the lack of sugar in our pantry, and Papa is finding excuses to avoid the mercantile. I think I'll have to be the one to brave the Cobbs."

Julia chuckled. "They aren't that bad. I was concerned at first, because they carry cookies and a few pies in the store, and I knew I'd be taking business from them. But once they heard the size of the order I placed for sugar, flour, and other things, Mrs. Cobb became almost cordial. *Almost.*"

They laughed.

"Well, I figured they'll have heard about the dress shop by now and *won't* be friendly to me. I don't intend to order through their store, or at least not for a while. I've brought all I need with me and eventually will probably order directly from my contacts in Chicago. Why pay extra to acquire merchandise from them?"

Julia tilted her head. "I hadn't thought of that. Well, I had, but I'd never had a business before moving here, and I didn't have contacts. Plus, there's been so much to do, what with getting the store ready and all the baking." Her eyes sparkled. "Then, too, I fell in love and got married—having a husband does take up one's time."

Constance laughed, grateful not to have a man diverting her time and energy from her business.

"Why, I've been so busy that it's easier to just have the Cobbs do the ordering."

"Speaking of busy...I haven't even opened my shop, and I can see I'll need a helper. Do you know of anyone?"

Julia shook her head. "I'd love to find a girl to help me in the shop before the baby arrives. I'm thinking of doing what Caleb Livingston did. He imported staff from Boston."

"That's what Felicity suggested."

"I think if I wrote to my friends back home, they could find someone for me. Of course—" Julia pointed upward "—then there's the difficulty of where to put her. Our living space only has one bedroom, and...." Color crept up her throat and into her cheeks. "We like our privacy."

Constance tactfully ignored the implications of Julia's blush. "I suppose I could write to my friends for a suitable candidate. Unlike you, I do have an extra bedroom." She couldn't resist teasing her friend. "As well as no need for certain kinds of *privacy.*"

Julia's blush deepened, and then she burst out laughing. "Constance, you wretch."

Constance leaned forward. "Blame the European influence on my thinking. People are not nearly so prudish in other countries, at least on the continent."

Julia sighed. "I envy you your travels. But at the same time...." She placed a hand on her stomach. "I wouldn't trade my happiness with Sam...the baby...my shop...for anything in the world."

"Perhaps someday you'll travel."

Julia shrugged, as if it didn't matter. "Sam's thinking of expanding again. Pushing out the back wall. We thought six tables would be enough, but sometimes, more are needed. I'd love more space in the kitchen. Then we could add a bedroom for when the baby is older, as well as space for our new employee."

"With extra thick walls." Constance joked.

"Of course," Julia said, deadpan.

They both burst into laughter.

Julia glanced out the window.

Constance followed her gaze to see several children heading down the street.

"School's out," Julia said in a low voice. "Let me wrap up your dessert before the mob descends."

"Do you really have that much business from the children?"

"A few. Some just like to look and wish. Ben Grayson, the nephew of Caleb Livingston, is quite generous when he comes in and buys for himself and his friends. Some of the other children sometimes have money they can spend."

Five girls of stair-stepping sizes filed in. Sisters, they looked to be, and all beautiful with their pale blonde hair, blue eyes, and sweet expressions. The oldest one held her hand closed, with the other hand underneath supporting it, as if she carried something very precious.

Julia tilted her head in the direction of the girls. "The Swensens. They come in to look from time to time. A poor family." She leaned closer to Constance. "If no one else is in the shop, I'll give them some broken cookie pieces or ones that are misshapen that they can split," she said in a low voice. "They don't care if a cookie doesn't look perfect, but I do."

"Mrs. Ritter, I have a penny," announced the oldest girl with a happy smile, her eyes wide.

"You do, Inga?" Julia moved toward the girls. "Today must be special."

"We've been helping Mrs. Gordon spring clean the schoolhouse, and she paid us each a *penny*, even Marta."

The littlest girl bounced on her toes.

"Mrs. Gordon didn't have to pay us. We like helping. But she said to come here and buy some candy." She opened her hand, picked up one coin and set the penny on the counter, closing her hand again. "We're taking the other four to the mercantile. I heard Ma and Pa talking about using credit there. They're worried about paying back the money. So, we're doing it for them." She beamed with pride.

Julia gave them a warm smile. "You are all thoughtful girls."

Whatever the parents owe the mercantile is probably far more than four cents.

Constance hadn't thought much about having children. But in seeing these girls, her heart opened and she tumbled into love. *I want to adopt them.* She imagined clothing them in frilly dresses, fancy pinafores, with big bows in their hair. *I wonder if their parents would notice if they didn't return home today?*

Julia glanced over, and Constance touched her chest and then her reticule, pantomiming that she'd pay for treats for the girls.

Julia winked and nodded. She leaned over the counter. "What would you like? Each of you pick what you want."

"We want to take something for Pa and Ma and Anneka and Lottie," the second oldest said earnestly. "Little Olaf can't have candy yet. He doesn't even have teeth."

Such dear girls. Constance held in a chuckle and placed a hand on her heart.

Julia nodded, her expression as earnest as the child's. "I'll pick something that's easy to carry. I know you have a long walk up the mountain."

"We have to stop and rest," Marta piped up. "That's cuz I have short legs."

Constance watched them each choose a cookie, and then Julia wrapped some candy for their parents. She stepped forward and pushed the penny back to Inga. "My treat, because you are such good girls, and I'm so pleased to hear how you helped your teacher." She placed several coins on the counter to cover their bill.

"Oh, thank you," Inga was starry-eyed. "Now, we can pay *all five cents* to the mercantile."

"Your parents will be proud," Constance assured them.

The other girls all chorused "thank you" and "good-bye" before filing back out the door, presumably to head to the mercantile.

Constance was tempted to follow them to the store and protect them from the formidable Cobbs, whom she'd heard so much about. *Surely, the most hardened hearts would melt in the face of such sweet innocence and their earnest desire to help their parents.*

Several cowboys entered, bringing in the smell of horses. With touches of their hats to her and shy smiles, they headed straight toward the counter.

Her nose twitched.

Rather than interrupt their business, Constance nodded to Julia and left.

When she stepped outside, farther up the street Constance could see the girls, walking like a gaggle of geese. *I wish Inga was old enough to work for me.* Since they were heading in the same direction, she decided it wouldn't go amiss to drop into the mercantile to make sure the girls were treated with respect.

The day had turned cool and breezy, and dust whirled into the air, making her wish she'd worn her half cape. The wind threatened to lift the straw sailor hat from her head. Hatpins kept it anchored, but not without a sharp yank at her hair. *I should have worn the heavier bowler.* She placed a hand on the crown to hold the hat where it belonged.

Tendrils pulled from her French twist and blew across her

face. Her skirt tangled in her legs, making her grateful she wore several layers of petticoats, else her lower limbs would be outlined for all to see.

A gust hit her face, flinging a speck into her eye. Annoyed with the primitive conditions of this town, Constance stopped to pull her handkerchief from her pocket. Lately, she'd taken to carrying the hanky that had been her mother's, making her feel connected with Mama. Being with Papa had brought back the ache of losing her.

She wiped the inner corner of her eye, luckily removing the speck. As she started to return the handkerchief to her reticule, a flurry tore it from her grasp and set the fabric dancing along the street.

With an exclamation, Constance hurried after it. The handkerchief landed on the dirt, the lace edges fluttering. Before the scrap of fabric could blow away, she stooped to grab it. But the tightness of her stays prevented her from leaning over very far.

She gasped for a breath. Before she could bend her knees low enough to stoop to the ground, the handkerchief took off again, making her chase the cloth skipping on the wind.

Knowing she was causing a spectacle made heat burn in her face and chest. *If that darn scrap of cloth weren't Mama's, I'd let it go and say good riddance.*

With one hand on the top of her hat to keep it steady and the other poised to grab the handkerchief, Constance had no way to lift her skirts, and, after a few steps, she tripped on the hem and barely caught herself, tottering forward and uttering an unladylike swearword. A strong hand grabbed her arm, hauling her upright.

"I believe dropping yer handkerchief is a time-honored way to attract a man's attention." His accent was Scottish, his tone angry rather than flirtatious.

She glanced up and saw Dr. Angus Cameron, who was *still* scowling at her, his blue eyes disdainful.

"If ye didn't have that ridiculous contraption imprisoning

your waist, ye could bend over *and* run faster. Ye'd have caught your handkerchief right away." Criticism dripped from every word. "Have ye no brains in yer head?"

Contraption? Shocked by the attack, it took Constance a few seconds to realize he meant her corset. *No brains? How dare he!*

From the corner of her eye, she saw her handkerchief take off in one sailing flight that carried it almost fifty feet away. She tried to tear her arm from the doctor's grasp, but his hand might as well have been an iron shackle.

"Let me go!" Enraged, she pushed her hands against his chest and yanked her elbow away.

He released her with an abruptness that caught her off guard, making her stumble back. Catching up her skirts, she rushed after the errant handkerchief, which fluttered down the street in the direction of a mucky puddle.

Oh, no. She increased her speed, panting, her corset too tight to get enough air.

Footsteps pounded behind her, and the annoying doctor raced past after the handkerchief.

The sight of him only made her angrier and determined to reach her precious keepsake without his help. But her heart pounded against her chest, and she couldn't breathe. Growing lightheaded, she slowed to a stop. She reached for a nearby hitching rail for support, but her hand met only air.

Dizziness overcame her. *Don't faint here!* Constance commanded herself. Through blurring vision, she saw the doctor grab her handkerchief.

He turned, and then he grimaced, obviously noticing her distress. "Oh, for crying out loud, woman!" He leaped forward and caught her just as she fainted.

After leaving the house, Angus had stalked down the street,

examining his new town and pushing aside a past he was unable to change. He saw Constance Taylor emerge from a shop with a sign proclaiming *Sugarplum Dreams* and waited so he wouldn't run into her. He wasn't in the mood to talk to the woman about rational attire. He only wanted to sit with a cup of coca in the sweetshop and let his anger and guilt pass.

But Angus couldn't help but watch Miss Taylor stroll away, torn between annoyance at the unnatural tininess of her waist, and the grace of her carriage and how the gentle, enticing way her bottom swayed as she moved. The fringes on her hem danced with each graceful step. *Fringes don't belong on dresses,* he groused, more to distance himself from his irritating reaction to Miss Taylor, than really caring about fringes, or the lack thereof.

Before he could enter the sweetshop, Angus saw the wind tear Miss Taylor's handkerchief from her grasp and how the restriction of her corset prevented her from bending all the way to catch it. The wind lifted her skirt enough to expose high-buttoned boots with two-inch heels instead of sensible footwear. Although tempted to watch her comical attempts to regain her possession, in such situations a gentleman must give aid, instead of standing in place and rolling his eyes at the show.

He started forward and, seeing her stumble, leapt to grab her arm. As Angus held her, he couldn't help making a sarcastic crack about her attire. A mistake, he realized, for she tried to pull away. Fearing the woman would topple over, he held tight, only to have her turn into a wild thing and attack by pushing against him.

Angus released her and watched in shock as she hurried after her handkerchief. *She'll do herself harm.* He bit off a curse and raced to catch the handkerchief before she tripped and broke her fool neck. He could see the headline now: *Doctor's Intervention Causes Woman's Death.*

I shouldn't have goaded her. I must learn to govern my tongue.

He ran past Miss Taylor, scooped up the handkerchief, which had come to rest on the top of a rut above a puddle, and turned to hand her the scrap of dirty fabric.

She tucked the handkerchief inside her cuff. As she tried to catch her breath, her bosom heaved. Tendrils of hair had come loose around her flushed face. Sweat beaded her forehead, and her hat was tilted askew. Her face paled, and her green eyes grew unfocused.

Recognizing the signs of an impending swoon, he stepped forward just in time to catch her as she crumpled and lifted her up. He stepped forward and tripped over her dress, trailing on the ground. Afraid he'd drop her, Angus squeezed Miss Taylor as carefully as possible against his chest, trying to find his balance, and biting off more mental curses.

Angus glanced around, not knowing what to do with the benighted woman. He could hardly lay her down in the street.

"In here." A large, dark-haired man emerged from the doorway of what looked like an office building and beckoned Angus forward. "I have a padded bench you can lay her down on," he said in a deep, gravelly voice.

Angus walked over, taking kicking steps to keep the blasted skirt from underneath his feet. *What a comical sight we must make.*

The man extended long arms in an offer. "You want me to take her?"

Although Angus was more than middle height, the man towered over him. As angry as he was with Miss Taylor, Angus felt an odd reluctance to give her up, especially since he'd contributed to her condition. He shook his head and followed the man into an office. A sign over the door read *Sweetwater Springs Herald*, which meant the man was Anthony Gordon. On occasion, Fergus had enclosed some of the reporter's articles with his letters.

Glancing around, Angus saw a long padded bench, and he bent to gently lay Miss Taylor on the leather top. Her arms draped over the sides. He stood and pulled the curtains of the front window closed so no passersby could see inside, and then leaned to touch her neck to take her pulse. *Rapid, which is to be expected, given her antics on the street.*

"I have water and brandy, Dr. Angus," Mr. Gordon offered. "Or whisky, if you'd prefer."

He wondered how the man knew his identity. "*I'd* prefer whisky, but it's not a drink most ladies appreciate. If you'll bring a glass of water, and then step outside so I can see to my patient in privacy, I'd appreciate it."

"Consider it done. Would you like me to fetch her father?"

Angus unfastened the first button at the top of the bodice. "Perhaps after Miss Taylor is herself again. I believe she's fainted due to overexertion while wearing this ridiculous clothing. She'll be fine soon, and there's no need to worry her father." He took the glass of water the man held out and set it on the floor next to the bench. "But if you can fetch Mrs. Cameron, I'm sure Miss Taylor will feel more comfortable with a woman present."

He plucked the hatpins from her sailor hat and dropped them on the floor. The hat fell off.

Footsteps, the clink of keys, and the click of the door told Angus the man had left. He rose and locked it, preventing entry by another.

He knelt on one knee and quickly unbuttoned the rest of the woman's bodice grateful she'd gone for big decorative buttons rather than the myriad of tiny ones a doctor sometimes had to fumble through. The bodice opened, exposing the top of beautiful, firm breasts pushed up by her corset and barely covered by a low-cut, lacy camisole.

Reminding himself that he was a professional, Angus averted his gaze from her breasts and groped for the ties to release her skirt, so he could reveal the bottom of the corset. Frustrated by the layers he needed to burrow under, he eased the skirt a few inches to expose the bottom of the restrictive garment. *Thank God, a front-tying corset.*

A glance at her face told him Miss Taylor remained unconscious, although her breathing was even but shallow from her diminished lung capacity.

The corset strings were doubled knotted, of course, and he

had to pick at the knot, which seemed to take forever to release. Then he worked to loosen the strings and pull apart the two edges of the corset.

Her ribcage expanded as her body took in much-needed oxygen.

He looked around for a blanket, and finding none, removed his coat and covered her.

Miss Taylor still hadn't regained consciousness, and he reached for the reticule on her wrist, opened it and rummaged around inside, looking for smelling salts. Most females carried them, especially if they were foolish enough to wear tight corsets and give themselves fainting fits, thus needing to be revived. He pulled out a crystal vial, uncapped the top, and waved the sharp scent under her nose.

Miss Taylor stirred and opened her eyes, glancing at him without recognition.

He capped the smelling salts and dropped the vial back into her reticule.

"Wha…?" The dazed look slowly cleared from her eyes. A slender, white hand fluttered to her chest and touched his frockcoat. She pushed away the covering and felt the lace of her camisole. An expression of horror crossed her face.

Angus braced himself. *Naturally she'll be upset, but as soon as she realizes I'm a doctor and am assisting her, all will be well. Hopefully, she won't recall my contribution to her plight. She'll feel grateful for the rescue.*

But even as Angus reassured himself, doubts came.

Or so I hope.

Chapter Eight

When she awoke, Constance had the sense of a man intimately close. Fear flooded her, and she flinched, her hand going to her chest, only to feel the heavy wool of a coat, then her camisole underneath instead of the gabardine of her basque. She gasped and, holding the coat to her chest, tried to sit and cringe away from the man at the same time.

"Dinna fash yerself, Miss Taylor. Hold yerself still." A hand on her shoulder pressed her back.

She recognized the accent and the man at the same time. "How dare you!"

"Steady, Miss Taylor. I'm a doctor. Ye fainted, and I'm tending to ye."

To be exposed, viewed by the man in such an intimate way! Embarrassment turned into anger. "Stop tending me," she snapped. "Go away so I can dress." She looked around, recognizing the newspaper office and wondering where Mr. Gordon was. *Hopefully, he's not in the room.*

"Gonnae' no dae that." His tone brooked no refusal. "Yer still peely-wally."

Has my brain been injured? "Wh—what?"

"White as a sheet," he translated.

She let out a breath of relief. *His accent was the problem, not my mind.*

"Let me help you sit up, so you can drink some water."

96

Underneath the shelter of the coat, Constance held the plackets of her basque tight and allowed him to assist her to a sitting position, feeling her stays shifting with her movement. *He loosened my corset!* The coat slipped off one shoulder, exposing far too much skin. Heat flooded her chest.

He pulled the coat over her shoulder, picked up a drinking glass, and held it out.

She transferred the plackets to one hand, reached for the glass, and sipped the water. She took a deep inhale and drank some more. Aware she owed him an apology for her defensive reaction, as well as gratitude for her rescue, Constance opened her mouth to thank the doctor.

"You're getting some color back in your face," he said in an obviously self-satisfied tone. "See how much better you can breathe when your lungs aren't held hostage by that corset."

His condescending tone spiked her anger. She snapped her mouth shut, and all thoughts of expressing appreciation fled. "What is it with you harping on my corset? You shouldn't even *mention* my corset to me."

"I'm a doctor, so I can mention female undergarments. That *corset* was what caused ye to faint. What would ye have done if I had na' been there to catch ye?" His accent burred until she could barely understand him. "Pitched forward into the dirt street, breaking yer pretty nose or an arm, that's what." As he spoke his voice rose.

Constance remembered the ridiculous spectacle she'd made chasing after the handkerchief, then fainting. He had a point. But now to awaken half naked and endure a scolding from the cad. *Why couldn't I have fainted in the arms of someone nice? Handsome and nice*, she amended. *The doctor was handsome enough but definitely not nice.*

"Ye might be still in the muck and mire, unless of course ye were rescued by some drunken cowboy or farmer, one who was coming out of the saloon and tripped over ye."

"Don't be ridiculous," she retorted. "Now you're dramatizing the situation."

"Yet, there's truth in what I'm saying."

She thrust the glass at him. "Turn your back."

Shaking his head, he sighed. "May I remind ye that I'm a doctor? Ye have *nothing* I haven't seen before."

Another flush of heat went through her. "You haven't seen *my* nothings before."

The very thought of him seeing her, maybe touching her breasts, made her body flood with sensual energy, and she tugged the plackets of her basque tighter, as if to contain her feelings.

His mouth quivered, as if he repressed a smile. But he obeyed, thankfully without them brangling further.

As Constance tried to button the basque, she couldn't stop her hands from shaking. The bodice proved impossible to close without first tightening her corset. She stood and had to grab her skirt and petticoats to keep them from sliding off.

At this rate, I'll be practically naked before him. Telling herself that the doctor had seen plenty of almost naked or maybe all the way naked females didn't help ease her discomfort.

With his back to Miss Taylor, Angus allowed himself a smile at her petulant response. "I didn't actually *see* yer nothings," he pointed out in a more reasonable tone. *Although I wish I had.* "Yer *nothings* are covered by a camisole." *Barely.*

He couldn't stop the vision of laying her back on the bench with her breasts exposed, of him touching her in a manner that wasn't at all professional, and his groin tightened. Yet at the same time, his improper reaction to a patient made the heat of shame burn up his neck.

A knock sounded on the door. "Angus? Miss Taylor?" Alice called. "May I enter?"

Not sure whether to be relieved or disappointed by the interruption, Angus strode over to the door, unlocked it, and held it open enough for Alice to slip through, closing it after her.

His sister-in-law glanced from him to Miss Taylor. "Is everything all right?"

"*No.*" Miss Taylor sounded as though she were gritting her teeth. "Everything will be quite all right once *that man* leaves."

Alice gave Angus a speculative glance.

"Miss Taylor overexerted herself and swooned," he explained, his tone stiff. "But now, she seems recovered. If you'd be so kind and aid her to dress...?"

Alice made a shooing motion. "Outside with you, and then you can escort Miss Taylor home in case she becomes weak again."

"No need," Miss Taylor said sharply.

"There is every need," Alice said in a tone as firm as Miss Taylor's was sharp. "We can't have you fainting in the street. You'll ruin your beautiful dress," she teased.

"You make a good point," Miss Taylor said in a grudging tone.

Angus rolled his eyes, opened the door, and stepped outside, hoping his sister-in-law would take the opportunity to point out to the patient that she shouldn't wear her corset so tight.

"Over here." Mr. Gordon's voice came from the left.

Suddenly feeling exhausted, Angus walked down the hall in that direction to see the man sprawled on the stairs, leaning back on his arms, his long legs spread out in front of him. A ring of keys, a crystal decanter, and two small glasses were on the step beside him.

Mr. Gordon sat up, raised one crooked eyebrow, and hefted the bottle in an apparent question. "Whisky, as promised. I went in the back door to retrieve my supply."

"Thank you, Mr. Gordon. I believe I'm in need of a medicinal draught."

"Need to settle your nerves, eh?"

Angus grimaced, bracing one hand on the bannister. "That's one way to put it."

"Call me Ant. Almost everyone does."

"Because of your diminutive size?"

He shot Angus a crooked grin. "You could say that. My appearance can make people feel intimidated. The nickname of a small insect makes me seem more approachable—an important requirement in my profession."

"My brother tells me that thickening our brogue does a similar job."

"I've seen that work with Doc Cameron quite successfully."

Ant pulled off the stopper, poured the amber liquid into a glass, and handed it to Angus. Then he poured a drink for himself and scooted all the way to the side of the staircase, leaving room for Angus to sit beside him. He raised his glass. "To new adventures."

"I'm not sure if I need any more adventures just now."

Ant shot him a crooked grin. "A man always needs adventures or else he gets stale."

Angus chuckled and took a seat. "To new adventures, then." He sipped, expecting to taste the familiar smoky flavor of Scotch, but this distillation lacked the bite along the edge that he expected. He held up the glass, looked into the liquid, swirled it around, and sniffed the woody, sweet scent.

"Bourbon, not Scotch," Ant instructed. "Made from corn, not barley. Made in America, not Scotland. Spelled with an *e*. W-h-i-s-k-e-y."

"Ah." Angus took another experimental sip, liking the taste better the second time, now that he knew what to expect.

Ant sipped his. "I have a dilemma—one caused by owning a small-town newspaper." He lifted his glass to indicate the ceiling. "And being the owner of this building."

"What might that dilemma be?"

"What just happened—Miss Taylor chasing her handkerchief, fainting, and you catching her—I saw it all through the window, and it is newsworthy in the sleepy town of Sweetwater Springs. Yet, Miss Taylor is my tenant, and therefore, I have a vested interest in her emotional sensibilities and the success of her enterprise."

Angus didn't see the problem.

His puzzlement must have shown on his face, for Ant began to explain. "When I was a reporter for a big New York newspaper, the only rules were to report the facts—newsworthy facts and protect the privacy of my sources. Of course, there were requirements for *how* I wrote the article." He held up an enormous hand. "Who, what, why, where, and how." He ticked off each point on a long finger. "Writing the article with the most important news first, down to the least important news so if the story needed to be chopped to fit the pages, paragraphs would come off the bottom."

The sound of the deep voice laying out the terms for reporting made Angus relax. He took another sip of his whiskey with an *e*.

"For the *Sweetwater Springs Herald*, though, I have other considerations. By now, I know most people here and have friendships of varying depths with many. My life, and that of my wife and nephew, is very intertwined with the folks here. Thus some of my articles can cause resentment that impacts our relationships. Then, too, what if I report something that hurts the reputation of a friend? Not—" he said hastily "—that in this case what just happened would hurt either of your reputations. If I report the whole truth as I saw it, then I'll have to write that Miss Taylor's efforts to rescue her handkerchief were impeded by her fashionable clothing. And since she is a dressmaker...."

"Ah. I see your dilemma. Perhaps—" Angus said slowly, thinking through the situation. "You can place the emphasis on how the wind blew the handkerchief. That scrap certainly led us on a merry dance. And it's not uncommon for women to faint when upset or under physical exertion. You don't need to mention her—" *corset* "—clothing. That kind of situation is well known and goes without saying."

Ant gestured with his glass for Angus to go on.

"Emphasize my rescue, casting me in the role of a hero. After all, doctors are supposed to be heroic." Angus chuckled. "For Miss Taylor's sake, I will make the sacrifice and set aside my natural inclination to remain out of the limelight."

Ant's laugh was as deep and gravelly as his voice.

"There. Dilemma solved."

Before Ant could refill both glasses, the door to the newspaper office opened, and the ladies came out.

Probably just as well we didn't drink a second round.

Setting the glasses on the steps, the men stood and walked to meet them.

Miss Taylor avoided Angus's eyes, looking past him to her landlord. "Thank you for the use of your office, Mr. Gordon."

She had a faint blush of color in her cheeks, but in Angus's opinion, she still looked too pale.

Alice handed him his coat and patted Miss Taylor's shoulder. "Our Angus will escort you home."

He expected another argument, but she merely nodded and moved toward the outer doors.

Angus shrugged into his coat and buttoned the front, thanked Ant for his assistance, and hurried after the woman, wondering if he'd have to chase up the street to catch her. But once outside, to his surprise, he saw that she'd waited for him.

Miss Taylor faced the other side of the street, her spine ramrod stiff.

She's probably terribly embarrassed. He walked to her side and extended his elbow.

Without looking at him, she wrapped her hand around his arm. "Don't say a word to me." She tugged on his arm to get them walking in the direction of the livery.

"Miss Taylor, there's something I must discuss with ye."

"Not another word," she said through gritted teeth. "I will

drop your arm and storm away. I don't care if I draw attention by doing so. I've already made a public spectacle of myself today, so I can hardly do worse."

He let out a frustrated breath but obeyed. *I'll find a better time to broach the subject.*

All the way to the livery, they walked in a silence charged with hostility.

Chapter Nine

Although she refused to look at him, Constance was very aware of the man at her side. Without turning her head, she could see him from the corner of her eye, walking as straight-backed as her. Doctor Angus wasn't a large man, but he was of good height, three or four inches taller than her.

Uncomfortable with his presence, Constance wished she could hurry away. But she'd promised Mrs. Cameron that she'd allow the doctor's escort, and, as much as she hated to admit it, she was grateful for the support of his arm. The strength of her earlier anger had drained away, leaving her shaky, feeling oddly vulnerable, and on the verge of tears.

When they reached the livery, she released his arm and glanced up at him before lowering her eyes. Politeness bade her speak. "Thank you for your escort." To her ears, her voice sounded flat, although she hadn't intended it so. She glanced up.

His gaze searched her face. "It is not uncommon after endangerment or such exertion as ye have undergone today to have a...drop in mood." His voice was unexpectedly kind.

Constance looked away lest she lose her composure.

"Your limbs may feel weak, as if you lack your normal vitality. After exertion followed by a swoon, women often experience tearfulness."

Ah.

"Rest and nourishment can go a long way to restoring your

spirits." He hesitated. "I...uh...I apologize for my part in today's mishap. I was wrong to speak so critically to you."

Surprise froze her tongue. Before Constance could respond in kind, with a slight bow, he left her at the big open doors of the livery.

She could almost feel him striding stiff-necked down the street, as if to remove himself from her vicinity. *Good riddance*, she should have said but instead felt a strange sense of emptiness.

I need to talk to Pa. Compelled by a necessity she couldn't identify, Constance rushed through the doors and into the barn, feeling like a young girl searching for her father. *Pa, where are you?* She frantically glanced down the double row of stalls and spotted him in the fourth one on the right, grooming a brown horse with a white blaze on its nose.

Rex, curled up outside the stall rose and loped over to greet her.

Constance sidestepped his rush, rubbed the dog's head, and kept going, her heels clicking on the wooden floor. She pulled open the stall door and stepped inside, the fresh straw cushioning her feet. Automatically, she stroked the horse's nose, disregarding her gloves.

Her father raised his eyebrows and smiled. "Eh, Connie, girl, what be botherin' you?"

The story spilled out—the scowling doctor; the chase of the handkerchief; swooning; the doctor's rescue.... She skipped the details of her state of undress but continued listing all ways the man in his arrogance had offended her. Then, to cap off her litany of complaints, just when she'd become quite determined on his character, he'd softened, leaving her unsettled and not knowing *what* to think.

All through her recital, her father continued running the currycomb over the horse's back and flank, with an occasional intent glance and nod, showing Constance he was listening. "You always did have a temper, Connie girl."

"Me?" She reared back, shocked he'd say such a thing. "I do

not!" *Isn't he supposed to take my side?* "How can you even say so, when you haven't seen me for years? Aunt Hannah always said I was a biddable child."

"So she wrote, which had me doing a fair bit of worryin', cuz I didn't recognize my stubborn, hellcat of a daughter in her description."

"I'm very even tempered," Constance said in a firm tone.

He just grinned and shook his head. "Many's the time you'd blow up at your ma, and her back at ya, which wasn't surprising, being that you git your temper from her."

Constance made a quick search of her old memories but couldn't imagine what he was talking about.

"Guess where you'd end up? In a stall with me. We'd groom a horse, and you tell me all about how your ma did you wrong."

"I remember no such thing." She didn't like being accused of having a temper. *Why, Victoria and I traveled throughout Europe, and we rarely had a cross word between us. Nor did I ever argue with Aunt Hannah. Protest a bit, yes. But that's natural between two people who are close. Not everyone can always agree.* Constance wished she could remember more about the time before her mother died. *Papa's gotten old. Maybe he remembers wrong.*

"I assure you, I'm quite a calm person." Intent on convincing her father of her amiable disposition, Constance almost didn't notice the horse wuffing in her face, as if trying to nibble her hair.

"Stop, Annie Bee." Without taking her gaze off her father, she gently pushed aside the mare's head a few inches.

He raised his bushy eyebrows. "That ain't Annie Bee."

"What?" Constance shook her head, as if the gesture would help her see reality. She blinked and realized she was right next to a *horse*—a place she could never recall being before—and stroking the creature's neck. With a gasp, she raised her hand and took a step back.

"That's Annie Bee's granddaughter."

Her throat tight, Constance glanced from her father to the

horse, seeing the mare, but also having a burst of memories—being small and standing in a similar stall to this one, talking to her pa about her childish upsets. They would groom one of the horses. Annie Bee was her favorite next to her pony Gilda. Pa sometimes let her ride the mare—astride, of course—provided he was right there with her.

"I...I...." Tears welled and dripped down her face. "I forgot!" she wailed. "The hurt was so bad I made myself forget. I couldn't bear to look at a horse, because I'd miss Gilda and Annie Bee so much. I wanted desperately to go home to you and Mama and the horses."

Her father's eyes grew damp. He shoved the currycomb into his pocket and touched her shoulder. "Makes sense now. I couldn't understand why you didn't go to the horses first thing after you greeted me. I wish I'd done different by you, Connie girl."

She wiped away tears. "What happened to Gilda and Annie Bee?"

"I sold Gilda to another family with two little girls. Then Annie Bee and the other horses and I moved here to Sweetwater Springs, and I opened the livery. Annie Bee lived to a ripe old age."

Constance sniffed. "I thought after our talk that I felt better about you sending me away. Past is past, and I turned out just fine."

"Might be *thinkin'* that's the problem."

She tilted her head in askance.

"Seems to me what's needed about your past is *feelin'*." He flicked a hand between himself, her, and the horse. "Our talk the other day was more about *thinkin'*. Don't get me wrong—" he said hastily. "You said what needed sayin."

Annie Bee's granddaughter snuffled Constance's hand, as if searching for a treat.

Her father reached into his pocket, pulled out a carrot piece, and handed it to her.

Constance took the carrot and held out her hand to the horse, palm up.

The mare daintily lipped the treat, her mouth velvet soft. She crunched the carrot, then searched for more.

The familiar ritual felt comforting, as if she'd done this a hundred times before. Memory stirred. *I probably did.* "What's her name, Papa?"

"Annie Dee, Annie Cee being her dam."

Constance chuckled. "Of course. A logical progression."

"She's yours, daughter. I'd promised Annie Bee to you when you outgrew Gilda. With you gone, I decided to breed Annie Alphabets 'til you came home." He shuffled his feet in the hay and then reached into his pocket for the currycomb and began to work the very same area he'd gone over before. "Think you'll want a pair of my britches to ride in?"

"Papa!" She laughed, almost scandalized to even consider the idea.

His eyes twinkled. "Guess you'll have to make yourself a divided riding skirt, then. Truth be told, that's what most ladies wear if they ride to town. Although out on their own places, they sometimes wear britches."

Britches are out of the question. But a divided skirt instead of a riding habit?

Constance began envisioning how she'd design such a garment. It would have to be made of durable yet comfortable material that could take the dust. "I'll have to pay attention to what I see other women wearing. Then I'll make one for myself and even carry them in the store."

Her father placed a hand on the mare's rump, and then walked around her backside to move to the horse's head. "Hear that, Annie Dee? Our Connie will be riding you, just like I promised." He began to comb her mane.

"Might be a while, Papa, before I have the time to sew something for myself."

"Annie Dee will be awaitin'."

Constance rubbed the mare's nose then leaned forward to drop a kiss on the white blaze, remembering when she had to pull down Annie Bee's head to reach this spot. Sudden tears filled her eyes—of gratitude this time, not pain—and she turned her face to press a cheek against the mare, absorbing the comfort that love between a gentle horse and a human could bring.

As much as she wanted to, Constance couldn't hold the position long, for her corset cut into her skin and made breathing difficult. With another kiss, she straightened.

Combing the coarse hair of the mane made sounds like a broom over floorboards. Her father kept at it.

She glanced around and saw a bristled brush on the crosspiece of the stall wall near the door. Picking up the brush, she began to work the mare's shoulder and withers, moving in short strokes.

"You're gonna get all dirty," Papa warned.

Constance glanced down at her clothing, already looking worse for wear. *Right now, I don't really care.* "Guess so." She continued brushing.

"Doc Cameron used to keep his surrey and his gelding here. Usually, I'd do the groomin' of his Morgan. Cookie, the gelding's name is. Sometimes, he joined me like this, as if he needed a menial task to take his mind off the doctorin' he'd just done." He shook his head, white hairs swaying. "Ain't an easy job patchin' up people and often times watchin' them die off."

Constance smiled across the horse's back at him. "I'd rather patch up clothing." She kept on brushing, inhaling the now-familiar smell of horse.

Papa didn't return her smile. "The doc...he'd sometimes talk about what was on his mind. Wasn't ever sure if he was talkin' to me or to Cookie, the horse and I being just as silent and good for listenin'."

"You *are* a good listener, Papa."

He nodded but continued on with his story, his hand moving all the while. "One of the things weighin' on the good doc's mind was his brother." He shot her a questioning glance. "You know where Doc Angus was practicin' before he came out here?"

She shook her head, not sure she wanted to know more about the man.

"East End London."

"But…that's a dangerous area." Constance tried to recall what she'd heard of the place. When she and Victoria had stayed in London, they'd received strict warnings not to venture near that part of the city.

"Workin' with the poor in miserable conditions, Doc Angus was. And him fresh out of medical school." Her father paused. "What do you think that doctorin' under those circumstances might do to a man?"

Constance didn't want to reason out the answer to her father's question. She lowered the brush. "You always did this to me when we talked," she burst out.

He raised one white eyebrow.

"Made me *think*. Made me see Mama's point of view." But she couldn't be annoyed with him. Having her memories back was too precious.

He gestured to the horse with his chin. "Annie Dee's awaitin'. She ain't got all day to get polished up."

Constance laughed, raised the brush to the mare's back, and set to her task. *I'll do my thinking about Doctor Angus later—much, much later.*

Four days later, Constance stood in her new shop, clasped her hands to her chest, and gave a girlish twirl. *Finally, everything's finished!* Yesterday, Pepe and Lucia had helped her hang the curtains at the windows and the paintings on the walls, as well as spread the large Persian carpet on the floor.

Over the last few days, the couple had become good friends

as they worked with Constance to finish the shop. While Pepe
had concentrated on the physical aspects such as painting, Lucia
ironed the readymade skirts and shirtwaists that Constance had
whipped up all week, knowing she needed a basic inventory as
soon as she opened her doors to the public. She was so grateful
for their efforts and promised Lucia a new dress in return—one
that could expand with her pregnancy and be taken in after the
baby's birth.

On the back wall a cabinet made by Mr. O'Reilly rose floor-
to-ceiling. Each narrow shelf held one bolt of fabric, arranged by
color, with plenty of practical, pretty cottons as well as wool,
velvet, chiffon, damask, black crepe, and other materials. On the
other side of the door leading to the back room, a wardrobe
stored intimate apparel.

The rack of readymade garments hung on the wall near the
entrance. On the other side of the door was a petite Sheraton
desk Constance bought in England and shipped to America. She
planned to sit there to write up orders or receipts. A bench
covered in blue, green, red, and silver damask matched the
curtains at the windows.

A shallow cabinet held trims, each spool of ribbon or rickrack
on a peg or in a cubby. Midway along one wall, a display of hats
in stands stood on a glass counter, simple ones of straw or felt
toques with ribbons or artificial flowers. When she had a chance,
Constance planned to make more elaborate ones. Inside the glass
counter, her lace collection, some antique and others new and
machine-made, lay in ripples of rich vanilla, white, cream, as
well as various colors.

Per Felicity's advice, colorful remnants draped over several
bars. The poorer women in town might not afford the price of a
new dress or hat, but they could buy a piece to use as trim for
their best dress or hat or maybe as a pillow covering to brighten
up their home.

On the plaster of Paris mannequin set on a dais in the middle
of the room was the *piece de resistance*—an evening gown made of

purple shimmering silk shot through with silver threads. The gown was designed more simply than one she would have displayed in Chicago and was cut in a large size so it could be easily taken in. She'd pinned the sides smaller to better fit the mannequin. Four rows of lace edged the square bodice, and the puffy sleeves, banded in velvet and lace, ended above the elbows. The bottom of the V-shaped basque had a small double ruffle.

Instead of decorating the hem, she'd kept the skirt plain, so it could be taken up or lengthened depending on the buyer's height, with a small gathering in the back, leading to a bit of a train. If the buyer wanted more trim, she could add velvet and lace for an additional fee. The beautiful gown made her feel proud; women would come to the shop just to look at that dress.

Unclasping her hands, Constance strolled into the back room, where she had marked off a large dressing area with painted screens and a full-length mirror. Behind another painted screen was a jumble of goods that needed to be organized: bolts of fabric that had too much material to be a remnant, but not enough to display in the front, some hat stands, a box of antique fabrics from Europe that she didn't know what she'd do with but had loved each piece enough to buy it, and another box of odds and ends, such as scraps of fabric, bits of ribbon, loose flowers, and stray beads.

A long cutting table, a ruler glued to one side and another across the foot, took up the space in the middle of the room. Aunt Hannah's sewing machine was by the window near a comfortable chair that Constance had brought from Chicago for when she needed to work on something by hand. She'd taken her own sewing machine upstairs and set it up in the spare bedroom.

Constance walked over to touch the wheel of the sewing machine, and grief rose in her, tightening her chest. *How I wish you were here, Aunt Hannah.*

She swallowed down the lump in her throat. *If Aunt Hannah were still alive, I wouldn't be here, I'd be in Chicago.* To her surprise, Constance realized she wouldn't change Sweetwater Springs for

Chicago. Aside from one confusing doctor, whom Constance had decided to ignore, everyone she'd met had been welcoming.

She glanced at the clock on the wall over the sewing machine. *Ten minutes before I open.* A squiggle of excitement fluttered in her stomach.

A knock sounded on the door of the front room.

An early customer?

She hurried into the other space and opened the door to see Ant and Harriet Gordon. He had his hand on his wife's back. She'd met the schoolteacher a few days ago and had thought the Gordons made an odd-looking couple—he so tall and angular, and she petite and pretty. Then Constance caught them exchanging a fond glance and realized that they were perfectly matched in love.

Mrs. Gordon held out a vase of lilacs. "A gift from us to wish you success."

Constance accepted the arrangement with a wide smile, feeling the sharpness of the cut glass pattern beneath her fingers. She took a breath of the sweet-smelling lilacs.

A generous gift, indeed. Constance's eyes blurred with unexpected tears. "How kind."

"Well," Mr. Gordon drawled. "It *is* in our best interest to see you succeed."

"Anthony Gordon!" his wife said in a reproving tone, looking as if she wanted to elbow him in the side, although she'd have to raise her arm to do so. "Miss Taylor isn't familiar with your sense of humor."

One eyebrow lifted in that upside down V characteristic of Mr. Gordon's expression. "What did I tell you?" he said to Constance with mock seriousness. "Scolding, always scolding."

As if asking for patience, Mrs. Gordon raised her gaze to the ceiling and shook her head. Then she smiled at Constance. "Pay him no mind. I try to do so whenever possible," she said in a joking tone.

Constance chuckled. She shifted the vase to one arm and held out a hand to Mrs. Gordon. "I do believe I understand *and* appreciate your husband's humor. I like a man who can make me laugh."

Mrs. Gordon squeezed and released Constance's hand. "So do I, although—" she shot her husband an amused glance "—it took a while for the appreciation to set in."

He lightly tapped his wife's nose with one long finger. "That's only because when I found you, you were lost, hurt, and soaking wet."

"Exactly!" She grabbed his finger. "Who jokes at such a time?" She shook her head, released his hand, and then smiled at Constance. "I wish I could come in and see everything, but I need to run or I'll be late for school. I'll be by later and hope you still have something I can buy." Her wistful gaze lingered on the purple gown. "If not, I'll have you make me something."

Constance walked over and placed the vase on a small doily on the desk, and then came back to her visitors, who were teasing each other.

"There you go, spending my money again," Mr. Gordon complained and winked at Constance.

Mrs. Gordon tilted up her chin. "Then I'll spend my own."

"What's mine is yours, love, as well you know." With a smile of farewell and a press of his hand on his wife's back, Mr. Gordon turned to escort her down the hall to the front doors.

Constance heard the sounds of their footsteps and then a pause before the front door opened. She had no doubt they'd exchanged a kiss. *That show of affection must be one of the nice things about marriage—kissing hello and good-bye.*

Not, of course, that she wanted to get married. *Even for kisses.*

Mr. Gordon's footsteps returned in her direction.

Lest she be caught eavesdropping, Constance pretended to busy herself straightening the already-neat rack of clothes, until she heard Mr. Gordon open the door to his office and go inside.

She fluffed the full sleeve of a white shirtwaist and then stepped away from the rack, meaning to close the door. With an abrupt change of mind, she decided to leave the door open to invite people in. Still thinking of the Gordons' loving relationship, Constance did one more slow perusal of the shop and allowed herself to feel satisfaction. *My dream of the last few years is about to be realized.*

Hearing the outer doors opening, she perked her ears and moved to stand near the desk, wondering if her first customer was about to arrive. But when a man's footsteps sounded, Constance figured he must have business with Mr. Gordon.

Instead a man in a frockcoat and bowler hat stepped through the doorway.

"Welcome," she began warmly and then realized Dr. Angus Cameron stood there, directing his familiar scowl her way. *If he didn't have such a dour countenance, with his auburn hair and a face of character, he might be an attractive man.* She wondered what he'd look like with a smile and a kind expression in his blue eyes.

I wonder if I'll ever know.

Why should I even care?

Dr. Angus took off his hat. "Miss Taylor," he said, with a stiff bow. "I came to wish you good fortune with yer enterprise."

Before she could thank him, he glanced around, noticed the dress on the mannequin, and stiffened.

Constance's cheeks heated. When she'd originally bought the mannequin, which had a much more realistic female figure than did a dress form, she hadn't counted on men being in her shop. *He's such a prude.*

"I bought the figure in Italy," she said in a tone of ice. "A replica of an ancient statue—one of the Roman goddesses, I believe." She glanced out the front window and saw a pair of ladies crossing the street, seeming intent upon reaching the store. "I'm expecting customers. Please leave."

"Miss Taylor, I must counsel ye about...." He waved a hand at the mannequin.

"Really, Doctor, it's hardly your place to criticize. My mannequin is *not* one of your patients, and neither am I."

His expression tightened. "Ye mistake me, Miss Taylor."

"Do I? Then you are not here to criticize me?"

The doctor hesitated, his gaze searching her face. But he didn't deny her accusation.

The nerve of him! And here I was wondering if I'd misjudged him. She pointed at the door.

"Let me at least give ye this." He fished in his pocket and pulled out a pamphlet. "Once ye read it, we can discuss the contents. I'm sure ye'll find it quite educational."

She glanced down and read, *Women's Rational Dress Society.*

Aren't they the women going around in those ugly knickerbockers?

"Good day, Doctor," Constance said in as polite a tone as she could manage. "In the future, I'll be happy to serve you as a customer who is intent on *purchasing* something."

Chapter Ten

Frowning over his failed attempt to talk to Miss Taylor, Angus walked into the office entrance of the house just as Fergus emerged from the kitchen.

"Good, you're back. Alice and I were just talking," his brother said with a head tilt toward the office. As he talked, he kept going across the hall.

Angus followed his brother into the office, inhaling the scent of herbs.

Fergus went over to his frock coat, which he removed from the hook and donned. Then he placed his hat on his head. "Things have been quiet here for the last couple of days. There are no babies due, no one is seriously ill and in need of my care, and no one is near death. As we know, this situation can change in a minute. But I think we should take advantage of the current state of peace, drive out to the Sanders's ranch, and look over their horses."

"What a grand notion. I'll get my kit." Just the idea of such an outing lifted Angus's spirits. He grabbed his doctor's bag from the shelf and set it on the bed.

"Yer learning quick, laddie, to always have yer bag with ye." Fergus grinned, strode over to the shelves, and brought down his own.

Alice entered, wearing an apron over her dress, and carried a jar of what looked like coffee and a parcel wrapped in waxed paper and tied with string. She held them up and smiled at Angus. "I have no doubt the Sanders will feed you plenty while you're there. But you never know what can delay you along the way." She handed him the food. "Just in case."

He was a city doctor and had only thought of the travel distances, not about running into other problems. But now, Angus could imagine being delayed on the journey by a tree blocking the road or a river too high to cross.

Fergus tugged on leather driving gloves. "For the same reason, Noem will throw a fur robe in the back of the surrey. Montana's weather can change at the drop of a hat. Just so you know, *bràthair*, there's a rifle under the front seat."

"A rifle?" He frowned.

"My Winchester," Fergus said with a serious expression. "We'll have to get you one as well. I've a catalogue around here somewhere. I'll show you a few possibilities. But first, we'll start with the horse."

Angus had never been near guns unless he counted the collection of weapons, including a medieval sword, mounted on the wall of Sir Henry Vail's house—an inheritance from his wife's uncle. "Have ye ever had to use yer rifle?"

"Aye. A few times. Bears, panthers.... More times still I was glad to know it was there, in case of need. I'll teach you to shoot." Angus picked up his bag and walked to his wife, giving her a kiss on the cheek. "Many thanks, *hen*," he said, using a Scottish endearment. "We'll see you tonight."

Alice placed a hand on his chest and looked into his eyes, a loving expression on her face. "Safe journey, husband."

Angus thought he might be witnessing a well-established ritual—one different than their parents' conservative good-byes. He remembered the rifle. *Journeying in the wilds of Montana isn't like driving the streets of Edinburgh—far more dangerous.* He hefted the packet of sandwiches. "Thank ye for these."

"Give my greetings to Elizabeth and Nick." Alice stepped back. "Safe journey."

He and Fergus walked out to where Noem had the surrey waiting. With the warm weather, Cookie's winter shag had started to shed and his sorrel coat gleamed through in patches. He stamped, apparently impatient like Angus, eager to be going.

With the bags and the food stowed in the back, they climbed into the front seat.

Fergus took the reins and released the brake. "I'll let you drive home. You have a problem with the surrey?"

"Can't be much different than the gig," Angus said, referring to their father's vehicle.

"We drove that plenty."

They exchanged grins. From the time they were young adolescents, both had worked with their father, although Fergus had already immigrated to America by the time Angus had started his informal apprenticeship. When their father was tired, he handed over the reins to his son to navigate home.

As they drove through Sweetwater Springs, Angus looked around with interest. He hadn't yet explored this part of town, comprised mostly of houses built of clapboard or logs, which became fewer as they reached the outskirts.

Soon, they drove through a forest. In many places, the rutted dirt lane was barely wider than the surrey. Often, tree branches overgrew the road overhead and blocked the light. Secluded clearings showed small cabins. The isolation made Angus uneasy, and he wondered how long it would take him to become accustomed to traveling through the back woods.

At first, Angus gazed at everything, the wilderness being so different from Scotland. But soon, he found himself thinking of Miss Taylor and his confusion and, aye, *frustration* with the woman.

Ought I tell Fergus what happened this morning? That I failed his assignment to educate her. "I had a—" Angus hesitated, thinking about how to phrase the meeting "—less than optimum encounter with Miss Taylor today."

"Oh? I hope her shop is ready. Alice plans to go over when

Craig's napping, and Mrs. Krutsky can keep an ear out for him."

"I went intending to wish her well and to take her a pamphlet on the rational dress society."

"Today?" Fergus asked in a sharp tone and annoyed sideways glance. "The day she's worked so hard for, dreamed of? Why would you think she'd even want to listen to you today of all days?"

Angus cringed, realizing his brother was right.

Fergus shook his head. "Are you so maladroit with all women, or just this particular one?"

The question stung. Angus had always considered himself a progressive thinker about women's suffrage and the rights of females. *I'm trying to keep women safe and healthy!*

Fergus guided Cookie around a branch protruding onto the road. "Remember I told you I didn't talk to Alice about corsets until after we were married and she was wanting a new dress?"

"Aye."

"I didn't have that conversation when we were courting, nor even as soon as we got married. I did it at a time after she'd gotten to know and trust me—as a loving husband and as a physician. You started out on a negative footing with Miss Taylor. Now, the more you try to make her see what you want, the more resistant she'll be."

Angus gripped the edge of the seat and growled in frustration.

"Do you really want your Miss Taylor to listen to you with an open mind and an open heart?"

When did she become my Miss Taylor?

"You've already ruined the topic beyond the point where the mere recitation of logical facts will fix the situation. Now, she'll have to get to know you and come to trust your judgment. Until then, she's not going to give you the time of day, laddie."

Angus sat back in his seat and crossed his arms. "It's not like I'm marrying the woman." *Although that thought isn't as abhorrent as it should be.* "How can I get her to trust me?"

Fergus let out a how-can-you-be-so-dense sigh. "Start off by refraining from criticizing her. Try being *complimentary* for a change." He hesitated. "One of the things Alice taught me was the importance of compliments to females. You gotta think on how we grew up."

A bird flitted across the road, making Cookie toss his head.

Angus wasn't quite following and turned to Fergus with a questioning expression.

"A lot of love, a lot of pride, but not a lot of showing feelings. Our parents are good people. We know they have a felicitous marriage. But do you remember Da complimenting Mama?"

He thought back. "Sometimes the meals."

"Aside from that."

Angus scrolled through the years, searching for an example but was unable to think of any. He shook his head. "Maybe if we'd had sisters...."

"I doubt it. The behavior is fairly engrained. I was the same as our father, of course. Although I did manage some compliments and a little flirtation during our courtship, else I doubt Alice would have married me."

Flirtation? Bestowing compliments is hard enough. "I'm *not* flirting with Miss Taylor."

Fergus lifted his eyebrows and gave him a bland stare. "Did I say so?"

Angus frowned and made a carry-on flick of his hand.

"I made the assumption that Alice would know how I felt." Fergus picked up his narrative as if they'd never taken a detour about flirtation. "That I found her beautiful, and I found her kindhearted, and I found her generous, and I found her loyal. I enjoyed hearing her laugh and marveled how a woman who wouldn't hurt a fly stood staunch when confronted with the worst injuries of my patients. Yet, she could not read my mind. The lack of my approbation caused her pain in the beginning of our union and led to some...some marital disharmony—that took a while for us to figure out and work through."

Might as well gain from Fergus's experience. "What kind of compliments?"

121

"For example, when Alice wears my favorite dress, I *notice* she looks lovely. In the past, I didn't say so, but now, when I *think* a compliment, I open my mouth and let the words out. It became a matter of paying attention to my appreciative thoughts and then expressing them, which—" he made a scoffing noise "—sounds far easier to do than the process actually was—at least in the beginning."

Angus wasn't at all sure of his brother's advice. "What if I don't think anything complimentary?"

"Then, laddie, yer not paying attention to life." Fergus lifted his chin in the direction of a flowering tree they drove past. "Did ye notice the beauty of that?"

"Aye."

"See, you notice *nature's* beauty. We compliment nature's beauty. We write about nature's beauty, sometimes effusively. Why do we not do the same for humans, especially those we care for?"

That answer, at least, was easy. "So we don't make them vain."

"Do you think such a thing is really possible? Granted, pride is a sin, but from my study of human nature, I believe what the Bible really warns about is *conceit*—vanity, if you will. But do you really think some heartfelt compliments to someone you love will make her vain?"

The surrey rolled over a bump, jolting him. "But what if she already is vain?"

"Are you referring to Miss Taylor?"

"I suppose I am."

"Why would you think she's vain?"

Angus made the hand flourish that would accompany a bow to royalty. "Look at how she dresses. Like she's going to tea with the queen." That comparison wasn't really fair. He'd seen Anastasia Vail in much more elaborate outfits.

"Angus," his brother said in an exasperated tone. "You know one's outer garments don't always correctly reflect one's inner state of mind or personality. You're making an unfavorable judgment about Miss Taylor, which, I remind you, the Good Book says we are not to do."

The truth of Fergus's lecture made Angus wince.

"You and I are both wearing the frock coats common to our profession. Any other doctor we encounter probably also will be. But does the coat say anything about our personality, our values, or our *competence?*"

Angus wondered if he could have dug himself any deeper into a hole.

"Your Miss Taylor might very well be vain and shallow," Fergus commented in an abrupt about-face.

"That's going too far, Fergus." Despite Angus being the one who believed the woman was vain, the statement made him bristle. *Why do I feel the need to defend Miss Taylor?*

But what can I say in her defense? I only have a brief acquaintance with her.

"We canna' know."

Fergus gave him a quick smile of agreement as if he'd not just said Miss Taylor could be vain and shallow. "It's certainly not fair to condemn her."

He grumbled agreement. Miss Constance Taylor had his thoughts so tangled, Angus wasn't sure he could unknot them. No woman had ever before bowled him over like this. *This transition to my new life must have impacted me more than I thought and has scrambled my wits.*

Apparently done with his lecture, Fergus fell quiet, and Angus wasn't about to bring up another topic of conversation.

Leaving the valley behind, they passed some time in silence. The road began to climb, heading toward a mountain pass.

Fergus transferred the reins to one hand to gesture ahead. "When we crest the hill, you'll see the Carter Ranch. We won't descend all the way, but we'll head along the edge of the valley toward the Sanders's ranch, which is our destination. Nick Sanders and his wife Elizabeth have one daughter, Carol, who is about...." He drew his eyebrows together. "Almost two and a half. Carol's age is easy to pinpoint because she was born on Christmas. Most deliveries I've done are a blur. Carol's arrival forced her mother to miss the Christmas pageant that she'd spent a month organizing." He chuckled. "Therefore, I missed it, too."

Angus thought of Maeve's stillborn baby and clenched his jaw. *Some births are memorable in the opposite extreme.*

The conversation lagged. Only the jingle of harness, clop of horse's hoofs, and rattle of wheels broke the silence.

The surrey reached the top of the pass and began the descent. Angus could see the Carter ranch spread out below them, with a river running through the grasslands. The place looked to be a substantial enterprise—a large, white house, a big barn, several other houses and outbuildings, and fields of cattle. White caps crowned the distant purple-gray mountains, and the vivid blue sky arched overhead—a truly stunning vista. *My brother is right. Nature is easy to admire and to praise.*

Fergus nodded toward the valley. "The Carter Ranch is one of the oldest hereabouts. John Carter and his wife Pamela are among the leaders of our community. They have three children, Mark, Sara, and Lizzy. Little Lizzy has always been frail, and we almost lost her a few years ago when we had an outbreak of influenza."

"I remember you writing me of the epidemic. Several patients died, I believe."

Fergus let out a slow breath. "Yes. Lizzy was saved by Elizabeth Sanders's idea to immerse the child in the icy river, which broke her fever. An herbal concoction prepared by the local Indian healer also helped the child's recovery."

Angus turned to him in amazement. "Ye used heathen medicine?"

"Who better than the herbal woman to know the local flora and what has worked for their people for generations?"

"But ye prescribed—"

"*I* didn't," Fergus interrupted in a wry tone. "Good Earth

Woman went directly to the Carters, and they made the decision." He shrugged. "The concoction worked, so now I keep the mixture on hand. I'll show you later and give you a list of ingredients. You'll also want to look through my notebook of the local remedies and what they're used for. Yarrow, for example...."

His brother entertained Angus the rest of the journey by detailing some of the local plants and their medicinal uses. The road rose again and then descended into another valley—smaller than the Carters', with a round blue lake like a sapphire in the middle. Horses, some with foals, dotted the green pastures.

As they drew closer, the Sanders' home surprised him—a big Victorian, complete with a round tower and large porch. Not what he'd have expected out here in the wilderness.

Fergus must have seen his reaction. "Mrs. Sanders comes from a wealthy Boston family."

"How did she end up in Sweetwater Springs?"

"The story goes that John Carter was in need of a wife, and no suitable women were available. So he traveled to Boston where his family originated in order to find a suitable match. He married Pamela, who was best friends with Elizabeth. Many years later, Elizabeth came to stay with Pamela. Nick Sanders was one of John's ranch hands."

"Quite a misalliance then—an heiress and a ranch worker."

"Perhaps by city standards," Fergus said in a reproving tone. "But here, it's obvious that Mr. and Mrs. Sanders are right for each other. You'll see."

"I guess...I just made a judgment without knowing them."

Fergus gave him a glance of obvious approval. "Yer learning, laddie," he said in a thickened burr, repeating what he'd said before they left the house. "But that's to be expected. We Cameron lads are supposed to be quick-minded."

Angus chuckled. "Aye."

The road curved to a stop between the barn and the house.

A man in denim pants and a blue shirt stepped from the front door of the Victorian, clapping a hat on his head—the kind the cowboys wore—and strode across the porch. He must have recognized Fergus, because he trotted down the steps and loped over to the surrey, a grave expression on his face. Fresh blood stained the front of his shirt.

Angus's stomach tightened, knowing something was wrong.

"That's Nick Sanders. Looks like we came at the right time." Fergus parked in front of the barn, setting the brake and tying off the reins. He stripped off his leather gloves and tucked them into his coat pocket.

Angus climbed down, grabbed his bag, and walked over to join Fergus, just as Sanders reached them. He was younger than Angus expected—maybe a little older than himself—with a stocky build. His nose was slightly crooked and obviously had once been broken.

Nick Sanders pushed back his hat. "Doc! Am I glad to see you! I was just about to send one of my hands to town. Ramsey was in an accident, and the men just brought him in. I don't know what the heck happened. The men found him unconscious with a head wound and a broken leg. His horse is all torn up from barbed wire."

Mr. Sanders's shrewd blue-green eyes assessed Angus. "You must be Dr. Cameron, the younger."

I need to squash that nickname immediately. "Dr. Angus will do, Mr. Sanders."

"Call me Nick." He gestured toward the Morgan. "One of the men will see to Cookie. Let me bring you straight to Ramsey." He tilted his head in the direction of the house and started them walking. "We've assumed he'll need a quiet space for his recovery, so we've put him in the downstairs bedroom instead of the bunkhouse."

Fergus nodded. "You assumed correctly. Do you know how long he's been unconscious?"

Nick shook his head. "Ramsey was working alone. Could be as little as half an hour or as long as two." He sighed. "His thigh bone is broken."

Angus exchanged concerned glances with Fergus. The thigh was a more difficult adjustment. They'd need to do considerable manipulation to overcome the strong contraction and shortening of the muscles and stretch the leg into the proper position.

"Good that you're here," Fergus said softly to Angus as they followed Nick toward the porch. "Always harder guiding an inexperienced man through this particular process."

"To be sure, my instructors at medical school never changed Da's way of setting bones."

"Right, laddie, right. We'll be fine."

Nick reached the porch. "I'll take you in through the front, which is closer and will give you a chance to first wash up in the bathroom."

With raised eyebrows, Fergus grinned at Angus. "The Sanders have a bathroom on the first level *and* one on the second story. Enjoy the luxury."

The double doors had round stained-glass windows in a flower pattern and led into a vestibule. They walked through a second set of doors into the spacious entry. The inside was as grand as the outside, with blue and silver wallpaper above paneled wainscoting, a Persian carpet over herringbone floors, and a grand staircase sweeping up to a second story. A huge chandelier dripped crystals.

They stopped to remove their hats and placed them on the hooks of the mirrored hat rack.

Nick led them down a hallway and stopped by a door. "The bathroom." He turned the glass knob and gestured for Angus to go inside.

The bathroom was indeed a luxury, grander even than the one at his brother's, with white hexagonal tile on the floors and paneled half-walls. A big tub took up one wall, and, next to the toilet, a sink was set into the marble countertop of a white cabinet. The small radiator would make bathing comfortable in the winter.

Angus quickly used the toilet, and then thoroughly washed his hands, grateful for the plentiful hot water. After he emerged, Fergus took his turn. Angus joined Nick in the hall.

A blonde woman exited a room from farther down the corridor.

"My wife," Nick said with a proud smile and a tilt of the head in her direction.

Elizabeth walked briskly toward them. Up close, she proved to be a beauty—perhaps a few years older than her husband, with even features and blue eyes. She wore a ruffled blue shirtwaist and—since she hadn't squeezed herself almost in half—a sensibly-tied corset.

He gave a satisfied nod.

Mrs. Sanders's navy-blue skirt swished as she walked. A gold cross necklace and small gold earrings lent elegance to her simple clothing. She looked at Angus, and her eyebrows drew together. She gave a little shake of her head, as if puzzled.

Before he could introduce himself, Fergus emerged from the bathroom and stepped around him.

The woman's expression broke into a relieved smile. "I thought I was imagining things." She held out a hand to Fergus. "Dr. Cameron, thank God, you're here! How did you know we needed you?"

Fergus took Mrs. Sanders's hand and shifted to present Angus before releasing her. "My brother, whom I told you about. We intended to visit and inquire about a horse for him."

"What a miracle." She smiled at Angus. "Welcome to Sweetwater Springs. We've been looking forward to your arrival."

"I'm sorry we have to meet under such circumstances, Mrs. Sanders."

"It's Elizabeth, plain and simple. We don't stand on ceremony here." She gestured toward the door behind her. "Ramsey is in there."

They followed her into the room. Two windows, the damask curtains pulled back, let in plenty of light. A fire in the green-tiled fireplace kept the temperature warm. A wooden chair with a green velvet cushion was next to a chest of drawers. A rough table that looked like it belonged elsewhere held towels, bandages, a bowl of water, and a sponge.

Their patient lay on a four-poster bed. Blood was starting to seep through the thick bandage wrapped around his head. From his wrinkled forehead, the lines along his long nose, and the gray hair around his ears, he appeared to be in his early forties.

Elizabeth sent an anxious glance toward the injured man. "I washed the wound with iodine, and I've continued to layer on bandages as they became blood-soaked."

Fergus pulled back the bedcovers, studying the leg. "Although for this procedure it's good that he's still unconscious, after all this time, I'm concerned that there's a more serious head injury."

"A concussion, certainly," Angus stated.

She shuddered. "Knowing you'd be here at some point, I didn't try to stitch it or anything. If I even could."

"Ye've weathered plenty new situations living here, as have we all," Fergus assured her. "Ye'd have managed, if need be." He set his bag on the table. "We'll address the head wound after we've set the leg."

Angus noted his brother's brogue was back, which seemed to ease her worries, for Elizabeth gave him a small smile and her shoulders relaxed. *Guess he's right about the potential uses of our accent.*

He set his bag on top of a chest of drawers and opened it to pull out splints, strips of cotton, and a bag of gypsum powder— all things he regularly carried because broken bones were a common reason for his services. He walked over to hand the plaster to Nick. "While we examine the patient, please mix this casting paste for us." He detailed what the man needed to do.

Fergus gave Angus an approving nod.

Warmed by the gesture, Angus took a towel from the stack and unfolded it. "It's good he's still out cold."

"Aye, 'tis." Fergus gently raised the leg so they could spread the towel under the limb. After lowering the leg, he pulled out a bottle of iodine from his bag, poured the liquid on a cloth, and gently went over the whole area. Even though the bone wasn't through the skin and no cuts were visible, best to clean the area to prevent any infections.

Fergus dropped the cloth on the table and leaned to grip Ramsey's upper thigh above the injury as close to the hip as possible.

Angus grasped the leg above the knee.

With a do-it-now nod that reminded him of their father, Fergus held the leg steady while Angus began a slow pull in the directional plane of the bone.

Ramsey groaned but didn't come to.

Gradually, Angus pulled harder and harder until he realigned the bone into as close to the original position as possible.

Moving quickly, Fergus laid the splints along each side and used several cloth strips to tie them in place.

Angus maintained his hold on the leg, while Fergus wrapped the gypsum powder-soaked strips around the splinted area. He gently lifted so his brother could reach underneath until the leg was encased in the plaster cast.

Once they'd immobilized the leg, they washed their hands in the bowl of water before going to the bathroom for a more thorough scrub. Then they returned to treat the head wound. Fergus unwrapped the bandages until reaching the bottom layer, which was sticking to the wound. With a raise of his chin, he motioned to the iodine bottle.

Angus poured some onto a clean cloth and handed it to Fergus.

His brother gently dabbed at the gaping laceration until the bandage loosened, exposing a three-inch gash. He glanced up. "Well, shall we spare Mrs. Sanders the mending of Ramsey's wound and have you do the honors?"

Angus took out small locking forceps and a curved suture needle. He hesitated. This procedure was his first medical challenge in America. His reputation would be established. *I'd best get it right.*

Then taking up the needle, he threaded it and, pouring some iodine on a cloth, swabbed the needle and silk thread as well as his hands. Then he moved toward Ramsey's head.

Fergus stepped away to give him space to work before shifting to stand where he could closely examine Angus's work.

Angus studied the wound, pinched the edges together with his fingers, and suddenly everything and everyone in the room faded. Before him was only the patient and the healing that needed to be done. He began to sew, using the forceps to help manipulate the needle through the epidermis and dermis, and tying off each stitch with a common reef knot and snipping off the thread, swabbing the blood as he went.

When he finished, Angus dabbed more iodine over the row of neat, black stitches and reached for a bandage to pad the wound. Then he took longer strips to wrap around Ramsey's head to hold the bandage in place.

Without being asked, Fergus lifted the man's head and angled his hands so Angus could complete the process around the circumference. At last, he lowered Ramsey to the pillow.

After checking the man's pulse and breathing, Angus stepped back to survey his handiwork with satisfaction. *As good as can be.*

Fergus smiled. "Well done. Go wash up. Then I will, and we'll talk to the Sanders about Ramsey's recovery."

Angus set the bloody needle and the forceps on a towel, rinsed his hands in the basin, and dried them. Then he left the room and walked down the hall to the bathroom, conscious that his legs were a little shaky and sweat beaded on his brow. He was tired but also somewhat exhilarated. The process of setting the bone and stitching the cut had been more nerve-wracking than normal, due to knowing that Fergus assessed his every move.

But all had gone well, the two moving as partners, as if they'd trained together for years, unlike his normal experience with working alongside another doctor or with nurses where he had to issue verbal commands—sometimes more than once for every step. *Our apprenticeships with our father were invaluable.*

When he returned to the bedroom, Fergus had already tidied the towels and bandages into a heap on the table and tucked away the iodine bottle and bag of gypsum powder. The forceps and suture needle lay on the towel. "I left them out so you can sterilize them while we eat. I try to do that before I leave a patient's home, rather than waiting until I get back to the house. Sometimes, I'm called to another emergency before I even reach home."

"Makes sense."

Nick and Elizabeth entered the bedroom and stood near the doorway. She reached for her husband's hand, as if needing comfort, and leaned into him.

Nick glanced down at her, his expression tender.

In that small exchange, Angus saw what Fergus meant about the couple being right for each other, and he felt a strange sort of envy. *Will I ever feel that way about a woman?*

The image of Constance Taylor came to mind. He couldn't imagine the infuriating attraction he had for her evolving into a loving relationship like the Sanders had, or one like his brother and Alice's.

Fergus placed a gentle hand on the patient's shoulder. "Now that Ramsey's been made more comfortable, perhaps he'll regain consciousness in the next few hours. I want someone to sit with him for the next two days because he must not move his leg until the plaster completely dries. Keep the fire burning so he stays warm and the plaster dries faster."

Nick glanced at the fireplace. "We'll make sure of that."

"Toss that water outside." Fergus gestured at the table holding the bowl. "Gypsum powder will clog your pipes."

"Can't have that," Nick said with a grimace.

Angus glanced toward the patient. "As I said earlier, Ramsey will certainly have a concussion," he instructed, looking at his brother with a raised eyebrow for permission to continue.

Fergus made a slight go-ahead motion with his hand.

Angus took a step closer to the couple. "Although a concussion doesn't look as serious as a broken leg, the brain is also in need of healing. The trauma the brain sustains during a concussion and the symptoms it creates—including headaches, dizziness, confusion, and fatigue—usually resolves within two weeks but might take weeks or even months longer. Normally, I'd say Ramsey must take it easy and avoid ana' physical activities that could reinjure the brain. However, given his broken leg, he'll be forced to rest ana'way. He'll need peace and quiet for a spell."

Nick nodded. "We'll see to it."

Mrs. Sanders smiled. "The two of you must be famished. The cook has kept dinner warm."

Angus became aware of his empty stomach. "Aye."

Nick gestured in the direction of the barn. "If you'll remain with Ramsey for a few minutes, my dear, I'll send one of the men to stay with him." He squeezed and released his wife's hand.

"Good idea. Carol will be waking soon." She glanced at Ramsey and then at Angus. "Dr. Angus, you have no idea how much it means to the citizens of Sweetwater Springs that you've joined your brother's practice. We are excellently served by him, but he is only one man, and to have a second doctor will make a big difference."

Although Fergus had said much the same thing, this time Angus was able to hear the sentiment without guilt and to accept he was finally right were he needed to be. Something that had been tight and sore-hearted in Angus since his time working in the East End eased.

Angus walked down the hall with Nick and Fergus. *Next on the program, buy a horse.* He was eager to get outside and look over the prospects.

As they approached the entryway, the sound of low male voices reached him.

"If that cut gets infected, might have to put Zeus down."

"Think the boss would sooner shoot Ramsey than that horse."

"Goes without sayin'."

When Angus reached the entry, he found two cowboys—one short with a long, drooping mustache and the other half a head taller and white-haired—standing at the foot of the staircase, obviously waiting for them.

"Doc...." The taller man gave Nick an uncomfortable sideways glance. "Sorry about Zeus, boss. He's tore up."

Nick nodded curtly and frowned, clearly unhappy.

The fellow made a motion toward Fergus that suggested helplessness. "Doc, how do?" He jerked a thumb over his shoulder. "Ramsey's horse, well, Zeus isn't *his* horse, 'xctly. His reg'lar mount tossed a shoe, so he was riding the young Morgan when he had the accident."

The short man elbowed the tall cowboy. "Jerry, git to the point."

Jerry hung his head, looking sheepish. "The horse is cut awfully bad. Tony's holding a pad on him. Do you think you could stitch him up? We was going to do it, but since you's here, we held off."

A horse? Does he think we're veterinarians? Angus waited for Nick to object to the imposition, or for his brother to explain that treating an animal wasn't possible.

Nick's jaw clenched. "Putting the horse down isn't an option."

"We'll take a look," said Fergus. "Ah, Bob. Jerry." Fergus swept a hand in Angus's direction and shot him a mischievous glance. "This is my brother, Dr. Angus Cameron," he said, his brogue thick. "He'll see to the Morgan."

Memories came back to him. That kind of look had never boded well for wee Angus, and he doubted much had changed, though the brothers were both grown men.

Angus clenched his jaw on a sound of protest for his

uncertainty about treating a horse. *I'm a city doctor, not one experienced with animals.*

Nick's gaze bore into Angus's. "If you can save Zeus, I'll be in your debt."

Fergus, who was proving too good at brotherly mindreading, winked and clapped Angus on the shoulder.

The cowboys exchanged looks of relief.

Angus held himself still. He wasn't a young boy to rebelliously shrug off his brother's hand.

"This is one of those times when it's good there're two of us," Fergus said, humor in his eyes. He glanced at Nick. "With your permission, I'll take one of these men to watch over Ramsey, give him instructions, while Angus looks over Zeus."

Nick nodded his approval. "Jerry—" he hooked a thumb in Fergus's direction "—assist Dr. Cameron."

"But—" Angus frowned.

The men turned to him.

He didn't want to get their expectations up. "I'm afraid my experience is in the treating of humans. Horses were rare in the slums of London's East End."

"Same as what ye'd do for a human." Fergus tilted his head in the direction of the sick room. "Come on, let's get yer bag." They went down the hall together.

Panic made Angus's heart beat faster. "But I don't know ana'thin about treating horses," he said in a low voice. "Driving them, aye. But not doctoring them."

"Use a bigger suture needle." Fergus grinned. "I'm sure Elizabeth will keep a plate warm for your dinner."

With a whole new understanding of why the biblical Cain might have wanted to commit fratricide, Angus paused before entering the room. "I've no time to sterilize my locking forceps. Can I use yours?"

"Of course."

Only slightly mollified, Angus continued into the bedroom.

Inside, Elizabeth had moved the chair next to Ramsey's

bedside, where she sat mending a man's shirt. She looked up and smiled. "Back already?"

Angus nodded at her. "Just needed some things. How's the patient?"

"About the same. He moaned in his sleep."

"That's to be expected."

Elizabeth nodded.

He opened Fergus's bag and paused, observing how his brother had arranged the contents in almost the same way Angus did—the system their father had taught them—only Fergus looked to have a few more bottles of medicine and small bags that probably contained dried herbs.

Making a mental note to write a thank-you letter to his father, Angus extracted the forceps, closed Fergus's bag, and grabbed his own, opening it to place the instrument inside. He rolled the edges of the towel around the bloody locking forceps and suture needle he'd used on Ramsey and took them along. Saluting Elizabeth, he eased around Fergus and Jerry, who were entering the room, and strode down the hallway.

Only Bob awaited him near the staircase. The cowboy pointed to the second story. "Nick heard the young 'un and went to her. Be back with us shortly."

A few minutes later, Nick came down the steps with a small blonde girl in his arms. He'd changed out of his bloodstained shirt to a green one. His daughter's curly head rested on his shoulder; his hand protectively cradled her back. "Someone just woke up." His eyes, looking greener from his shirt, radiated pride.

Angus leaned forward so she could see his face. Carol was a miniature version of her mother and, he suspected, probably had her papa wound around her little finger. "Hello, lassie."

"Say hello to Dr. Angus," Nick coaxed.

She scrunched a face and turned her head.

Angus laughed and straightened. "Leave her be. With sixteen nieces and nephews, I well know how the wee ones are upon first awakening from a nap."

"Sixteen, eh? I can't imagine." Nick kissed his daughter's head. "Let me take her to Elizabeth, and then I'll be right with you."

Bob waved for Angus to follow him. Instead of going out the front door, they continued on down the hall and into the kitchen.

The spacious room was made homey and serviceable by a big rectangular table, plenty of cabinets with marble countertops, a pie safe, and an icebox. A tall, thin woman with an apron over her black dress stood at the huge, six-burner stove, ladling food onto a dish.

Stew, Angus supposed from the aroma. His stomach grumbled.

The woman looked over and frowned. She had a hooked nose, dark hair streaked with white, and sharp black eyes. "Doctor Angus, I'm Mrs. Jirtis. Mrs. Sanders told me to hold dinner for you and Doctor Cameron. You must be famished."

"That I am, Mrs. Jirtis. But it's a doctor's lot in life to see to the needs of others before his own—in this case, the needs of a horse." Angus held out the towel with the used suture needle and forceps. "I'm in need of boiling water to sterilize my instruments."

The cook gestured to a pot behind the one holding the stew. "I've been keeping hot water going for your use. Thought you might need it for Ramsey. Will this amount be enough?"

"Aye." Angus walked around her to slide the needle and forceps into the steaming water.

She hovered a hand over the pot. "How long do you need these boiled?"

"About fifteen, twenty minutes. If you don't mind, I'll leave them here while I see to the horse."

"No bother at all." She reached for a roll in a wicker basket on the counter, broke it open, and ladled a bit of stew inside. "Here, doctor, take this with you to tide you over." She handed him the roll and frowned at Bob. "Don't stand there like a lump, Bob Simpson. Take the doctor's bag so he can carry the food."

Suppressing a smile, Angus gave Bob his satchel.

"And some coffee." Mrs. Jirtis bustled over to a rack of tin cups and back to the stove, where a coffee pot sat on a burner. "Won't be as hot as it should. Just started brewing a new pot."

Angus, who'd drunk plenty of cold coffee over the course of his studies and first year of practice, was grateful for the bracing brew. "Ana' temperature will do. Bless ye for yer thoughtfulness."

The woman beamed. "Just doing my job." She poured coffee into the mug and handed the brew to him.

"Thank ye kindly." He jerked his head toward the door in a message for Bob to lead the way and bit into the stew-filled roll. The food tasted as good as it smelled.

Nick entered, carrying his hat. "Ready?"

Angus raised his roll. "Mrs. Jirtis has taken care of me."

Nick winked at the cook. "That's her specialty. Mrs. Jirtis takes good care of all of us."

The cook affected a stern look, but a smile pulled her lips up. "Get along, all of you. No sense wasting your flattery on an old woman when a poor horse needs tending."

Bob, carrying Angus's bag, walked to a hat rack near the back door of the kitchen. He removed his brown cowboy hat from a hook and snugged it on his head.

Angus gave a thought to his own bowler hanging in the entryway but figured he didn't need to wear a hat in the barn.

Nick and Angus followed Bob outside, across a back porch with several wooden rockers and small tables like the one in Ramsey's room, and down a dirt path toward the barn. Cookie grazed with other fine stock in the fenced pasture beyond.

Alternating between sips of coffee and bites of the sandwich, Angus tamped down his building anxiousness. "Tell me of the injuries and what's been done so far."

"Zeus has a slash across his chest." Nick demonstrated by angling a hand over his body. "We washed it out with iodine."

"Woo-ee—" Bob interjected. "He didn't take kindly to that."

"He danced some, poor fella," Nick said. "Can't get any

bandage on there, though. Got Tony holding a pad on it, but Zeus is pretty restive, so that's not working well."

Bob tugged on the ends of his mustache. "Pity, the scar that'll leave—if Zeus lives. He's a showy one, he is, and, best of all, sound and good tempered." He released his mustache and sent Nick a sidelong glance. "Well-trained of course, like all our horses. Would have fetched a pretty sum from someone wanting a looker."

Nick clenched his jaw, his expression grim.

They entered the barn, a cavernous space smelling of horses and straw, with rows of empty stalls and a large hayloft. Angus caught a glimpse of a dark horse in the nearest stall, a cowboy next to him.

"Zeus's in there with Tony." Nick pulled a latch, and the stall door swung open. "We've got him tied in a box stall. I'll get a twitch on his nose before you begin."

The Morgan had a proud head and a hide so dark brown he looked almost black. He was nicely muscled around his shoulders and hindquarters.

The gelding looked at Angus with large, expressive eyes, and his small ears twitched.

Angus gulped back worry that he might not do justice to this fine, apparently trusting, animal.

A dark-complexioned fellow—Tony evidently—pressed a blood-soaked pad against the wound.

Bob handed Angus the bag. "I'll cover the rest of the chores, boss. Don't worry about that."

Nick dipped his head and turned his attention to the horse, running a hand over Zeus's neck and withers. He began talking in a low voice, almost a croon.

While Nick soothed the horse, Angus moved to study the laceration. From what he could see, the slice looked about a foot long, the edges jagged.

He placed his bag on a nearby bale of straw in the corner of the stall.

Two buckets of water stood nearby.

"The bucket on the right has iodine mixed with the water," said Tony.

Angus nodded in acknowledgment, opened the bag, and removed a pair of scissors, a bigger suture needle than the one he'd used on Ramsey, the iodine bottle, Fergus's locking forceps, some small towels, and the spool of silk thread. He cut off several lengths of thread and then swabbed everything with the iodine, laying each item on a strip of clean cloth.

By the time he'd finished his preparations and looked over at the horse, Nick had a loop of rope around the Morgan's nose, attached to what looked like a two-foot long wooden handle. Using the twitch, he'd angled Zeus's head away from Angus's activities, giving him room to work.

Tucking away his concerns about mending horseflesh and focusing on the misery the beast must feel, Angus slowly approached Zeus. "Ah, yer a braw laddie." He rubbed the horse's head. "I know yer hurtin'. I'll get ye fixed right up right and tight, aye?" He cleaned the wound again with the iodine water, then bent to the laceration and dabbed with a pad soaked in iodine to clear away some of the blood to better see. "Easy now, laddie." He probed the depth of the wound.

Zeus shuddered, but the restraining twitch kept him in place.

One corner was deeply cut, probably the impact point of the wire, but a good half of the laceration trailed off to a surface slice that didn't penetrate the muscle.

"How's it look, Doc?" Nick peered around Angus's shoulder.

"Not as bad as I thought."

Nick nodded, still looking concerned.

Standing to the side in case the horse kicked forward, Angus leaned to cut away the edges of loose hide so he could have an even line to stitch the wound. Then he straightened and went back for the suture needle and forceps, leaving the bloody scissors on the towel.

Angus grasped the threaded needle and the locking forceps.

He took a deep breath and stepped up to do his duty, willing his hands to be steady. He made a ninety-degree stitch at the edge of the deepest end of the laceration.

Zeus squealed and jerked back.

"Stand, boy." Nick commanded, tightening the twitch. "Easy, now."

Rolling his eyes, the gelding tried to shy away from Angus, but Nick held him steady.

He used the same technique and vertical stitches on the gelding as he had with Ramsey's laceration, although he utilized the locked forceps even more to pull the suture needle through Zeus's hide.

Even with being tied and the twitch, the horse still was restless.

By the time Angus tied the last reef knot and snipped the thread, his arms were trembling, his muscles ached from holding himself in a contorted position, and he was sweating. *If I'm to work on horses, I'll need to trade my coat for an oilcloth apron.*

With a huge sense of relief, he straightened and stretched, before moving back to the bale and setting the forceps and needle next to the scissors. He dipped his hands into the water bucket to wash off the blood. Then he picked up a towel and dried off his hands.

Nick had removed the twitch and was rubbing Zeus's nose. He smiled. "Well done, Dr. Angus. Now you can add veterinarian to your shingle."

Angus reached out a hand to Zeus and patted the gelding's neck. "I think I'll stick with humans. Although I was glad to help him." He studied the black stitches, not quite as neat as the ones he'd done for Ramsey, almost blending in with the horse's hide. "Will this scar affect his value?"

"Somewhat." Nick shrugged. "More important to me is that he'll be all right."

"Should be. Let Zeus stay in the stall for a couple of days. Send for me if the wound doesn't seem to be healing."

"Will do."

Angus rubbed around the Morgan's ears. After what they'd just been through, he felt rather attached to the horse. *What do you think, boy? Can we work together?*

As if reading his mind, Zeus turned and nuzzled Angus's face.

For the first time in hours, he fully relaxed. *Guess that's my answer.* He grinned at Nick. "I'll buy this fine fellow. Ye can deduct the veterinary bill from his price."

Chapter Eleven

In church on Sunday morning, Constance tried to focus on the sermon, but two things distracted her. The first was the sight of Dr. Angus Cameron sitting next to his sister-in-law and his brother several rows ahead and to the left. *I should have chosen a different pew, one where I can't see that infuriating man.*

She'd selected the middle right of the church, because the spot was where she and Aunt Hannah had usually sat in their church in Chicago. But today she was alone, even though the pew on either side of her was full.

Her father sat in the very back row because he needed to slip in late and leave early because he was busy tending to people's horses. Pepe and Lucia attended the earlier Catholic service. Felicity was working at the hotel today, and Julia and her husband Sam also sat in the back, so they, too, could leave for the sweetshop the moment Reverend Norton concluded the benediction.

Constance's second dilemma stemmed from a woman stopping her before church to ask if she'd open the dress shop today after the service, like the mercantile and Sugarplum Dreams.

Haven't these people heard of a day of rest? We aren't supposed to work on a Sunday. The very idea was scandalous, and she was surprised the two ministers condoned the practice.

Opening on Sunday didn't tempt Constance one single bit.

She was exhausted from the preparations for her home and the shop, as well as having plenty of business from yesterday. Instead of working, she desperately needed quiet and rest.

Yet, she couldn't help thinking about the women who could only come to town on Sundays. *Don't they deserve a chance to order new clothing or buy fabric?*

How can my conscience be arguing back and forth? I thought a conscience was supposed to argue with the part of you that's being tempted.

A baby fussed.

In the pew ahead, Dr. Angus leaned toward Mrs. Cameron, which brought Constance's attention back to the arrogant man. She glared at the back of his red head, and then, remembering where she was, smoothed her face into pious benevolence.

He took the baby from Mrs. Cameron and held him in front of his chest with both hands.

Constance could see the boy's blue eyes open wide before his expression crumpled. She braced herself for the scream the little one was sure to let out.

Dr. Angus jiggled the baby.

Instead of crying, the little one gave him a big smile.

The sight of Dr. Angus taming a fussy baby melted some of the ire she held toward the man. *Perhaps I have been overly hasty in judging him.*

Back and forth. To her annoyance, Constance couldn't seem to settle on an opinion of the doctor. *Why does it even matter what I think of him?*

Because you're attracted, her inner voice suggested.

Nonsense! Straightening, she forced herself to stop thinking about Angus Cameron and focus on the sermon. But in spite of her best efforts to pay attention to the elder Reverend Norton's wise words, Constance found her thoughts straying to the dilemma of whether to open the store after church. *Maybe just for a few weeks until the novelty wears off.*

She let out a sigh.

A stout woman on the other side of Constance, wearing a black dress about five years out of date, sent her a reproving glance.

Realizing the woman must have thought she was sighing from boredom, Constance gave her an apologetic smile and strove to keep her attention focused during the remainder of the service.

At the conclusion, Constance was no more decided than before. After the Nortons walked down the aisle, the others in the pews exited out the middle and sides. For a moment, she stayed put, thinking. Although many leaving the church gave her curious glances, smiles, and nods, no one stopped, and she tried not to feel lonely or to wish for someone with whom to discuss this decision. With a sigh for no one to hear, she picked up her reticule, stood, and moved to the end of the pew.

The younger Mrs. Norton, who'd walked outside with her husband, Reverend Joshua, reentered the church and headed toward Constance. A striking woman with delicate features, she had olive skin, hazel eyes, and a hint of red in her brown hair. Unusual for a minister's wife, she was dressed in the height of fashion, in a well-cut gown of ocher silk with balloon sleeves. She wore matching amber beads in her ears and around her neck.

"Miss Constance Taylor, I believe?" the minister's wife asked in a soft Southern accent.

Constance nodded.

"I'm Delia Norton. Welcome to Sweetwater Springs."

"Thank you," she said, pleased the woman had sought her out.

Mrs. Norton leaned closer. "I know from experience that moving to this small, frontier town from a big city can be quite a challenge. Although Chicago to Sweetwater Springs isn't as much a stretch as New Orleans to Sweetwater Springs. At least you're used to cold weather!"

"I should say so, although I've been spoiled from residing in Italy for two winters."

Mrs. Norton's smile charmed. "If need be, we can commiserate together. Oh, and please call me Delia. Much easier to distinguish me from my mother-in-law that way."

The woman didn't sound like a minister's wife any more than

she looked like one. Not that Constance minded.

Delia slipped her hand around Constance's arm. "I'm so sorry I missed your opening yesterday. Reverend Joshua and I drove out to the Dunn ranch, and we didn't return until almost nightfall. But I heard a rumor that you'll open today after church for a few hours."

Who said that? "It's only…well, I was raised to eschew commerce on the Lord's Day."

"Hmm," Delia mused, nodding. "Many people believe that. We were not so strict in New Orleans. My husband and his father approach the issue with a practicality that those living in the outlying areas appreciate—Sunday being their only day in town—if that. Some families live so far and have no means of transportation, so they only come to town a few Sundays a year."

I can't even imagine living that far away. "So you're saying your husband and his father don't object to business owners working on Sunday?"

"Remember the Sabbath day to keep it holy," Delia quoted. "Reverend Joshua says the commandment doesn't delineate *how* we're to keep the day holy. If we attend church and hold God in our hearts and minds throughout the day…." She shrugged.

"Hard to do when I'm dealing with customers." Constance smiled and held up her palms. "Can you imagine if I'm sizing a gown on some poor woman and thinking about God instead of what I'm doing? I'll stick her with a pin."

"Oh, dear. I see your point. But you can hold God in your heart even when you're not actively thinking about him." Delia fingered her beads. "Anyway, Reverend Norton has asked the Cobbs, the Ritters, and your father, that they spend time later in the day after their businesses are closed reading the Bible and praying, so I'm sure that request will apply to you, too."

I guess that solves my dilemma. "It's a practice I often do on Sunday evenings."

Delia gave Constance an impish smile. "Tomorrow, I'll visit your shop and bring my mama-in-law. For most of her life, she's worn secondhand clothes made over from those in the mission barrel. Not until my husband came home from his missionary work in Africa did that change...he bought her—both his parents, really—new clothes."

Constance had met gentle Mrs. Norton when she and her husband came to call. Her dress had been simple, but the fabric was good and the cut modestly fashionable. "Making do with old clothing must have been hard for her."

"I doubt it." Delia shook her head. "My mama-in-law is the kindest, most unselfish woman I've ever met. She and Reverend Norton are genuinely good and put the needs of others before their own. They give away most of what they have to others and keep only enough for their basic necessities. Joshua has to go to great lengths to get them to accept his gifts."

Constance glanced at Delia's elegant gown and her expensive jewelry. "Do they think you should give away everything, too?"

Delia shook her head. "They don't cast judgment. Besides, it's not so easy to give all one's money away, even if my papa would allow it."

"How can that be?" She shook her head in disbelief.

"The majority of the people here are proud. They don't take charity. Indeed, Reverend Joshua and I sometimes must force money, food, clothing, or medications upon people. What usually works is saying that it's for the good of their children. But other times we need to get creative to find ways to help people without denting their pride—especially when that's all they have."

"But what about the minority who'd gladly accept handouts?"

"My in-laws have lived here a long time. They know who's greedy, who'd seek to take advantage as opposed to those who are truly in need and willing to accept help. Papa has some long-term plans to benefit the community, but I won't say more because he wants his projects to be a surprise."

"Then, I'll look forward to hearing about them when the time is right."

Delia took Constance's hand. "I'm going to have a small

dinner party next Saturday. Please say you and your father will attend."

Constance had heard the younger Nortons lived in a mansion newly built by Delia's father. She couldn't imagine Papa being comfortable in such surroundings. "I'd love to. I can't answer for my father, but I'll let you know tomorrow when you come to the shop."

"Splendid." Delia nodded and moved away.

With a bemused smile, Constance stared after her, wondering if she'd just made her fourth female friend in Sweetwater Springs. She gave herself a little shake. *I'd better hurry out of here if I'm expected to open the shop.* Luckily, while she'd been talking with Delia, everyone had exited the church. She quickly moved down the aisle, out the door, and down the steps, only to see Dr. Angus angle in her direction.

Too late to avoid him.

"Yer in a hurry, Miss Taylor." Dr. Angus glanced at her waist as if judging the tightness of her corset.

Her cheeks heated. "I have customers awaiting me," she said coolly.

"Today?" he said sharply. "On the Sabbath? The Sabbath's not a day for labor."

"Oh." She raised one brow. "And if someone has an accident or becomes ill today, you won't treat them?"

"Dinna' be so foolish. 'Tis not the same, and ye know it."

"You're sounding very Scottish again," she said in a light tone intended to goad.

With a sound of frustration, he clenched his jaw.

Was that a growl? Constance suppressed a smile of satisfaction at succeeding in jabbing the insufferable man. "Good day, Dr. Angus." Wanting to keep her advantage, she strode away, weaving through the members of the congregation who lingered outside, and headed up the street toward the shop.

"You opening today, Miss Taylor?" a woman asked, waving.

Several ladies stopped to hear her answer.

"In a few minutes," she called loud enough to be heard by all of them.

"I'll be right there."

Last night, Constance stayed up late, sewing two more seven-gore skirts, although she left the hems raw. Easier to tailor the length exactly to a customer's height, rather than to let down a hem or bring it up. Good thing she'd delivered the skirts to the shop before she'd left for church.

Once inside the building, Constance took the key from her reticule, unlocked her door, and entered, pulling out her hatpins, which she tossed in the drawer of the desk along with her reticule and the keys. She yanked off her gloves, dropped them next to the keys, and shut the drawer.

As she walked into the back room, Constance removed her bowler, propping her hat on the wheel of the sewing machine, and then took off her half-cape and draped it over the back of the chair. She just had time to go behind the screen and check in the mirror to make sure her hair was smooth when she heard the tapping of heels out in the hall.

Quickly, she moved into the other room, just in time to greet a flurry of ladies—none of whom she knew—coming into the shop. "Welcome."

As they entered, Constance received a stream of introductions and tried to keep the ladies straight by matching names to the hats—not necessarily the best long-term solution. But most women of moderate means wore the same hat all season.

Constance walked from one to another, answering questions and directing the women where to try on the readymade garments. Within what seemed like moments, she sold two hats, a shirtwaist, and several feet of trim and ribbon. She measured and cut yards of material for women who intended to make their own outfits and pinned up the hems of the two skirts she'd made last night, promising the buyers that she'd have them done by next Sunday.

Although Constance was warm with exertion, she enjoyed the

happy bubbling of women's voices and the unexpected monetary boost to her business.

One dark-haired young woman, perhaps sixteen or seventeen, just seemed to be there to look. Sometimes, she reached out a tentative finger to touch the fabric, but mostly she kept her hands clasped behind her back as she studied each bolt. From the state of her shabby dress and the faded sunbonnet she carried by the strings, she badly needed a new outfit from head to toe but apparently couldn't afford them. Like many farm girls, she didn't wear a corset.

Constance noticed the girl's crocheted lace collar and the embroidery on her cuffs and wondered if she'd done the work herself.

Just in case she was a potential customer, once the rest of the ladies left, Constance walked over. "Can I help you find something?"

The girl was pretty, with pansy-brown eyes, a freckled snub nose, and a wide smile. "Oh no, Miss Taylor. Everything's so lovely, though. I'm trying to look my fill so I'll remember all the details when I go home. Who knows when my father will bring us back to town." She leaned forward, shifting her gaze from side to side as if wanting to impart confidential information. "We work the farm on Sundays, just like any other day of the week."

Charmed by the young woman, Constance smiled and gestured in a circling motion to indicate the whole shop. "Apparently, so do I."

"I'm ever so glad." She bobbed her head. "I have a good imagination, and I can create a new dress." She waved toward the mannequin. "One like that would be wonderful but not realistic. My leg-of-mutton sleeves won't be that big." She pointed at the dress and made a curving motion. "I'd make them half way between fashionable and practical."

"Sounds sensible. I prefer not to use the term *leg of mutton*. I sound too much like a butcher."

"Full sleeves, then."

"That will do, or if you want to sound fancy and Parisian, *gigot* sleeves."

Her brow furrowing, the young woman repeated the word. "*Geego*. What does that mean?"

"Leg," said Constance dryly.

Giggles erupted, so infectious Constance couldn't keep from joining her.

"*Geego*. I'll remember that." The girl extended a hand, stopping just short of touching a bolt of blue gingham. "I've chosen this fabric."

"Do you need me to help you figure out how much fabric you'll need to buy?"

The girl let out a long slow sigh. "Only in my dreams. But I tell you, Miss Taylor, that dreams are important out on the prairie when you don't have much else."

The girl's wistful expression gave Constance a sudden idea. With a spurt of hope, she asked, "What is your name?"

"Elsie Bailey."

"Miss Bailey, are you interested in dressmaking?"

She blushed. "Call me Elsie, please. That's what I'm used to answering to. Making a dress is just a dream."

"Doesn't have to be. Would you be interested in a job?" She waved around the shop. "As you can see, I have more work than I can handle. I'm looking to hire someone."

Elsie's brown eyes lit with fire. "I'd love to, Miss. I can sew a fine seam by hand, embroider, tat, crochet. I make patterns from old newspapers, but I don't actually use them on fabric, since I don't have any material." She shrugged. "Every scrap we have is already put to use."

Constance smiled. "You sound very talented."

The zeal in Elsie's eyes dampened. She sighed. "But what with needing two hours to drive to town and another two home..." She shrugged. "Don't even know how long I'd take to walk to town. Wouldn't have enough hours in the day to actually *work* for you, although maybe in the summer when it stays light for a long time, I could give you a few hours and maybe even take sewing home with me."

Eager and hardworking. "Housing comes with the job." Constance pointed upward. "I have a suite on the third floor with an extra bedroom. You can live with me."

Her eyes widening, she sucked in a long breath. "Really? You're not pulling my leg?"

"*Limb*, Elsie," Constance chided in a mock plummy tone. "Ladies use the term *lower limb*, not leg."

"You're not pulling my lower limb, Miss Taylor? My *geego*?"

"Why, Elsie, you learn so quickly." Constance chuckled. "I wouldn't be so cruel as to pull your *gigot*."

Elsie clapped her hands together. "I'd like nothing better than to work with you. I'll ask Pa and Ma right now. They're at the mercantile." She whirled and headed out the door.

"Wait," Constance called after her. "You don't even know how much I'll pay you." But from the click of the front door, the girl was already gone. She crossed her fingers. *Here's hoping Elsie's parents say yes.*

After Constance straightened up the shop, she grabbed her bowler from the wheel of the sewing machine, put it on, and turned off the light, grateful for the ease of flicking a switch instead of having to blow out the flame of a kerosene lamp. *No oily, smoky smell, no filling the bases with oil every few days, and no cleaning the glass chimneys!*

She hurried into the other room, moving quickly before a late customer could arrive, and readied herself to leave. Turning off the electric light, she left the shop.

After locking the door and dropping the key into her reticule, she glanced longingly down the hallway to the staircase, wanting nothing so much as to go upstairs to her suite and take a nap. But

Elsie hadn't returned, and Constance had a feeling the young woman's parents might be reluctant for her to accept the job.

Not that I blame them. She'd be leaving the security of her home to live with a stranger.

Elsie seemed perfect for the job—bright and eager, with imagination and a sense of humor.

I need that girl and can't let her get away. These kinds of intuitive thoughts had come to Constance before, and she'd learned to act on them.

With a tired sigh, she moved toward the outer door of the building. Once outside, she walked at a brisk pace—or at least as quickly as possible, given the restrictions imposed by her stylish outfit. She didn't want to arrive at the mercantile appearing out of breath or overheated.

Good thing Dr. Angus isn't around. He'd be giving me the stink eye. The thought made her giggle, even though Constance knew if the annoying man saw her and cast judgment, she'd quickly become furious.

The mercantile was a brick building with a big window in the front. Constance studied the display, noting the pale blue, two-piece gown on a dress form in the window. Nothing special, really—a frilled front, full sleeves ballooning to just above the elbow, a gored bell skirt. On the floor by the dress was a straw hat with a matching ribbon and daisies dyed in the same shade.

In an odd juxtaposition, farming instruments were propped on the other side of the window—a plow, a hoe, and a shovel, with a bucket on the floor. Constance shook her head and went inside.

The store looked empty of customers. Probably most had already come and gone.

A vinegary scent from the crock of pickles near the left of the door greeted her. A large basket of potatoes, one of carrots, and another of apples, lined up next to the crock. A quick glance around showed a baker's rack on the right with some cakes, pies, and cookies, mostly picked over by the after-church crowd, she guessed. On the left, tall rows of shelving ran almost the full width of the room. Between the door and the counter the empty space showed worn wide plank floors.

No clothing in sight. *Perhaps in the back.*

The short, plump woman behind the counter focused her attention on a basket of eggs. She removed each one, examined it, and put the egg in another basket. She wore on an unbecoming shade of gray with brown stripes and too much expensive trim. When she looked up, her close-set brown eyes narrowed, and she glared at Constance.

Ah, no doubt the notorious Mrs. Cobb.

Constance raised her chin to a regal angle and glided over to the counter. "I want to introduce myself—"

"I know who you are," Mrs. Cobb said in a snide tone. The woman swept a critical gaze up and down Constance's attire.

Go ahead. Try to find fault. Constance kept her features impassive instead of flashing the condescending smile she wished to bestow. After all, the woman clearly needed Christian compassion.

The shopkeeper sniffed in evident derision. "You're the daughter of the livery stable owner. You're living in the barn with him."

Constance's temper flared, but she held in her ire, refusing to let the woman goad her, and kept the benign expression on her face. "Your information is out of date, Mrs. Cobb. I'm living in a suite of rooms in Mr. Gordon's building."

Mrs. Cobb huffed. "A woman living alone is no better than she should be. You're a scandal to the community, that's what."

She caught her breath at the insult. *Don't allow this woman to get the best of you.* "Well—" Constance gave in the tiniest bit to her temper and offered Mrs. Cobb a honey-sweet smile "—I'll have to run your opinion by Reverend Joshua and Mrs. Norton. I've just had a conversation with *Delia*." She stressed the intimacy of being on a first-name basis with the wealthy minister's wife. "She intends to visit my dressmaking establishment tomorrow. In addition, she has invited my father and me to dine with her and Reverend Joshua at their home."

The shopkeeper frowned and crossed her arms over her chest, then evidently thought better of the gesture, for she smoothed out her expression and lowered her arms. "Is there anything I can help you find?" The words came out stiffly, as if the woman begrudged having to issue the invitation.

"Thank you," Constance said in that still-sweet tone. "I'll just have a look around and see what your establishment has to offer." She turned and strolled down the aisle that ran alongside the wall. A glass display case similar to the one in her dressmaking shop held lace and jewelry, and hat stands stood on the top. None of the hats looked inspired.

She glanced down the rows of shelving as she passed. Canned goods of all sorts. Baking supplies. A row of all types of folded clothing, pants, shirts, shawls, shoes, boots, and stacks of men's hats.

She found Elsie toward the back, a basket on her arm filled with some goods. She stood with her parents, a brother about fifteen, and a sister of twelve or so. All of them had similar looks—brown hair and eyes, and shabby attire. They milled around a rack of farm implements. Mr. and Mrs. Bailey were debating the merits of a long-handled shovel with a flat bottom edge versus a round-bottomed, pointed spade.

Shopping with very limited funds must be worrying, indeed. Every purchase carefully weighed against what else was needed and how much everything cost.

Elsie saw Constance, and her eyes lit up. She hastened over. "I told them about the job, Miss Taylor," she said in a low voice. "But they haven't given me an answer. I thought we best get the shopping over with before I press my case."

The Baileys turned and stared at Constance. They both had a similar shape—tall, thin, and broad-shouldered, with weathered, square faces, softened by the same big brown eyes they'd passed to their daughter, and gray-streaked brown hair. Mr. Bailey wore a long beard. Luckily, Elsie hadn't inherited their shapes, being smaller and rounder, but her poor sister was built along the same spare lines as her mother.

155

Constance suspected Elsie's parents were younger than they appeared. Their hard life had probably aged them. She wondered if they were related, cousins, perhaps.

Elsie touched Constance's shoulder. "This is Miss Taylor, whom I told you about. Miss Taylor, these are my parents, Anne and Richard Bailey, and my brother, Ricky, and sister Mary."

Constance stepped forward and offered a hand to Elsie's mother, who took it. "Your daughter was so eager to tell you about the job that she didn't stay for more information." She released Mrs. Bailey's hand. "I'm sure those details are important to you, such as how much your daughter will be paid."

Mr. Bailey cleared his throat. "An offer in hand is important."

"I'll pay fifty cents a day with free room and board—living with me, of course, so your daughter will be chaperoned." She thought of the disparaging comment Mrs. Cobb had cast. "We'll chaperone each other. A day off every other week. We can figure out when. Perhaps, Sunday, so if you come to church, Elsie can spend time with her family."

Elsie sucked in a breath, her eyes wide.

Her parents exchanged thoughtful glances.

"In addition, I will train her in dressmaking, so she'll be learning important skills. I'll give her a discount on all fabric and other goods."

Elsie clasped her hands together, a pleading expression on her face.

Constance couldn't see how the girl's parents could resist that appeal. "Why don't we give this arrangement a try? Say a month? Then, if the situation doesn't suit Elsie or you, or me, for that matter…."

Her father sighed. He pushed back his hat and rubbed his head. "There might be times when we have the sore need for another pair of hands. The harvest…."

"I see no reason she can't go home for a week or so." Constance didn't know what else she could offer to entice them. She sent up a little prayer for divine intervention.

"Please, Pa. Ma," Elsie begged. "My wages could really help out, and I'll be able to make everyone new clothes."

Mr. Bailey shifted his feet and shook his head. "We couldn't take all your money, daughter, generous though the offer is."

"Half, then. I insist. You need new boots, Pa." She placed a hand on his arm. "Please, I *want* to help my family."

He glanced at his feet and then at his daughter. "You're sure about this?"

"Oh, yes, Pa." Her head bobbed.

He held up a hand in apparent resignation. "All right then."

Elsie gave a little bounce. "Oh, thank you!"

Mr. Bailey looked at his wife and shrugged before turning back to his daughter. "Barring bad weather or some unforeseen circumstance, we'll make sure to attend church in a few weeks to see how you do."

Feeling as if a weight had tumbled off her shoulders, Constance relaxed and sent up a prayer of gratitude. She smiled at the girl. "Can you stay and start tomorrow, or do you need to return home and pack your things? If you stay, I can lend you the necessities," she offered, anxious to put the plan in motion. "Or, if you wish, you can take a nightgown, undergarments, a skirt and blouse, from what I have in stock. We'll deduct the cost from your wages."

"I think you should do that, Elsie." Her mother spoke up for the first time. "If you work in Miss Taylor's shop, you'll need to be dressed well." Her cheeks reddened. "Everything you have at home is even shabbier than what you're wearing. As for the rest of your things, we can bring them with us next Sunday."

"That's settled, then." Constance smiled. "I'll leave you to finish your shopping, and then Elsie, why don't you bring your family to the shop? We can show them around and go upstairs so they can see where you'll live."

"We're finished here." Mrs. Bailey glanced at the basket over Elsie's arm. "If you don't mind waiting just a minute, we'll buy these and come with you."

Constance didn't glance at the basket, already having seen the pitifully small amount of supplies inside. She tipped her head in the direction of the counter. "Shall we?" She turned and walked toward Mrs. Cobb, the Baileys following, and then moved back from the counter so the family would have privacy to finish their business.

Mrs. Cobb gave Constance a hard stare but then ignored her, taking the basket Elsie handed over and setting it on the counter.

Mr. Bailey leaned the shovel handle against the counter.

One by one, Mrs. Cobb removed each item from Elsie's basket and set them in two stacks. She held her hand over one pile. "The eggs will only cover these. You'll have to pay cash for the rest." She sent a malicious glare Constance's way. "No credit."

Mr. Bailey frowned.

Constance heard the door open behind them and the sound of footsteps crossing the floor, but she didn't dare take her attention from Mrs. Cobb to look to see who'd entered.

"No credit," Mrs. Bailey echoed, her hand going to her chest, a stricken look on her face. "Why ever not? You've always extended us credit before."

"We've paid back every cent," Mr. Bailey said gruffly.

"Yes, but repayment took far too long. We're not a bank."

Mrs. Cobb's doing this to get back at me. Dismayed by the realization, Constance reached for her reticule to pay for the goods, hoping she carried enough money with her. Then she stopped, instinctively knowing the Baileys were one of those prideful families Delia had told her about. With a sinking feeling, she knew any offer of payment would shame them and just make matters worse.

"Well, if credit is needed?"

From behind her she heard the words of a familiar Scottish brogue.

"I have nae problem with extending some."

Relief went through her, and she turned to give Dr. Angus a wide smile.

He caught her look and nodded, a corner of his mouth quirking, before he shifted his attention to Mr. Bailey.

The man stiffened. "We have no need of charity." He handed the shovel to his son. "Put this back."

Dr. Angus raised one eyebrow. "I have na' offered charity. *Credit* was the word I used. Doctors are used to extending credit." He held up a palm and offered a slight smile. "We are good at judging when someone will do his or her best to repay us."

The boy paused, holding the shovel like a staff, and looked from his father to the doctor.

At Mr. Bailey's puzzled look, Constance stepped closer to the couple. "Mr. and Mrs. Bailey, you probably haven't met Dr. Angus Cameron yet. He's newly come from Scotland."

Mr. Bailey's hard gaze relaxed. "I heard you were coming, doctor."

Mrs. Cobb let out a huff and reached up to finger the gold flowered brooch pinned to her basque. "Perhaps I spoke hastily."

Constance was grateful she wasn't on the receiving end of the scowl Dr. Angus bestowed on the shopkeeper. In fact, knowing the power of that expression, she rather liked seeing him direct a disapproving look Mrs. Cobb's way rather than toward her. She pressed her lips together to keep from smiling.

Angus waited a beat without relaxing his stern expression. "Does that mean yer reconsidering offering this family credit, Mrs. Cobb?"

The shopkeeper fluttered a plump hand. "Of course, since you practically vouched for them."

Dr. Angus looked at Mr. Bailey. "Ye might want to consider whether ye want to be indebted to the mercantile or not."

Mr. Bailey broke into an unexpected grin, showing a missing incisor. "Would rather not be indebted to anyone. But I can't be putting my problems on your shoulders." He turned back to Mrs. Cobb, the stern expression once again on his face. "We'll take the credit. We'll bring eggs whenever we come to town. After the harvest, I'll make good on what's still owed."

The shopkeeper harrumphed. "Very well." Ignoring the Baileys, she glanced at Dr. Angus and bestowed an ingratiating smile upon him. "Dr. Cameron, I'd heard you'd arrived in town. Please allow me to bid you welcome. Can I help you find something?"

He didn't return the smile. "Nae, Mrs. Cobb, ye canna. I came in to see the store—'tis a fine establishment—and now that I've done so, I'll be about my business." He gave them all a little bow, turned, and left.

Bravo! Constance smiled at the Baileys. "I'll wait for you outside."

Mr. Bailey nodded.

With an unhurried pace, Constance sedately crossed to the door, not wanting Mrs. Cobb to think she was chasing Dr. Angus. Otherwise, the next she knew, the unpleasant woman would be spreading gossip that Constance was setting her cap for the new doctor. *As if I'd wear something so old fashioned as caps!*

A smile played about her lips. *Who would have thought I'd feel grateful to Angus Cameron!*

"Wait, Dr. Angus!"

Constance. He could no longer think of her as *Miss Taylor.* His heart stuttering, Angus turned to see her heading toward him, the pretty smile she displayed at odds with her determined stride. She looked so beautiful, he had an impulsive wish to take her in his arms and kiss her. The reaction shocked him—not entirely in a bad way, but enough to keep Angus from grinning back.

Now's the perfect time to pay her a compliment. He heard Fergus's voice in his head. *But I can hardly tell her she's beautiful. That would sound strange coming from out of the blue and might make her uncomfortable with me.*

Without him offering, she took his arm. The breeze blew the

smell of her rose perfume his way and teased tendrils of her hair into dancing around her face.

"Thank you for what you did in there for the Baileys." Her eyes sparkled.

Lovely like emeralds. Should I say so? What if that's often said to her? She's been in Italy and is probably used to suave and debonair men, who drop compliments like a tree sheds leaves.

"Quick thinking on your part, Dr. Angus. Quite impressive— the perfect rescue."

He straightened his shoulders, feeling a foot taller from her praise. *This is what Fergus means.* "'Twas nothing."

"Hardly nothing. Generous and clever. I wouldn't have thought to offer them credit." She huffed out an annoyed sound. "Mrs. Cobb is *such* a nasty woman."

He gave up the effort of figuring out what to say, shoving the dilemma on the back burner. "I couldna' let her treat those people so poorly. Being arbitrary about credit for nae reason."

"Oh, Mrs. Cobb had a reason, all right," Constance said in a wry tone. "My dressmaking business has put her nose out of joint, and she let me know of her disapproval when I first entered the store. In fact, she told me that as a woman living alone, *I was no better than I should be.*" She mimicked the shopkeeper's voice.

He stiffened. "Why, that auld biddy. To slur yer character like that."

Constance laughed. "You're sounding very Scottish again. I can barely follow you." She shook her head. "Mrs. Cobb must have heard me talking with the Baileys and offering Elsie a job. So she took her pique with me out on them. So unfair!"

"My brother warned me about the Cobbs, including that they'd respect my profession and treat me obsequiously."

"And she *did*. I've never seen such fast back-tracking." Constance chuckled. "I'd been warned of them, too. How horrible to be the type of people others caution against."

"With, as we've just seen, justification. Often people don't deserve the reputations they are tarnished with." Angus remembered his earlier judgment of Miss Taylor and felt ashamed.

"Do you think the Cobbs understand how others see them? Or care?"

"Maybe we'll know in time." He shrugged. "Maybe we'll never know." He glanced down at her. "I saw ye reach for your reticule. Ye were going to pay for their supplies."

"I wanted to but knew they are prideful people. My offer would only have made the situation worse."

"I think yer reasoning was sound."

Her eyebrows lifted. "Are you paying me a compliment? Or, actually—" her eyes danced "—*sort* of a compliment?"

"I'm na good with flattery," Angus said stiffly. *Although I'm trying.* He didn't say so, not wanting Constance to think he was practicing on her.

"Well, *that* puts me in my place," she teased.

He started to protest, but then the Baileys streamed out the mercantile door, the girls each carrying a basket and the boy the shovel. Everyone stopped before Angus and Constance.

Mr. Bailey held out a hand to Angus.

Constance released his arm.

The two men shook.

"Thank you for your help in there, Dr. Angus. I don't know what ruffled Mrs. Cobb's feathers, but I'm glad you were able to smooth them down."

Angus was careful not to look at Constance for fear of laughing. "'Twas nothing."

Mr. Bailey pointed down the street. "We'll load everything into the wagon and drive over to your place, Miss Taylor. Would you like a ride?"

"The day is so fine, I think I'll stroll." Smiling, she glanced up at Angus from under her eyelashes. "That is, if the good doctor will lend me his arm."

Her choice surprised and pleased him. "The good doctor will be more than willing," he said, crooking said arm. "Come along, Miss Taylor."

As the Baileys sought their wagon, he and Constance ambled down the street, empty now of the church crowd and looking quieter than he'd so far seen. He was acutely aware of the woman at his side—of the feel of her hand around his arm, the swishing sound of her skirt, the scuff of her footsteps—and felt pride in his lovely companion.

They were silent until out of earshot of the Baileys, and then Constance giggled, sounding like a girl. "Oh, dear." She covered her mouth with a gloved hand. "I didn't *dare* look at you for fear I'd burst out laughing—not that ladies *burst*. Dear me, what shocking language. Pretend you didn't hear me say that."

He couldn't help but grin at her. "I'm a feather-soother. Who ever would have thought it?"

"That you are. But I suppose it's an important skill for a doctor to have."

He chuckled. "Aye."

She squeezed his arm. "I didn't want the Baileys to think I was laughing at them. So unmannerly! I had a hard enough time persuading them to let Elsie work and live with me, and I can't risk them changing their minds." She grinned. "I'm rattling on, aren't I?"

"A wee bit," he teased.

"I must blame the influence of my best friend Victoria, with whom I grew up and traveled to Europe. She could chatter for an hour about nothing. *Someone* had to be the sensible one of the two of us. But now that I'm not around her—"

"Well, ye have me to be the sensible, perhaps even *dour*, one, so blather away."

She laughed. "That's true."

"I'm not implying—" he hastened to add "—that yer really not an intelligent woman." *Is now the time to mention that she doesn't dress sensibly?*

Her cheeks pinked.

No, he decided, not wanting to ruin the moment. *Moments of*

163

laughter and accord don't mean she trusts me yet. "How are ye adjusting to life in Sweetwater Springs, Miss Taylor?"

She hesitated. "Living here is very different from what I've known. Frustrating in many ways, but wonderful and...*healing*, actually, in others."

"Healing?" he questioned, intrigued. "If I may ask...in what manner?"

"I was five, going on six, when my mother died—quite suddenly, really, of influenza. My father sent me to live with my aunt in Chicago. I so mourned for my parents and my beloved horses that I refused to even look at another horse. In fact, I completely forgot I loved them and avoided the creatures as much as possible."

"Forgetting childhood pain is more common than ye think. I believe there's a protective value in so doing."

Her forehead crinkled. "That makes sense. I also didn't retain many memories of my father and, in fact, felt abandoned by him."

"I can imagine so," he murmured.

"Papa did the best he could and, as I've recently told him, I'm grateful for the opportunities I had in Chicago, including the loving relationship with my aunt and how she taught me the dressmaking business." She grinned. "I'm making a divided riding skirt, and Papa will teach me to ride. I'm hoping somewhere in here I remember—" she tapped her forehead under the brim of her hat "—so I'm not quite an awkward novice."

"Perhaps he can teach me, too." The words were out before Angus had a chance to think through the implications.

She glanced askance at him.

"Yesterday, I purchased a horse. Zeus is his name. He's a gelded Morgan who was lacerated by barbed wire, and I sutured him up. I'll take possession of him in two weeks. He's broken to ride and drive, and I'm a capable driver. But I haven't ridden at all. My brother assures me riding is a skill I need to acquire."

"I didn't know you were also a veterinarian."

He grimaced, hunched his shoulders, and looked around as if in mock fright. "Don't say that aloud."

A bow-legged cowboy sauntering by gave him a confused look.

Angus straightened. "I happened to be present, so the horse's owner asked me to see to his injury. Actually, one of his cowboys asked *Fergus* to see to him, and my annoying brother sicced me on the four-legged patient."

She made an amused sound. "How brotherly of him."

"Aye," he said in a wry tone. "I was a tad irritated with Fergus at the time, but it turned out well. Do na' tell him I said so, though."

She touched a gloved finger to her mouth. "My lips are sealed."

His gaze lingered on her mouth, ripe for kissing. He made himself look away. "I ordered a surrey yesterday from a coach builder in Crenshaw. I'm hoping since I want a simple version, no fringe or other—" he almost said *ridiculous* to the woman wearing fringe on her gown "—embellishments, that he'll have one in stock and not have to construct the vehicle from scratch."

"This must be such an exciting time for you—moving here, starting a practice with your brother, a new horse and surrey...."

And ye. But Angus could hardly admit that each time he saw her a surge of excitement went through him.

They reached Ant Gordon's office building and paused in front of the door.

Angus could see the Baileys approaching them—hear the jingle of harnesses and clop of hoof beats. He only had another minute. He gathered his courage. "When my surrey arrives and my horse is accustomed to the vehicle, would ye do me the honor of going for a drive with me?"

Have I just committed to courting her? His stomach knotted. *In fear? In excitement?* Then he saw the surprise—or was it dismay in her expression? In that moment, he regretted the impulse that had made him speak.

Chapter Twelve

The following Saturday, dressing in her bedroom for the Norton's dinner party, Constance stood in front of the full-length mirror that was placed next to her massive wardrobe, checking her appearance. She wore a dinner dress of pale green duchesse satin, with fichu folds of velvet around the square-cut low neckline, butterfly bows at the shoulders, and rounded puff elbow-length sleeves. Her only jewelry was the double strand of Aunt Hannah's pearls.

She placed her hands around her waist, stretching her fingers to measure, and feeling pleased with her hourglass figure. With a swish of her skirts, she emerged from her room to see Elsie already waiting.

"Oh, Miss Taylor!" Elsie's eyes widened. "You look like a princess."

Constance smiled and smoothed her skirt.

The girl had refused to borrow any finery from Constance. She insisted her new rose-colored shirtwaist and skirt would be sufficient and were far nicer than anything she'd been accustomed to wearing.

Keeping that Bailey pride in mind, Constance didn't insist. But she did convinced her assistant that pinning a fall of lace and a cameo brooch at the collar of her blouse and some tortoise shell combs to fancy up her hair wouldn't come amiss.

Elsie promised, with as much fervor and solemnity as a vow, to return everything undamaged to the shop.

"It is enjoyable to dress up for parties, but I'm sure Delia will outshine me."

"Mrs. Norton is beautiful, too, in a completely different style."

"You've learned your lessons in tact and praise very well this week." In fact, the girl had absorbed everything Constance had taught her, even the use of the sewing machine, as if she were a dry sponge soaking up water.

Still, she would keep an eye on Elsie tonight, for the girl would be out of her element, and subtly guide her through the evening, so she didn't make any gauche mistakes.

Elsie clasped her hands together. "This week has been the *best* of my life."

Constance flashed a smile, enjoying the girl's enthusiasm. "One of the best of mine, too, even if we've worked long hours."

"But we caught up on ever so many orders and sold out most of the inventory. Do you think Mrs. Grayson will be at the dinner party and wear the lavender gown? Oh, I'm so nervous just thinking about tonight with all the *grand* people in the *mansion*."

Constance chuckled indulgently. "I don't know that Sweetwater Springs has many grand people."

"You're just saying that because you were in Europe and associated with lords and ladies and counts and countesses." She pinched the sides of her skirt and bobbed a cheeky curtsey. "For a girl who just a few days ago lived in a two-room soddy in the middle of nowhere, they're *grand*."

"Delia gave me a list of all who will attend. Mrs. Grayson won't be there, but her brother Caleb Livingston will be present. Hopefully we'll see Mrs. Grayson wearing the dress another time. You're already acquainted with most of the guests; there's no need for nervousness. Let me think. My father, of course, who'll probably be even more uncomfortable than you, although Lucia promised me she'd ensure he'd show up in his suit, even if the thing is a million years old. Now, you'd hardly call him grand."

"Your pa is funny. I like him."

She nodded in agreement. "You've met Dr. and Mrs. Cameron, right?"

"I know who they are. But all we've done is exchange hellos. Anytime we got sick, Ma did the doctoring."

"Dr. Angus, then. You've met him twice." A few days ago, the doctor had visited the shop to buy some lace as a birthday gift to send to his mother. She'd admired his thoughtfulness.

"The doctor was nice to me, but he really only had eyes for you."

Constance's cheeks warmed. Dr. Angus had seemed attentive, something she tried very hard not to think about. "Mr. Livingston, as I've already said, along with his fiancée Mrs. Baxter," she said hurriedly. "Delia's father Andre Bellaire. They'll soon be your new friends," she teased.

"Oh, no, Miss Taylor!" Her eyes were wide. "I wouldn't *dare* talk to Mr. Livingston or Mr. Bellaire. They're *rich*."

Constance laughed and patted the girl's shoulder. "Wealth isn't a curse, Elsie. I've only been introduced to Mr. Livingston, and I haven't met Mr. Bellaire, but I'm sure they are perfectly amiable."

"They may be, but I still won't dare open my mouth."

That's hard to believe. "You haven't met Felicity Woodbury or her friend Lars Aagaard, who's a logger. But you've heard me talk about Felicity. You two are close in age and she, like you, is far from *grand* and *rich*," she teased. "You both are intelligent, pleasant young women."

"I do hope Felicity likes me."

"Hmm, who else?" Constance tapped her chin. "Oh, yes. The sheriff. I've been looking forward to meeting her."

"Oh, I don't know, Miss Taylor." Elsie shivered. "I met Sheriff Granger once, and she scares me. Her eyes are so cold, like she can see right into you."

"Sounds just like how a sheriff should look." Constance glanced over at the grandfather clock and sucked in a breath. "Goodness, look at the time. We must be leaving. Elsie, I insist you borrow my green velvet cape. Your own shawl just won't do."

Constance watched the struggle with pride play over Elsie's expressive face.

The girl wrinkled her nose. "Very well. If you insist."

Constance returned to her bedroom, picked up the long gloves lying on the dressing table, and tugged them over her hands and up to her elbows. Then she took her evening cape from the wardrobe, swirled it around her shoulders, and tied the satin bows. Her reticule, fan, and the velvet cape were already tossed on her bed. She gathered them up, turned off the light, and went into the other room.

Elsie's eyes grew wide. "That is the most beautiful cape," she said in an awed voice. "What is it made of?"

"Swan's-down. Isn't it gorgeous?"

"I've never seen anything so lovely. You look like a winter princess from a fairy tale book." She extended a hand. "May I touch it?"

"Of course."

"So soft," Elsie said on a breath, her brown eyes dreamy. "Oh, Miss Taylor, do you think if I work real hard, I could have a cape like this someday?" She clasped her hands together and tucked them under her chin. "I'd love that more than anything."

Constance smiled warmly. "I think a swan's-down cape is obtainable, although I suspect you'll come up with new dreams to aim for."

The girl shook her head. "Oh, no, Miss Taylor." She touched the cape again. "One like this is enough."

Constance handed Elsie the velvet cape. "In the meantime, you'll have to settle for this one."

Elsie giggled. "Settle, ha! This one is nice, too. Just not *as* nice." She arranged the cape around her shoulders and picked up her reticule, a bag crocheted of several kinds of yarn, obviously left over from other projects.

With a shake of her head, Constance led the way out of the suite. After locking the door, she placed the key in her reticule—a beaded flower pattern against a gold background—and they moved downstairs. The door to the newspaper office stood ajar, and the click of typewriter keys sounded as they passed.

The day was mild, so Constance had chosen to walk with Elsie rather than have her father pick them up. This past week, they'd been so tied to the shop and their sewing machines they'd barely been outside, much less had any exercise.

They perambulated through the streets of Sweetwater Springs at a slow pace, their corsets too tight for anything brisker. The temperature was too warm, really, for their capes, but they would need the garments later this evening on the way home. Admiring glances—and in some cases, stares—came their way from the others who were out and about in the fine weather.

The Bellaire mansion was set back several blocks from the main thoroughfare, farther down on a street with two-story brick homes in the four-square design that had gained in popularity during the last few years. Nice homes, especially compared to the small log or clapboard houses populating much of the town. But the mansion appeared as a swan to their ducklings.

As they approached, Constance admired the three-story building's rough-cut bricks of Sioux quartzite that looked like brownstone except with pinkish rather than coffee-colored hues. On the left, a round tower with a cone-shaped roof rose above the steep slate roofline. A pergola perched in the front center. She suspected the third floor was probably servants' quarters. Copper trim edged the roof and the big window under the pergola. The metal was still bright and shiny. She wondered how long before the copper turned green.

Elsie sucked in a breath. "That house is *definitely* grand."

"I've heard that, although Mr. Bellaire was from New Orleans, his business was based in New York, and he traveled extensively in Europe. His house reminds me of a French *chateau.*"

"*Chatoe?*"

"A certain type of manor house." A walkway of the same rough quartz led to the entryway. To the right of the tower beside the stone porch that swept across the front of the great house, irregular piles of bricks showed the yard was still under construction. Constance wondered what else was planned— walled flowerbeds, perhaps.

Elsie placed a hand on her chest. "Oh, Miss Taylor, I'm so nervous!"

"Take a deep breath, my dear, and think of this party as an adventure. After all, you've handled every new experience that came your way this week. You'll see this one through, as well."

Elsie inhaled and exhaled. "You're right. Why just six days ago, I longed for adventures." She straightened her shoulders.

At the carved double doors, Constance reached for the doorknocker shaped in a lion's head. She tapped with the ring fitted into the center of the lion's nose.

Apparently losing her nerve, Elsie sidled behind her.

An elderly Negro butler in black livery opened one of the doors and surveyed them with calm brown eyes. His curly white hair was pomaded back from a high forehead.

She'd heard that, like Caleb Livingston importing hotel staff from Boston, Andre Bellaire transported the servants from his home in New York to Sweetwater Springs. Apparently, since he was a good employer and offered increased wages, most had accepted his offer.

Elsie stepped out from behind Constance and and gasped. "Why, he's...."

Constance glanced at her companion suddenly understanding the young woman had never before seen a man with black skin. "Elsie," she said in a warning tone, placing a hand on the girl's arm.

"Yes, Miss Taylor?" Elsie dragged her gaze from the butler.

Constance frowned and whispered, "Don't stare. It's rude."

Nodding, Elsie lowered her gaze.

"Miss Taylor and Miss Bailey," Constance announced.

With an impassive expression, the butler gave a slight bow and opened the door wider to allow them inside.

The entryway was wide with panels up to the chair rails and leaf-patterned green-and-gold wallpaper extending to the ceiling. The bannister of the staircase ended with a statue of a woman wearing only a short, sleeveless toga holding a flame aloft.

"She's partially naked," Elsie whispered. "You can see her lower limbs!"

Constance held in a laugh. *She'd be shocked by some of the statues in Rome.*

An older woman in a black maid's uniform waited in the hall. She, too, looked as though she had Negro blood and, from her prominent cheekbones, perhaps some Indian, as well. "If you will come this way, ladies." The maid's voice held the accent of the South, although not as strongly as Delia's.

The presence of Negro servants was sufficiently rare in Montana that Constance felt like she had entered a grand home in Chicago. She gripped Elsie's arm lest the girl say or do something else inappropriate.

The woman led them into a small room situated to the left, which turned out to be a big coat closet, with hooks running along two walls and shelves on which to set reticules and other paraphernalia. An electric lamp lit a floor-length mirror in an ornate gold frame.

Constance untied her swan's-down cape and handed the garment to the maid.

Elsie, who'd started to hang up the velvet cape, caught herself and gave it to the maid.

After setting her reticule on a shelf, sliding the fan's loop around her wrist, and checking her appearance in the mirror, Constance turned to the maid. "If I may ask your name? I know—" she hurried on, hoping she wasn't causing offence "—

in New York and probably New Orleans as well, servants are to be ignored as much as possible. But this is Sweetwater Springs where everyone knows each other."

The woman's expression broke into a broad smile. "Bless your heart, Miss Taylor. I'm Tilda. Tilda Mounier. My husband, Rufus, is the butler. He and I have worked for Mr. Bellaire for nigh on thirty years. We followed him to New York and from there to here."

"Then you're like family," Elsie commented. She placed her reticule next to Constance's.

"That we are, Miss Bailey, and our children work here, too. Does our hearts good to see Mr. Bellaire so happy. Now——" she waved toward a different door from the one where they'd entered. "We have a bathroom there if either of you need to refresh yourself."

"Oh, my," Elsie said, *sotto voce.*

"A newly built home contains so many conveniences," Constance commented. "If this were the French chateau the mansion is modeled after, in most cases, we'd have to make due with chamber pots."

Elsie giggled. "We only walked a few blocks. I have no need to freshen up, although I'm tempted just to experience the bathroom."

Tilda gave her a kind smile. "If you're ready, I'll take you to the parlor."

Voices in the entryway heralded the arrival of other guests.

"Just a minute, please." Tilda whisked out of the room to greet them, reappearing with Caleb Livingston and his fiancée, Maggie Baxter.

The hotel owner was an attractive man—tall with dark hair and eyes, even features, and an air of sophistication. His formal evening attire made him appear even more handsome than a regular suit.

The scent of exotic perfume trailed after Maggie Baxter. Although technically still within the mourning period for her late husband, she wore a high-necked red gown. The color enhanced her Slavic beauty and emphasized her olive skin, dark-lashed brown eyes, high cheekbones, and wide mouth.

Constance had briefly met the couple at church last week. They had attended with Mrs. Baxter's baby, so they left right after the service.

She cast a professional gaze over the dress, which was full at the shoulders but without puffs and had wide black lace over the lapels of the basque. Black braid trimmed the cuffs and collar. Fan-shaped black appliques embellished the skirt.

Constance wondered if the bright hue made a statement about the quality of the woman's marriage. *Some men aren't worth mourning.* She dismissed a piercing memory of Marcus's betrayal.

Mrs. Baxter removed her black lace shawl and handed it to Tilda, then turned to Constance. "Miss Taylor, how good to see you. I'd hoped to become better acquainted. Having a baby does tend to limit one's socializing." She didn't sound the least bit regretful.

Mr. Livingston touched her shoulder. "I don't know, Maggie." His tone was warm and teasing. "The way your daughter attracts admirers, I think she *enhances* your social life."

Mrs. Baxter gave Constance and Elsie an impish grin. "Charlotte has Caleb wound around her little finger."

Mr. Livingston caught her hand and raised it to his lips. "As does her mother."

The romantic gesture and loving glances the two exchanged made a lump rise in Constance's throat. She had to look away to regain her composure.

Elsie gazed at the couple, her eyes wide, probably spinning dreams of her own romance.

Constance wished her well of them—*not like with Marcus.* She shoved down another bitter memory of the man. *Not all love ends badly.*

Mrs. Baxter turned to Elsie. "I don't believe we've met. I'm Maggie Baxter."

"Elsie Bailey, Mrs. Baxter," she said with a dip of her chin. "I'm Miss Taylor's assistant."

"Please, both of you call me Maggie. My last name only has associations that are abhorrent to me," she said with surprising frankness. She glanced at Mr. Livingston with obvious affection before looking back at them. "Luckily, my daughter and I won't be carrying the burden much longer."

"So pleased for you both. I'm Constance, not Miss Taylor."

Elsie giggled. "I'm still not used to being called Miss Bailey. Until this week, I've only answered to Elsie, and that's just fine."

Mr. Livingston didn't invite them to address him by his given name. Aside from his relationship with Maggie, he didn't seem very approachable.

Maggie placed her black lace reticule on the shelf next to Constance's. "This evening will be the longest I've ever left my baby. I'm torn between worrying and enjoying myself."

Mr. Livingston shook his head. "My sister Edith and nephew Ben are watching Charlotte," he told them. "They adore her and chivvied us out the door so they could claim the baby for themselves."

"We've met Mrs. Grayson."

"That's right," Maggie exclaimed. "Edith purchased that lovely gown from you. She paid you the high compliment of saying the dress was stylish enough to wear when she moves back to Boston after our wedding."

As the four of them turned to exit the closet room, Maggie touched Constance on the arm. "I'd like you to make my wedding gown."

A thrill of excitement went through her. From gossip, Constance knew Mr. Livingston intended their nuptials to be quite *grand*—to borrow Elsie's word—and such a wedding gown would be the perfect advertisement for her business.

Mr. Livingston placed his hand in the small of his fiancée's back. "No expense spared, Miss Taylor. If it were up to Maggie, she'd try to safeguard my pocketbook and dress simply."

She elbowed him. "As if I could. Whenever I try to economize, you just go behind my back and purchase whatever you want for Charlotte or me."

Constance laughed, enjoying their banter. "Before we leave, let's come up with a time to meet and go over what you might like."

"Good idea."

Tilda led them into a sybaritic parlor, the floor covered in Persian rugs, and left them just inside.

The room looked like it ran the length of the house and could probably hold three or four times the number of guests invited today. At the far end, two clusters of people stood chatting, despite the plethora of places to sit. Balloon-backed needlepoint side chairs were scattered around two velvet sofas as wide as beds, with plump pillows and round arms on one end.

A quick glance showed Constance her father hadn't yet arrived. As they walked across the room to reach the other guests, she studied the decor.

Several bookcases lined one wall. A grandfather clock rose on another. Both a fireplace and a radiator could provide heat, although neither appeared in use. Constance admired a tilted black *papier-mâché* table with an inlay of pink roses in the center and a gold-painted border.

Among the group of guests, her gaze was drawn to Angus Cameron, and her stomach dipped.

He conversed with his brother and sister-in-law, along with Reverend Norton and Delia. Both doctors had eschewed their frock coats for suits, and Angus looked less rigid than when clad in his professional attire.

He glanced up and saw her. A smile lit his solemn face.

Her heartbeat increased, and heat flooded her body. She smiled back, and then snapped open her fan to cool her cheeks. With effort, she tore her gaze from his and continued her perusal of the room.

Felicity and her powerfully-built friend, Lars Aagaard, moved to speak with Dr. and Mrs. Cameron and a man she hadn't met. Her friend looked pretty and fragile in the black dress Constance made for her but not as wan as when they'd first met. Just this week, she'd let out an inch from the seams of the mourning gown because Felicity was finally eating more and regaining some of the weight she'd lost grieving the death of her fiancé.

The thin, older man she didn't know detached himself and approached.

Andre Bellaire, Constance guessed from the few auburn streaks remaining in his white hair. Delia had his hazel eyes. She snapped shut her fan and released it to dangle from her wrist.

She'd heard he had a weak heart, which had kept him home from church the last few weeks. Indeed, his heart attack on the train had stranded him and Delia in Sweetwater Springs over a year ago.

Constance smiled to herself, realizing how much she already knew about the people at the party, even though she was barely acquainted with most. *Well, pinning a woman into her dress for the correct measurements is rather time-consuming. So, of course, the customer wants to chat.* She'd certainly heard a lot, although fortunately, since she usually had several pins in her mouth, wasn't expected to contribute to the flow of gossip.

Mr. Bellaire took her hand and gracefully bowed. "Miss Taylor," he said with charming warmth. "I'm Andre Bellaire."

"We are delighted to be here," she said.

He released Constance hand, reached for Elsie's, and bowed. "And you must be Miss Bailey." He let go of her hand.

Elsie went pink with obvious pleasure.

A male servant approached with a tray of champagne glasses.

"Would you like some champagne?" Mr. Bellaire gestured toward the man. "Dr. Cameron has forbidden me the drink of the gods, so I must content myself with fizzy water." He contorted his face into an expression of distaste, making Elsie laugh.

Constance leaned close to her assistant. "Just one glass," she said in a low voice. "I doubt you'll like it. Champagne is an acquired taste. After that, stick to water." She lifted a glass from the tray.

The girl nodded, took a glass, and sipped. She wrinkled her nose, making Mr. Bellaire and Constance laugh. Then her gaze strayed to the bookcases, and she sighed. "I've never seen so many books in my life. And here I thought Miss Taylor had enough to keep me reading for years."

Constance suppressed a smile and sipped her champagne. Elsie didn't realize she'd actually spoken with the *grand* man. *So much for her nervousness.*

"These are Delia's," Andre said, with a languid wave. "You can go look at the books if you'd like. She would tell you to feel free to borrow any that take your fancy. Mine are in my library on the other side of the house. Perhaps I can give you a tour after dinner."

"Yes, please. Excuse me, sir, Miss Taylor...." Elsie drifted toward the bookcases.

Tilda entered, carrying a tray with more glasses. "These are just water," she announced to the room. "Fizzy water."

Andre let out a dramatic sigh and claimed a glass. "A crime, really, not to drink champagne on such occasions."

"I'm sure your health is more important."

"You are absolutely right, Miss Taylor." He sipped his water. "I'm glad to meet you for yourself, but also because of your dressmaking skills. One of my joys is to spoil my daughter." He shook his head. "None of this business about being a preacher's wife and dressing plainly. I won't stand for it. Luckily, her husband allows me my way."

Constance laughed. "Delia is fortunate in her father."

His expression turned serious. "I'm fortunate in having my daughter. She's my greatest blessing."

"Then you both are blessed." Her gaze wandered and she spotted her father. Mack had arrived when she wasn't looking and was speaking with Reverend Joshua.

He saw her glance and gave her a shy grin and slight wave before continuing his talk with the minister.

Constance wondered if her father felt similar feelings of love and gratitude about her.

Mr. Bellaire tracked her gaze. "Your father and I have had a conversation about our girls. We have in common our love for our daughters. We have to forge relationships with our young women. Different from having our girls by our sides all their lives as they grew into ladies. I'm not sure who had it worse—Mack, who had his girl for five years and then suffered the agonies of being away from her—or me, who didn't know about my girl, and experienced many empty years without her."

Tears pricked Constance's eyes. To her chagrin, one spilled over.

Suddenly, Dr. Angus was at her side, extending a handkerchief and taking her glass from her.

Where did he come from? "Thank you." Constance accepted the handkerchief and dabbed at her eyes. "I don't know what came over me." She gave Dr. Angus a tremulous smile and then blew her nose. "I appreciate the rescue." Glancing down at the used handkerchief, she made a face, unsure about returning it.

"Here." Angus plucked the handkerchief from her fingers and tucked it into his pocket. "Doctors are used to the need for them. I always carry several."

Constance snapped open her fan and waved it to cool her hot cheeks.

Mr. Bellaire patted her shoulder. "No more tears, young lady, or you'll have me weeping."

"Whose fault would that be?" Constance retorted, feeling as if the man had already become a dear friend.

His eyes twinkled. "I'll take all the credit." He looked beyond them toward the doorway. "Now—" he said with a small bow "—if you'll excuse me, I have new arrivals to greet." He left them.

Dr. Angus handed Constance her champagne glass and beckoned Tilda over to take one of fizzy water from her tray.

Constance supposed a doctor needed to always remain in an alert state of mind. *Or perhaps he and his brother take turns. Maybe at the next party Dr. Angus will have champagne.*

"You're always there to rescue me," she said in a low voice for the doctor's ears only, her tone flirtatious. "I believe that is three times."

"Then the next time, ye'll have to rescue *me*."

Constance felt the power of his smile all the way to her knees, which trembled. Not wanting to betray her reaction, she waved her fan and glanced around the room.

The Nortons both took glasses of water from Tilda's tray. Delia wore a gown of bronze figured silk with a heart-shaped décolletage, framed on the shoulders and back by a deep velvet collar edged in spangled trim, which draped over the puffs of the sleeves. Her delicate filigree pearl, emerald, and enamel necklace had matching earrings.

Constance wondered again at the dichotomy in which the two lived—a minister and his wife who must balance affluence with the requirements of their faith and their roles in the community.

Sheriff K.C. Granger stood a few feet away from the group, observing the gathering with her cool gray gaze. Although not a beautiful woman, she had strong features and an air of confidence that lent her an unusual kind of attractiveness. The sheriff shook her head when the server offered champagne but accepted a glass of water.

Constance studied the lawwoman's mannish gray suit, looking for the gun belt she'd heard the woman habitually wore. But she couldn't see it. Perhaps, the sheriff had removed the belt and left her pistols in the closet.

She caught sight of ten-year-old Micah Norton stealing into the room. *Hopefully, the weapons are out of the sight and reach of a curious boy.*

Micah had the same crystal blue eyes of his father Joshua and grandfather, although his hair was a darker mink-brown and his features more rounded. With a mischievous expression, he hid behind a chair. He caught her watching him and shook his head, placing a finger against his lips.

She smiled and winked.

The butler entered the parlor. "Dinner is served."

Dr. Angus crooked an elbow and extended an arm. "Allow me to escort ye."

Constance fluttered her eyelashes to tease him. "My pleasure, kind sir."

The dining room, like the parlor, was immense—similar in size to the one in Count Armodo's villa in Italy—and beautifully decorated. A long table covered in a lace cloth, with gold-rimmed, pale green china at each place and two enormous silver candelabra in the middle, could seat sixteen guests. Tonight, though, the numbers were uneven at only fifteen attendees.

Constance glanced around, admiring the ornate gold mirror over the carved fireplace mantle, the mural of a Chinese scene of cherry blossoms on one wall, the ceiling-high olive-green curtains with gold trim, the large China cabinet, and a marble-topped sideboard.

The table was set with little place cards. Constance found hers near the head of the table to Reverend Joshua's left and saw with pleasure Mr. Bellaire was next to her. She wondered why he wasn't taking the host's seat. *After all, this is the house he'd built for himself and his daughter's family.*

Perhaps, she thought of his frail health, and goose bumps shivered along the skin of her arms, *he sees the mansion as belonging to his daughter and son-in-law because he might not live long.* She hoped that situation wasn't the case.

Sheriff K.C. Granger sat across from Constance, giving her plenty of opportunity to covertly study the unusual woman. The gray of her suit enhanced the color of her eyes, and she wore her brown hair in a long braid down her back.

Idly, Constance envisioned the style of gown she'd create for the lawwoman. Gray was a good color for the sheriff, perhaps with black accents. A military cut, nothing frilly. *Could I persuade the sheriff to commission a dress?*

As soon as that speculation came to her, Constance had second thoughts. The sheriff needed to respond to trouble at all times. What if she couldn't restrain a criminal or help someone else because a corset restricted her breath and movement, or her lower limbs tangled in her skirts? A dress simply wouldn't be practical. Both her own safety and that of others could be affected. The idea of causing such a calamity made her shudder.

Her father sat on the sheriff's other side. As Lucia had promised, Mack was slicked up, his face cleanly shaven and his hair pulled back into a neat tail.

With a feeling of guilt, Constance noted his ill-fitting, old-fashioned suit. *I should take better care of him.* She made a mental reminder to tailor him a new suit as soon as she'd filled the initial rush of dressmaking orders, and also when things slowed with her business, to set a regular day every week to have him over for supper.

Felicity sat next to Angus with Lars on her other side. Since their initial meeting, this party was the first opportunity Constance had to observe the two together. The big logger was clearly in love with Felicity, but her friend was still wrapped in a cloak of mourning. However, her manner clearly indicated she liked and trusted the man. *Perhaps love will follow.*

Not for the first time, Constance wondered how she could champion love for others but not for herself. *I'm not actually opposed to falling in love. I just don't want to. My life is ordered just as I've dreamed, and I don't want anything to upset my plans.*

Falling into unrequited love would be almost as bad in Sweetwater Springs as in her Chicago neighborhood. She'd be forced to see the man on a regular basis, which could prove unbearable.

Still, Constance couldn't help sneaking a glance at Dr. Angus, who was deep in a discussion with Delia. While Caleb Livingston was far more classically handsome, something about the doctor attracted her—maybe it was the intelligent glint in his blue eyes, or the way his voice, with the sensual Scottish accent, seemed to curl around her spine and pull her toward him.

To break the attraction before it became obvious, she glanced around the table at the other guests. *How wonderful to find so many special people in my new home. This will be a good life.*

Angus called something across the table to his brother, his expression alight with laughter.

She tried to resist the tug on her heart. *A good life only if I don't do anything such as foolishly falling in love with an unobtainable man.*

As the meal went on, Constance was glad to relax and allow course after course to be placed in front of her. The past week, she and Elsie had been too busy to do more than the most basic cooking. They'd subsisted on a lot of bread and cheese. Apples. Cookies from the sweetshop. Hard-boiled eggs. She was determined to enjoy the special dinner and become better acquainted with her new friends, without allowing Angus to further beguile her.

The meal was delectable, and she enjoyed watching Elsie try unfamiliar foods, starting with the beef consommé and then to the chicken salad and the spiced beef tongue. The girl's expressive face gave no doubt of how she felt about each new taste.

Alice Cameron took a sip of her wine. "Sheriff Granger, I haven't had a chance to hear about your latest trip to the Indian reservation. Have conditions improved?"

The sheriff grimaced. "Somewhat, because of the supplies we've been sending there. Far too many people still died over the winter. But more would have succumbed if our community hadn't helped out." She glanced at Dr. Angus. "Too many, especially the young and elderly, are not strong enough to combat the illnesses that sweep through the place."

Angus leaned forward to look at the sheriff. "I haven't heard about the Indians. At the risk of boring everyone who may be quite familiar with the situation, I'd like to know more about it."

So would I, Constance thought, hiding a shiver.

Sheriff Granger set down her fork. "To make a long story short, the Plains Indians, in our case the Blackfoot tribe, roamed freely and subsisted in great part on the buffalo herds for their food and other needs. Now, the buffalo are all but wiped out, and the people are confined to reservations."

While in Europe, Constance hadn't followed much of the American news, but before her travels, she and Aunt Hannah had avidly read the newspaper. "But isn't the government providing assistance?"

"Barely," the sheriff said, her tone clipped. "Not nearly enough and much of the supplies are stolen by unscrupulous agents—the very men who are supposed to see to the Indians' well-being. About a year ago, some of the young braves were stealing food from some of the outlying farms to help their families survive, which is how I discovered the appalling conditions the tribe lived in. The donations to the reservation have solved the problem of theft. But more problems remain. At least, though, for this visit, we were able to bring seeds and cuttings and help them get gardens planted—a whole new skill for a nomadic people to learn."

Angus exchanged a glance with Fergus. "I'd like to go along when ye next visit the reservation," he told the sheriff. "Perhaps, I can help with some doctoring. I could also learn more about the Indian's herbal remedies."

Constance sent an admiring glance his way, although with his gaze on the sheriff, Dr. Angus didn't see it. *I'll tell him later.*

For the first time, K.C. Granger's eyes warmed. "Dr. Angus, I appreciate that offer more than you can know. Your brother is tied by necessity to Sweetwater Springs. But with two doctors now...."

"Do ye know when ye'll be going again?"

"Not for a few months. As you can understand, some of the timing depends on what's going on here. Sweetwater Springs is usually a quiet town." Sheriff Granger pressed her lips together.

The expression made Constance wonder if the lawwoman had some concerns she didn't want to express.

"Speaking of natives." Mrs. Cameron smiled at Reverend Joshua. "I found your sermon two weeks ago for Mission Sunday quite interesting. Your stories about the Africans had me spellbound."

Maggie laughed. "And, of course, the stories about Micah and his friends—those little monkeys—were so amusing. How could we not open our purses and give to the missions after hearing that sermon?"

Reverend Joshua grinned. "Here my son has a whole new group of monkey friends, although luckily Micah has more supervision now and isn't getting in as much trouble."

"That you know of," Andre said wryly, one eyebrow crooked.

Everyone laughed.

Constance wondered where the boy was now. She wouldn't put it past him to be under the table and had to resist lifting the tablecloth and peeking underneath to check. Not that her corset would allow her to bend that far, anyway.

"Micah told me the last few weeks the church was packed full to overflowing," Mr. Bellaire said in a casual tone.

Reverend Joshua nodded. "Good weather always brings greater attendance, and the town has certainly grown, even in the short time I've been back from Africa." His eyebrows drew together. "My father and I are discussing having a second service. The problem is, the Catholics hold mass before ours. A later service will run into the dinner hour. Sunday dinner is usually a special time for families, and we don't want to disturb that tradition."

Mr. Bellaire took a sip of his fizzy water. "The time has come to build a bigger church. A grand one."

Constance met Elsie's gaze in shared amusement at the man's use of *grand*.

Reverend Joshua shook his head. "I doubt the community could afford a grand one, Andre. Maybe, somehow, we could extend the current building."

Caleb Livingston's eyebrows drew together. "I'd contribute to a new building. How fast do you think a church could be built?" He smiled at Maggie. "Not wanting to scandalize my Boston relatives, my fiancée refuses to wed before her official year of mourning is over. Maybe we could hold the ceremony in the new church."

Reverend Joshua frowned. "We'd first have to raise money—quite a lot of money."

Andre cleared his throat. "I'd be willing to contribute a considerable sum. However, a church belongs to the whole community, and it's only right that everyone feels he or she has contributed what they can to their house of worship."

"You could start a building fund," Constance offered. "When I was in Europe, I saw that some churches had locked boxes in the back where people dropped in money specifically for the needs of the building, new roofs and such."

Reverend Joshua nodded. "That would work nicely."

"We could have fundraisers," Alice Cameron suggested. "A bake sale, for example."

Maggie tapped the table with a finger. "How about a fundraiser that everyone can get involved in? A bake sale is usually organized by the ladies."

"Although the men appreciate eating their efforts," Mr. Bellaire quipped.

"In Grant Hills where I was sheriff before—" the K.C. Granger glanced around the table "—every year the church organized a harvest festival—a huge event—almost like a country fair. People donated livestock, chickens, or a suckling pig, or a calf or goat, and food—baked goods, of course, and other specialties—and handmade items or something from their business...." She looked at Constance. "For example, you could donate a dress."

Mrs. Cameron's eyes lit up. "I see what you mean. Women could donate quilts or doilies, baby clothes, tatting. In addition to livestock, men could bring furs or carvings, even furniture."

Delia smiled across the table at her husband. "This is a wonderful idea, and if we build a new Protestant church, the Catholics can have the old one. I'm sure Father Fredrick would appreciate not having to bring out the statue of the Virgin Mary and put her away again for every mass."

Reverend Joshua leaned back in his chair. "I'll discuss this suggestion with my father. But really, it's up to the community." He glanced at Mr. Livingston and wrinkled his brow. "As for the size and grandeur of the building...that can't happen quickly. Plans have to be drawn up. And how can we commission an architect when we don't know the funds we have to work with? I think you and Maggie better settle for a ceremony in our existing church."

"Well..." Andre drawled, sounding very Southern. "I might just have plans already drawn up and have engaged an architect."

"Oh, Papa." Delia's eyes sparkled. "Of *course* you have."

"And since this house is almost finished—" he made a circling motion above his head to indicate the mansion "—thank goodness, we'll soon have no more banging. We can transfer the workers to the church."

Mr. Livingston cocked an eyebrow. "And I suppose you've already bought the land—the section that was recently sold by the heirs of Anders Nuis to an unknown buyer." He narrowed his eyes. "In fact, two parcels were sold in town recently—in different areas. Did you buy both?"

With a wave of his hand, Mr. Bellaire dismissed the question. "Now, now, Caleb. Let's focus on the church, shall we?"

"Benevolent despot," his daughter chided.

Mr. Bellaire laughed. "Two years ago, I was a lonely man without a purpose and carrying a heavy burden of sadness and regret. I didn't have much to live for. "Now—" he raised his glass "—I have a daughter, a son-in-law, a feisty grandson, and a whole community to meddle in."

"'God moves in a mysterious way, His wonders to perform.'" With a wise smile, Reverend Joshua quoted from the poem of William Cowper. "I suppose you can say I was in a similar place before coming home to Sweetwater Springs, although I did have Micah."

The conversation made Constance reflect on what had brought each of them to this town. She wasn't sure of everyone's story yet, but, as she surveyed each guest in turn, she surmised Joshua Norton might be the only person at the table who was born in Sweetwater Springs. So different from her neighborhood in Chicago, where she'd been the newcomer among families who'd lived there for a generation or two.

Why this town? she mused. Constance certainly never would have come here if not for her father. She'd have to ask him what made him choose Sweetwater Springs after her mother died. Nor would she have come here if it weren't for Marcus. If that Christmas kiss hadn't happened, she wouldn't have fallen for her childhood friend and needed to leave when he loved another. She'd still be living in Aunt Hannah's house.

Constance glanced across the table at Angus, who appeared more relaxed than she'd seen him before, and wondered if his situation was similar. Had he come to this town merely because this place was where his brother's practice was situated? Or, like her, had something else driven him away from Scotland? *England*, she amended, remembering he'd been working in London.

I want to know more about this man.

Becoming better acquainted doesn't have to mean falling in love.

Still, when he looked over and their gazes met, Constance couldn't help but enjoy the warmth that swirled through her.

Chapter Thirteen

All evening, Angus had to work hard not to stare at Constance Taylor. He was coming to know her face in all moods—animated, upset, annoyed, flirtatious, determined, and serious. He sure there were more expressions to discover and found he wanted to learn them all. *A disconcerting idea to be sure.*

After the meal concluded with three kinds of cake and sherbet, the guests in the parlor sipped tea and talked in small conversational groups. As much as he wanted to remain glued to Constance's side, Angus couldn't exhibit such poor manners. Besides, he also wanted to become better acquainted with the other guests, and he made sure to move around and speak with everyone.

As the evening drew to a close, Angus observed Constance talking to Sheriff Granger. They stood near the bookcase, teacups and saucers in hand.

Two women could not have appeared more different. The sheriff's masculine attire and lithe, strong form starkly contrasted in dress and figure to Constance, the epitome of fashionable femininity. While the lawwoman's clothing was practical, safe, and probably should be adopted by all females, he couldn't help but admire Constance's modishness. *What does that say about how I live up to my beliefs and knowledge?*

Carrying his teacup and saucer, Angus moved to join the two just as Miss Bailey approached Constance.

"Miss Taylor," the girl asked with a look of appeal. "Would you mind if I left with Felicity and Lars?"

Constance smiled at her assistant. "Not at all. I'm glad the three of you are becoming friends. And it's fine with me if you invite them up to our rooms for a chat and a cup of tea. I don't think I'll be leaving here for a bit."

"You don't mind walking home alone?"

Constance turned to the left where Mack Taylor talked to Dr. Cameron, obviously intending to speak to her father.

Here's my chance. Before she could request a ride, Angus seized the opportunity. "I'll escort ye, Miss Taylor."

"There, you see," Constance said to Miss Bailey with a smile. She touched Angus's arm. "I'll be fine with Dr. Angus. Do you have your keys?"

"In my reticule." With a little wave, Miss Bailey left with her new friends.

Constance gazed after them, her eyebrows pulling together and causing a little V to form on her forehead. "I do hope Elsie doesn't fancy Mr. Aagaard. He certainly is a striking man. He looks like a Viking, and my assistant is an impressionable girl."

Jealousy squeezed Angus's stomach. *Surely, Constance isn't attracted to the logger?*

Constance looked from the sheriff to him. "I can tell Mr. Aagaard has eyes only for Felicity. Just between us, I'll say that I have hopes for a match between them."

His stomach relaxed. "Alice told me the story of the logging accident. Two men dead and another injured. Tragic."

Constance nodded. "From what Felicity relayed to me, Mr. Aagaard feels guilty, although apparently he heroically tried to save them."

"I know the feeling," he murmured. "Even though, ye've done yer best, there's often a feeling, no matter how illogical, that says ye could have—*should* have—done more."

The sheriff's gaze was on him. She nodded in evident understanding.

A sheriff likely has as many reasons as a doctor to feel powerless about changing the course of other people's lives...or deaths.

He gave a little shake, trying to slough off bad memories. *Constance is entirely too easy to talk to.* "A dinner party is na' the place to discuss such gloomy topics."

For a moment, the three stood in silence, drinking their tea.

Mr. Livingston and Mrs. Baxter came over to say good-bye, no doubt anxious to get home to the baby. She touched Constance's arm. "I've thought of a good time for us to meet to discuss my wedding dress. Charlotte takes a nap after her luncheon feeding. So around one o'clock would work."

"I can come to the house," Constance offered.

"Oh, I'm not home in the daytime. I manage the bathhouse now and bring Charlotte with me. But you can come to me there. I don't yet have an assistant, so it's hard for me to leave, even thought that time of day is usually pretty quiet."

"I understand the need for an assistant. I have no problem with going to the bathhouse."

Mr. Livingston touched Mrs. Baxter's back. They said their good-byes, and he gently steered her toward the door.

The sheriff nodded at Angus and Constance. "I'll say goodnight, then. Rounds to make." She stepped toward their host and hostess.

Alice and Fergus came over to take their leave. Angus knew they were anxious to see how baby Craig had done in their absence. He held up a hand to forestall his family from dragging him off. "I've promised to see Miss Taylor home."

"Wonderful." Alice reached out to take Constance's hand. "So lovely to spend some time with you, Miss Taylor." She shot Angus a conspiratorial smile and then turned back to Constance and released her. "You and your father and Elsie will have to come to dinner one night. Please let us know when you're available."

Angus wanted to roll his eyes at his sister-in-law's obvious attempts at matchmaking, but since he approved of her efforts, he kept his expression impassive.

Constance smiled. "I'll check with my father. But most evenings are fine."

"Of course, although I must warn you in advance that my dinner parties can oft go awry. More often than not, they are ill-fated. Fergus gets called away, leaving me to entertain the guests on my own." With a fond look, she slipped her hand around her husband's arm.

"We don't need him ana'way." Angus teased. "In fact, we can do without the man altogether."

Alice gave his arm a playful slap. "Get away with you, now, Angus." On a wave of laughter, the couple said their farewells to Constance and left.

Constance turned to him with a smile. "This has been such a lovely evening, and one, I must admit, I never thought to experience in a small, frontier town."

"I saw small frontier towns from the train, and I do na' think Sweetwater Springs qualifies as such ana'more. 'Tis neither small nor frontier."

"We'll have to come up with a better descriptor. Especially, since we now have two doctors."

"Almost-medium? A-little-more-polished-than-frontier?"

She laughed and tucked her hand around his arm. "I never would have thought you had a sense of humor."

Angus liked how her opinion of him was changing and becoming more positive. "Nae. Ye canna' be thinking that. Else ye'll be expecting me to keep ye in stitches."

"Ha." She released his arm, only to give him a smack on the shoulder. "Clever *double entendre.*"

"I have my moments."

"That you do." She held his gaze for a moment longer, stirring in him a longing.

For what? Physical intimacy? The comfort of home and companionship that Fergus enjoyed with Alice? Heat crept up his neck and into his face.

An answering blush made her cheeks pink. Then, as if

growing aware the other guests might notice, Constance broke the connection and glanced toward the doorway. "Are you ready to go?"

"I—" he cleared his throat "—I could use a walk after such a fine meal."

They thanked their hosts and hostess, she kissed her father's cheek, and they left the parlor to gather their things from the closet room. In the intimacy of the enclosed space, the atmosphere between them remained charged.

Angus gestured toward the row of women's outer garments. "Which one is yers?"

"The swan's down." She pointed.

He took the white one from the hook, the feather down soft under his fingers, and draped the cape around her. His hands brushed her shoulders. Bending, Angus inhaled her scent—rose perfume and Constance—a potent fragrance he'd never forget.

The butler showed them to the door and bowed them out of the mansion.

They stepped into the dusky evening, the distant mountains dark shadows against the golden sky. The orange undersides of the clouds rippled like a curtained ceiling.

They both looked up, admiring the beauty. Angus made a mental note to get outside at this time of evening more often. Such a performance by the Almighty shouldn't be wasted. *Even though 'tis the beginning of summer, the cold of winter will be here all too soon.*

Constance tore her gaze away from the heavens to smile at him. "The sky is on fire. What an amazing sight. I know the weather in Montana is often abysmal. But tonight, that's hard to believe."

"We are nigh on summer solstice."

She looked askance at him. "The longest day of the year?"

"Yes. Christian though we are, deep down we Scots have na' forgotten our pagan roots. Solstice was a time of celebration. I imagine 'twas quite an event."

"I was thinking earlier about how almost everyone at the party was not born in Sweetwater Springs—Reverend Joshua being the exception."

"Not like home, eh? My family has lived in Edinburgh for generations, and we've been physicians for just as long. America is such an unusual country. All this moving about in search of a better life."

They turned onto the main street, passing Hardy's Saloon, the windows bright with light. Tinny piano music followed them.

"Was there another reason besides your brother living here that brought you to Sweetwater Springs?"

Angus hesitated before saying, "Aye." He glanced down. "And what about ye?"

"Aye," she mimicked.

"Don't stop there, lass. Tell me."

She let out a long, slow sigh. "Foolish, really, when viewed with the wisdom of several years' experience. I fell in love with a neighbor and friend, instigated by a party kiss and some vague promises. His sister, Victoria, is my best friend. In retrospect, much of my feelings came from coveting his family, who were very dear to me. They'd taken me under their wing and made me feel loved and accepted. I wanted so desperately to belong to them, especially, since my Aunt Hannah had died not long before."

"He broke yer heart, poor lass." Angus clenched a fist, feeling an unaccustomed need to smash that man's face.

"Yes," she said simply. "But I'm not sorry. Because of that experience, Victoria and I traveled in Europe, and I changed. When I returned home, even though I no longer had feelings for Marcus, my old life was not a good fit." She shrugged. "So, here I am."

He forced his hand to relax. *Constance has her heart well in hand.*

"And you?"

"Although my circumstances were entirely different, the reasons were similar. I changed and no longer fit where I was."

She nudged him with her shoulder. "You'll have to give me more details than that, Angus Cameron. After all, I shared about my broken heart." She looked up at him, one eyebrow raised in a challenge.

Angus remembered the stillborn baby—bonnie wee Charlie—and the feeling of his heart breaking. "Aye, ye can say a broken heart drove me here, too." As they strolled, he began to tell her about his time working in the East End.

Constance proved to be an attentive listener, often giving him glances of empathy or squeezing his arm at a particularly poignant recounting.

Angus found himself describing his experiences and his *emotions* in a way he never had to anyone, not even Fergus. He talked all the rest of the way. Even though few people were about, the conversation seemed to cocoon them in their own little bubble. Their steps were slow, but they arrived at their destination far too quickly.

Reaching the entrance of the Gordon Building recalled Angus to his surroundings. He glanced up and down the street, wondering if there was a place somewhere in town that courting couples could go to talk. In his Edinburgh neighborhood, a fountain stood in a nearby square with stone benches on four sides. The place wasn't entirely private, which made it acceptable to sit there unchaperoned with a lady. But courting couples were still out from under parental eyes. His brothers had taken full advantage of the spot.

I'll have to ask Fergus. Angus frowned, knowing if he did so he'd reveal his interest in Constance. Actually, his brother already knew of his interest. But he'd have to confess to courting Miss Taylor. Angus wasn't sure he even wanted to admit that possibility to himself.

Constance paused at the door of the building, smiled, and let out what sounded like a happy sigh. "I wish this evening didn't have to end. I'd invite you inside, but after such an intimate conversation with you, I don't want to make social small talk with the others." She released his arm and fished in her reticule for a ring with four keys on it. She sorted through them to find the one she needed.

"Allow me." Angus took the key from her, unlocked the front door, and opened it, hearing laughter at some distance within. "There you go, *hen*."

"Did you just call me a *chicken*?" Constance asked in a shocked tone, stepping into the hallway as if to get away.

His neck burned, both from an endearment slipping out as if it were normal everyday speech, and choosing that particular one, which, of course, she'd misunderstood. He followed her inside, leaving the door open because the hallway was dark. "*Hen* is a Gaelic, uh, *endearment*. I don't know what it means, exactly. I've assumed 'tis like hon, for honey."

The stiffness in her posture melted. "Well, then," she teased, with a flutter of her eyelashes. "I think you should repeat the sentence, so I can properly appreciate what you're saying."

Against his volition, Angus stiffened, feeling awkward. Frustration and desire moved him to stop any more teasing. "Ye drive me mad." The words sounded angry, but his tone was full of longing. He reached out to take her hands and pulled her close, gazing down into her beautiful face. He let go of one hand to reach up and skim a finger along her soft cheek.

A terrible tenderness that he'd never felt for anyone in his life knifed through his reserve, opening him to the heavy mass of emotion inside—feelings he struggled to identify. The anger, at least, was familiar, with maybe a trace of fear underneath, all intertwined with lust. *Surely only lust and not anything deeper.*

He dragged his finger oh-so-slowly across her lips until they parted. An invitation, or so he took it, easing her toward him. Heart beating strongly, he pressed his mouth to hers.

Constance startled back a bit, and then relaxed and leaned closer. She made a little sound of pleasure.

Releasing a hand, he slid an arm around her waist, feeling the stiff bones of the corset, the unnatural curve of her body, and imagined her internal organs squeezing together in protest.

Disturbed by the image, Angus broke off the kiss. Before he could bend to kiss her again, he heard footsteps coming down the staircase and pulled back to a discrete distance, not sure whether to feel relief or dismay at the interruption.

Constance stepped out of his arms, her gloved fingers touching her reddened lips. Her gaze held his, unwavering. Then she lowered her hand and inhaled, as if coming back to herself. "Nice." Her smile and tone teased.

Nice?

Constance touched his arm. "Good night, Dr. Angus. Thank you for your escort home." She peered up at him from under her eyelashes and smiled flirtatiously. With a swirl of skirts, she turned and moved away, tossing a saucy glance over her shoulder, her eyes sparkling like emeralds. She strolled down the hallway, her hips swaying, the curves of her figure so enticing, so deadly.

With a mesmerized shake of his head, Angus watched her go and wondered how one beautiful woman had managed to upend his world.

What am I going to do about Constance Taylor?

In a state of bemusement, Angus walked out the door, took about ten steps across the empty road, and then his legs could go no farther. He stopped and stared almost unseeing at the sky. He was a praying man, of course, especially when he felt intervention from the Almighty might tip the balance of the scales weighing life and death. But, he seldom prayed for himself.

Now, he looked at the fiery sky, the shadows on the undersides of the clouds growing wider and darker, and sent up an inarticulate plea, not even sure what he was asking for. Angus just knew he needed guidance.

A breeze kicked up, swirling around him, and bringing the scent of earth. A leaf danced.

Behind him came the sound of the door opening. He took an unsteady breath and turned to see Miss Woodbury and Mr. Aagaard emerge from the building.

Miss Woodbury accepted Mr. Aagaard's arm. In contrast to his large frame, the young woman was thin. She didn't look healthy.

Angus had heard—he didn't remember where—that Constance had made Miss Woodbury's gown. Her tightly corseted waist was particularly tiny.

His doctoring instincts impelled him to move closer and speak to them. "Good evening, Mr. Aagaard, Miss Woodbury."

With pleasant expressions, they greeted him.

"Forgive me for the impertinence, Miss Woodbury," he began. "I must confess to a physician's nosiness." He didn't wait for a response. "Ye seem to be too thin, and I'm wondering if ye've always been so, or if this is a more recent occurrence? I know 'tis common during grief to lose yer appetite. Have ye been so affected?"

She glanced up at Mr. Aagaard and back at Angus, her expression drawn. "I was enjoying myself tonight. Truly. I ate of the first several courses. Then I couldn't help but think I was at the party because of my changed circumstances, you know?"

"The accident." Mr. Aagaard nodded.

"If Johnny and I were still together, I wouldn't have been invited to… His death brought me to the attention of the Nortons." She waved a dismissive gesture. "I'm not saying they wouldn't have been kind to a member of their congregation."

"They are good people," Angus agreed.

"It's just that Reverend Joshua and Delia are new here and slowly becoming acquainted with folks. I don't know when—" she tapped her chest "—a hotel maid who only attends church every other Sunday would have caught their attention, much less been someone they needed to befriend. I felt guilty, knowing my good spirits in that lovely home were a result of Johnny's death."

Mr. Aagaard glanced down at her and frowned, his eyebrows pulling together in obvious concern. "Johnny, of all men, would want you in good spirits," he said fiercely, speaking with a slight Norwegian accent.

Angus nodded in understanding. "It's to be expected after such a loss that ye'll have times when the contrast brings both enjoyment and pain."

Miss Woodbury gave them a slight smile. "I didn't resist the sherbet." She placed a hand on her stomach. "I'm eating better than at first, Dr. Angus, really I am," she added hurriedly. "But sometimes, I feel like my stomach has a big knot inside. There's no room for food."

"Well, nourishment is still necessary. Try foods that are light, where ye don't have to do a lot of chewing. Soups, for example. Custards. Cottage cheese. Well-cooked oatmeal with honey and cream. Gruel. Dipping bread in soup or milk so it's soft, or a cookie into tea. That sort of thing."

"That makes sense."

"In addition to eating, the process of breathing in and out is very important for general health."

Miss Woodbury nodded, her blue eyes solemn.

"If I may be so bold.... Don't wear yer corset so tightly. Allow the flow of yer breath to go through yer body." With his hand, Angus made an up-and-down motion along his torso. "I've observed breathing deeply, from here—" he touched his stomach and then raised his hand, palm up "—helps bolster and calm the emotions. The pain is still there, but more...controllable."

"Thank you, Dr. Angus. I'll do as you say."

Mr. Aagaard gave him an I'll-see-to-it nod.

Angus wasn't sure what the man could do, given that the logging camp wasn't nearby. Something like a half-day's ride away, he'd heard. But the love and concern of a friend was important during a time of mourning. "If your appetite doesn't improve in the next few weeks, come see me."

"I will," she promised.

The couple said good night and strolled down the street toward the hotel—her hand in his arm, he bent protectively close.

As he watched the big man and waiflike woman disappear into the dusk, Angus realized he'd relaxed while talking to the young woman about her health. Yet, his worry about Constance hadn't been assuaged.

He walked home through the gloaming, remembering the feel of Constance's waist under his hand, and was disturbed. Whereas before, rational dress was sort of an ideological battle, now the topic had become much more personal. Angus knew he needed to speak with her.

He had a whole list of concerns—foremost, her health and well-being. But he also worried how she'd react to the information. Would she be defensive? Angry? Feel bad about the example she was setting and the dresses she'd made and was paid for? Reject not only *what* he was saying but *him*. He didn't want to think about how much that circumstance would hurt.

When Angus reached the house and, out of habit, went around to the office entrance and entered, he was no closer to easing his mind.

A glow from the kitchen made him step inside to find Fergus in his shirtsleeves, standing at the counter and looking out the window into the rapidly fading light. A lamp burned on the table. He caught the familiar scent of heated milk. "Here ye are now," he said to Fergus, thinking he might have a few words about his dilemma. "I didn't expect ye to still be up."

"Alice is feeding the bairn. She thought some warm milk would help us sleep after all the excitement tonight." He grimaced at the cups on the counter in front of him. "I made the milk too hot. Now, I'll have to wait until it cools, else I'll get an earful of teasing about how I canna' even heat milk."

"And so ye should," Angus teased with a mock stern expression. "'Tis a simple enough task." He chuckled. "I suggest ye stir the milk so it cools faster, and ye don't get that nasty skin on top."

Fergus shot him an older-brother, I'm-going-to-pummel-you look. Then his expression cleared, and a grin pulled at his mouth. "And how was yer walk home with Miss Taylor?"

"How did ye know——" Angus broke off the question and glared at Fergus.

His brother laughed. "Yer a Cameron, laddie. Ye'll contrive."

His scowl deepened. "I wish I could be so sure."

Fergus cocked an eyebrow and stirred the milk, waiting.

With a growl, Angus sank into a chair at the kitchen table. "I think we've arrived at that point of trust. Yet, telling her...." He shook his head. "Did ye know, the distinguished anatomist William Henry Flower published a book, *Fashion in Deformity*, in 1881, demonstrating by text and illustration, among other things, the deformities caused by corsets? Ironically, that information did not prevent his wife and four daughters from wearing them. If he could na' convince his own kin, how can I possibly hope to make any impact?"

Fergus abandoned the cups of milk and took a seat. "You do realize Flower specialized in primates. Perhaps his wife and daughters dismissed him because they thought he was comparing them to monkeys."

"What if I say things wrong? With such an important and delicate conversation, I could easily put my foot in my mouth and ruin the sweet relationship developing between us."

Fergus gazed at him with lowered eyebrows. "Aye, and ye probably will. If there ever was such a heavy-footed man around a woman, I ne're saw him." Fergus shook his head in obvious exasperation.

"Yer not helping," Angus growled, annoyed that he'd even opened his mouth about the problem.

Fergus let out a long breath. "Sorry, laddie. Guess, we're still brothers, aye, even though we're all grown up." He rubbed his chin. "Let me act as if we were strangers instead of family." He leaned against the table with an elbow. "Well, Dr. Angus," he intoned in a deep brogue. "If yer afeared of insulting the lassie, I suggest ye write her a letter. On a scrap of paper, ye can practice what ye want to say until ye have the words just right. Then ye can neatly write them out properly on a piece of stationary."

"That's not a bad idea." He flashed Fergus a mocking grin. "I might like ye better as a stranger."

Fergus laughed and stood, clapping Angus on the shoulder. "I'm off to bed, *bràthair*. I wish ye joy of yer composing."

Feeling gratitude well up, Angus clapped his hand over Fergus's and struggled to find the words to express his gratitude. "I've not told ye how much I appreciate ye having me here. I couldna' ask for a better brother." He winked. "Just don't tell the others I said so."

"Aye, they might travel all the way here, just to gang up on ye in one mad pile," Fergus joked. "Then what would we do with them?"

"Just what we need, more Camerons in Sweetwater Springs."

His brother's gaze softened. "Ye've given me a great gift in coming here, *bràthair*. Never forget that." He gestured toward the office. "Ye'll find the paper in the left-hand drawer of the desk. Scrap paper underneath the ledger with my notes and stationery under that." He moved to the counter, picked up the cups, and glanced out the window at the last vestiges of light. "I'll leave ye the lamp. Alice has one lit upstairs." With a smile conveying good luck, he walked out of the room.

Angus thought about seeking his bed but knew he wouldn't be able to sleep. Perhaps he should just get what he wanted to say out of his mind and onto paper. He could deliver the letter in the morning after church.

He picked up the lamp and walked across the hall into the office and over to the desk. Setting down the lamp, he removed his suit jacket and hung up the garment. He rolled up his sleeves and took a seat, opening the desk drawer.

Avoiding the scrap pieces, he reached under the papers to

remove a piece of stationery. *Hopefully, I won't need more than one attempt.* He picked up the pen, dipped it into the inkwell, and began to write.

1*Dear Constance,*

As he scratched out the salutation, Angus realized he hadn't asked permission to address her by her given name. He ran his hand through his hair. *Surely, if I've kissed the lass, I can call her Constance?*

Why must this task be so difficult? With a shake of his head, Angus dipped the pen into the inkwell and returned to writing.

I've tried unsuccessfully to communicate with you about rational dress but have ended up offending you each time. Yet, as our friendship has grown, so has my concern for you, motivating me to express myself through the medium of writing instead of speaking.

I want to make clear that I'm not disparaging your talent at dressmaking. I'm trying to convey concern. The tight lacing of corsets has well-known ill effects on the female body. These facts are not unknown to the public. The pros and cons of using stays to form small waists in girls and women are often debated in the newspapers and have been so for years.

He scowled at what he'd written, tempted to tear up the whole thing.

Well, in for a penny, in for a pound. He dipped the pen again.

While I'm not accusing you of vanity, I have experienced female patients blatantly lying about their waist size, asserting they did wear their stays loose, and their small waists were natural. I can assure you that the Lord who endowed women with the ability to carry a baby did not intend for that same area of the body to be artificially shrunken to such a great extent as fourteen to eighteen inches. As Victor Hugo wrote, "Fashions have done more harm than revolutions."

The ills of a tight corset are more than a restriction of movement, although that in and of itself can cause serious problems. Chasing after a handkerchief can be an inconvenience. But, what if you needed to run after a small child who'd darted into the street?

Living a restricted life works well for the hothouse flower of a woman in wealthy circumstances, who spends much of her time shopping, making and receiving calls, and other such frivolous pursuits. But a woman who wants a life of freedom needs the ability to move.

He underlined the word with a slash and dipped the pen once more.

The Lancet (a British medical journal) cites the female's lack of physiological knowledge as a contributor to the problem of the prevailing fashion. So, allow me to educate you with a list of ramifications. A tight corset:

Compresses lungs

Compresses and deforms ribs (sometimes even fracturing them)

Misaligns the spine

Crushes organs

Causes poor digestion

Causes hiatus hernias

Can deform a developing fetus

He turned over the paper and, with another dip of the pen in the ink, started writing on the other side.

In addition to the harm a tight corset can inflict on the wearer, there is the problem of toxic substances, such as mercury and arsenic, which are used in dyes. Take purple, for example, historically the hue of royalty. Tryanian purple was achieved through the ancient process of crushing the shells of a mollusk called Murex, making a rare and costly dye. This was a natural process, and to my knowledge, the dye isn't harmful.

In contrast, modern mauve dye contains arsenic, picric acid, and other substances injurious to the skin. Green, particularly in the shade of Schelle's or Paris green, can be poisonous. Other color dyes may also be harmful.

I'm not implying we go around in plain cotton. Here are some suggestions for minimizing the toxicity.

1. Soak materials in water, and then rinse them in running water before drying and using. Don't use any fabric, such as velvet, which cannot first be washed.

2. Use undyed cotton as lining to the colored fabrics.

3. Wear cotton gloves when working with materials, and tie a strip of cotton over your nose and mouth to avoid inhaling fumes.

4. Hang a gown made of velvet or other unwashable fabric outside on a windy day to air out but not where the fumes can affect humans or livestock.

I've not written this letter to cause contention between us. Quite the contrary. My primary concern is your health, that of Miss Bailey's, as well as your customers, and, indeed, all the women in Sweetwater Springs.

I'm available to discuss any of your concerns or to cogitate on other solutions.

Sincerely,

Angus Cameron, M.D.

He set down the pen and read what he'd written. Although he wasn't entirely satisfied with his composition, Angus didn't know what he could change or add to make the letter clearer. He waited for the ink to completely dry.

On a sudden impulse, he folded the paper and rummaged in the drawers for an envelope. Picking up the pen, he wrote *Miss Constance Taylor* across the front, tucked the letter inside, and sealed the flap. He rose, rolled down his shirtsleeves, grabbed for his jacket and shrugged it on.

Angus knew there was a three-quarter moon tonight, which would shine enough light to see him to the Gordon Building. He hadn't heard Constance lock the door behind Miss Woodbury and Mr. Aagaard, so hopefully he could slip inside and leave the letter in front of her door.

Tomorrow, I'll know her reaction.

Chapter Fourteen

The memory of Angus's kiss made sleep almost impossible for Constance. She kept replaying each delicious moment and every sensation, especially how he'd made her feel cherished and hungry to explore further physical intimacy. Luckily, she'd retained just enough presence of mind not to let him know her reaction and to end the evening on a playful note. After all, he might just be flirting, and the kiss, like the one from Marcus, meant little to him.

I'll not make the same mistake twice. While in Europe, she'd indulged in a few flirtations and kisses, none of which moved her as did the one with Angus, brief though that contact was. She'd been so careful to keep those former encounters light and pleasant but virtually meaningless.

In just a few moments, Angus had upset her careful plans of a life as a spinster, making her want more—or rather her body and her heart crave more. Her head, however, didn't agree. *I need to allow my head to rule and somehow prevent my heart from yearning.*

Even after arriving at a logical conclusion, she had a hard time falling asleep and awoke early, feeling tired and grumpy. Dawn was breaking, flooding rosy light into her room. She hadn't yet found time to make curtains. *Hopefully this week.*

Constance attempted to turn her thoughts to practicalities— the cut of the tricky sleeve on Mrs. Thompson's dress, the reminder to order more gold ribbon, the need to sew more skirts and shirtwaists, the unpacking that still remained. She eyed the trunks lining the wall under the windows. Once she emptied them, her father promised to store the trunks in the hayloft. *The sooner I complete the task, the sooner I'll have more room to move around my own space.*

Rather than lie in bed and circle around the same memories and wishes and regrets, she rose and put on a dressing gown, resolving to brew coffee and eat some of the cookies she'd bought from Julia yesterday. *Oatmeal cookies are practically breakfast, just in a more palatable form.*

Then she'd go downstairs and sew. *Goodness knows we can use the inventory,* she told herself to assuage her guilt about extra work on the Sabbath.

With the robe tied tight around her waist and in stocking feet, Constance let herself out the front door of the suite to go use the bathroom. She took a step into the hall, only to spy a letter on the floor. *That's odd.*

She stooped to pick up the envelope and read her name on the front, written in a firm, masculine hand. *A love letter from Angus?*

Her heartbeat sped up. Although she wanted to tear open the envelope and read the letter, remembering her resolve for her head to rule her heart, Constance moved back inside and set it on the table. Still, she couldn't help hurrying to the bathroom and rushing through her ablutions.

Back in the suite, Constance forced herself to wait while she stirred the banked embers in the stove and added wood. As the water heated, she removed the oatmeal cookies from the marble crock purchased in Rome and placed them on a plate. She made the coffee with the plunger filter bought in Paris and poured herself a cup, adding cream from the icebox and a lump of sugar.

Constance carried the cookies and cup and saucer to the table. Taking a seat, she picked up a cookie, dipped the edge into the coffee, and took a bite. Despite the deliberate manner, her anticipation built.

Only after finishing the cookie did Constance open the envelope, drawing out a single sheet of stationery. She turned over the paper to confirm the signature. The writing covered both sides. Angus had scrawled his name and title across the bottom.

With a smile curving her lips, she settled back in her chair, took a sip of her coffee, and began to read.

Before too many lines had passed, Constance realized this correspondence wasn't any kind of letter expressing romantic interest. With a huff of disappointment, she straightened, her annoyance growing the more she read.

When Constance finished, she threw the missive across the table. The paper floated up and then drifted down, almost back to where it had started. She rolled her eyes up toward the heavens, grabbed the letter, and began to read, more slowly this time.

The second perusal didn't ease her ire, but concern did start to grow, and her stomach tightened. Angus was correct that the information about corsets was well known. She'd read some of the articles and letters to the editor he'd talked about, which, she figured, were similar in both British and American newspapers.

She'd always found the whole debacle easy to dismiss. A corset gave a lady an hourglass figure and helped with straight posture. Those benefits had been more than enough for her.

She touched her stomach, feeling the softness of her muscles under her fingertips. Not wearing a corset felt odd because the rigidity of her stays was familiar. But she hadn't always felt so comfortable.

Aunt Hannah hadn't made Constance wear a corset until her sixteenth birthday, when she'd received one sized for eighteen inches, and, thank goodness, she never had to sleep in one. Even now, she remembered the pain in her waist and back that first month before she'd grown used to the restriction.

Then Aunt Hannah had presented her with a seventeen-inch corset, and the pain started all over again until her body adjusted. Six months later came the sixteen-inch version.

Victoria's mother had enacted the same routine with her daughter, and the two girls often commiserated about their discomfort. Yet, at the same time, they'd felt grateful not to be tortured at earlier ages, as were many of their friends whose mothers compelled them into stays when they were still girls. One neighbor had started at age seven and had to sleep in a corset at night that was only an inch less constricting than her daytime one. She remembered the girl's tears....

Her aunt had stopped at sixteen inches, allowing Constance to make the decision for herself about whether to go smaller. But not wanting to suffer more torture, Constance had never constrained her waist into fifteen, and definitely not fourteen inches, even though sometimes she'd felt guilty for not being a better model of fashion for her customers.

She carried smaller sizes in the shop but hadn't yet sold a single one. Nor did she stock any constructed for children, although, luckily, no one had asked for one. *Perhaps the ladies in Sweetwater Springs are more sensible.*

So deep in thought was Constance that she didn't hear Elsie moving around in her bedroom. Not until the girl approached the table did Constance pull out of her introspection.

Elsie was already dressed for church in her shirtwaist and skirt, without the lace and cameo she'd worn last evening. "Miss Taylor?" She cocked her head in askance. "Is everything all right?" She glanced at the letter with unabashed curiosity.

Constance gestured at the paper. "From Dr. Angus."

"Dr. Angus?" Elsie held up a hand to stop her. "Just let me nip off to the bathroom, and then you can tell me everything."

Constance glanced over at the grandfather clock, surprised by how much time had elapsed. She'd soon have to start getting ready for church. Now that the weather was warm, she had a delectable gown in Prussian blue, sure to impress one specific doctor.

She rose, moved to the stove, and gingerly touched the coffee pot. *Still warm.* She picked up the pot and poured a cup for Elsie.

The liquid wasn't piping hot, but she knew Elsie didn't care. The girl often expressed gratitude for being offered coffee, previously a rare treat. *Really, Elsie's cheerful, modest personality makes her a joy to be around.*

As she added cream and a sugar lump to the brew, Constance realized that not a day had gone by when Elsie hadn't made her feel grateful. Aside from her much-needed assistance, the girl served as a reminder for Constance to not take for granted the comfortable circumstances in which she'd grown up, as well as her current prosperity. *I need to remember to count my blessings more often.*

Does Dr. Angus count as one?

She frowned at the letter. *Right now, he feels more like a curse.*

That thought made her feel guilty. *I'm wrong to think of people as curses.* As annoying as Constance found the man, she knew without a doubt that he meant well. That realization allowed her to take a deep breath, easing the tightness in her stomach.

Elsie bounced back into the room. "That coffee smells wonderful! Just what I need to wake me up." Seeming to recall how she should be moving, she abruptly slowed to a glide.

Constance hid a smile. The girl had worked hard all week to turn herself into a lady. *I must make sure she doesn't go too far and lose her freshness and zest for life.*

Elsie patted her stomach. "Oh, Miss Taylor, I'm down an inch." She twisted from side to side, preening. "I've been sleeping in the corset for the last three nights. I had no idea how much it would hurt! But all the trouble was worth it. Look at me now!" With a big, bright smile, she waited for Constance's approval. "Maybe I'd better not eat breakfast, though I'll gladly take some coffee."

Oh, dear. "How did you sleep?" Constance asked.

Elsie scrunched a face. "Not very well. But I'm sure I'll get used to the constriction. 'The end justifies the means,' and all."

The girl's words hit Constance like a blow. *This is what Angus is concerned about!* He didn't list going without food as a consequence, but here was Elsie, a girl who loved to eat, ready to deny herself nourishment and sleep, as well as enduring pain, just for a smaller, more fashionable waist.

Have I done this to her? "Where did you get the idea to sleep in your corset?"

Mrs. Grayson told me that was what I needed to do."

"Mrs. Grayson?" Constance echoed. "When did you talk with her?"

"Remember when we were helping her try on the mauve dinner gown, and Mrs. Adler came into the shop for a hat? You left to go wait on her. I told Mrs. Grayson I admired her beautiful figure and graceful carriage and confessed to never having worn a corset before. She graciously told me if I slept in my stays I'd speed up the process of decreasing my waist. Wasn't that nice?" Elsie beamed, obviously gratified that such a *grand* lady had condescended to give her advice.

Oh, no. Constance glanced at the letter, thinking she might have to reread Angus's message with fresh eyes and an open mind.

Elsie tracked her gaze and gave Constance a knowing look. "That's a love letter from Dr. Angus, isn't it? He's sweet on you. I know he is. Last night at dinner, he kept glancing over when you weren't looking."

Heat rose in Constance's face. "In a way," she said slowly, thinking. "Perhaps this is a love letter. Just not in the traditional sense." She thrust the paper at Elsie. "Go ahead and read it." She rose. "I need to get dressed." She took a few steps, then turned and waved toward the plate of cookies. "At least have one. They're oatmeal. Better in a cookie than in porridge."

As she closed the bedroom door behind her and moved to the wardrobe, Constance realized she couldn't wear a looser corset to church, even if she'd wanted to. Her clothes were all sized to a sixteen-inch waist.

She pressed her lips together.

Angus will take one look at me and think I'm defying him. Did she care about his opinion? *Yes.* The thought she might hurt or anger him made her feel sick.

I'll just have to explain as soon as I can. Although, I don't know what I'll say beyond that I'll need time to let out the seams of my clothing.

To how much? Twenty inches? The thought made her cringe.

I need time to think through the information and make decisions on what, if anything, to implement.

Sunday morning, Angus awoke at dawn with a question on his mind. *Has Constance read my letter yet?*

His stomach knotted. *Will she even talk to me?* He imagined her turning a cold shoulder in his direction. Or maybe she'd say something cutting. Or maybe.... He forced himself to stop speculating. *I'll know the truth soon enough.*

He took in several long breaths, trying to relax and doze for a bit longer. Then, realizing he wanted to be early to church to speak with her—at least to judge her state of mind toward him, even if they couldn't communicate—Angus threw off the covers and rose. Walking over to the window, he drew back the curtains to see a sunny day.

Once dressed, he went downstairs to the bathroom, intending to do his best to hasten the morning's preparations for everyone so they could get out the door in a timely manner. However, his nephew thwarted his intentions.

Baby Craig was fussy, cutting a tooth, which distracted Alice and kept her from getting ready. As the minutes slipped by, Angus became more and more tense.

By the time Alice made the decision to stay home with the baby, the hands of the clock had moved perilously close to the top of the hour. Angus and Fergus had to hurry, else they'd arrive late to the service.

Walking down the street at a fast clip, well behind the

townspeople heading in the same direction, only made the knot in Angus's stomach tighten. He sent up a little prayer that all would be well with Constance, and not just the matters between the two of them. As a dressmaker, she'd be molding the attitudes and habits of the females in this town—affecting their health— for years to come.

The bell started ringing when they were still about a hundred yards away. As they approached, the crowd of people who'd been taking advantage of the fine weather to chat outside dwindled as they headed inside. He searched for Constance but didn't see her.

One by one, people filed past the two ministers and their wives, who stood on either side of the foot of the stairs, greeting the parishioners before heading into the church.

Angus and Fergus moved to join the line.

People smiled, nodded, and called out greetings.

His body tense, Angus tried not to be rude. He hid his impatience and responded in kind but still kept an eye out for Constance.

Angus saw Ant Gordon move aside, and Constance walked up the stairs of the church with Miss Bailey. The big man had blocked his view of them. She was wearing a dress he hadn't seen before, this one in a shade of blue-green, and her hat sported a peacock feather. His gaze lingered on the wasp-thinness of her waist—as tiny as ever—and his stomach curdled.

Constance turned and sent a glance around but didn't appear to see him—if, indeed, she was looking for him at all. Then she and Miss Bailey moved inside.

Angus let out a long, harsh breath. *Now, I'll have to wait until after the service.* An hour—or more if the minister waxed eloquent with the sermon—seemed interminable.

Fergus gave him a curious glance. "Do you plan to give Miss Taylor your letter today?"

"Already did. Left the envelope outside her door last night."

Fergus raised his eyebrows but didn't say anything more.

They reached the Nortons. Fergus chose the left, greeting the older couple.

Angus moved toward Reverend Joshua and Delia. "Thank ye again for the lovely evening."

Delia smiled at him. "We had a wonderful time." She glanced up at her husband.

"Certainly." Reverend Joshua nodded in agreement. "Although we didn't have a chance to speak much to you. To Miss Taylor, either. Perhaps, next time we'll keep to smaller numbers."

"I'd like that." *If the numbers include Constance.* Aware of the people waiting behind him, Angus nodded and moved up the steps.

Contrary to his expectations, the service wasn't interminable. The rituals settled him, easing his stomach and allowing his tight shoulders to relax. He was able to pay attention to Reverend Joshua's sermon and join in singing the hymns.

It helped that one selection was his favorite, "Lift High the Cross," even though the lyrics expressed in American accents made the song sound different. As Angus fervently sang the words, he also listened, half in enjoyment and half missing the familiar brogue of his homeland.

After the service ended, as people rose and began to leave, Angus was conscious of the cacophony of voices. His chest constricted, making it hard to breathe. He stepped from the pew.

Although Fergus was right behind him, for the first time since arriving in Sweetwater Springs, Angus felt adrift and alone in the midst of strangers. As he flowed with the stream of people down the aisle, his thoughts were far away.

He calculated the time in Scotland—seven hours ahead. His family had probably finished dinner and gathered in the parlor, talking over cups of tea. With a sudden, fierce stab of homesickness, he longed to be there.

Once outside, Angus blinked in the brilliant sunshine. The vivid blue sky looked bright to the point of harshness, the dirt streets and wooden buildings primitive—nothing like the stone masonry and cobbled byways of Edinburgh.

An elderly woman in black approached Angus and his brother and started describing her rheumatism symptoms.

Since she mainly addressed Fergus, without moving his head Angus allowed his gaze to slide past her. He found Constance and Miss Bailey engaged in conversation with Mr. Aagaard and Miss Woodbury about thirty feet away.

Angus knew from some remarks he'd overheard at the dinner party last night that the logger had spent last night at the livery. Apparently, Mack Taylor charged cheap rates for the corner of the hayloft where a person could toss down his bedroll and sleep.

Constance shifted and faced his direction, although her attention remained on her friends.

As he watched her animated expression and the graceful sweep of her hands as she gestured, something inside him anchored—to this land, to her—and Angus was able to breathe again.

Mr. Aagaard and Miss Woodbury smiled and nodded in farewell. They moved away, heading in the direction of Sugarplum Dreams, probably to indulge in some treats.

A man about Angus's age approached Constance and Miss Bailey. He wore the shirt, vest, and trousers common to both farmers and cowboys' Sunday best and engaged the two women in conversation, his expression admiring as he looked from one to the other.

Constance's open stance and the way she responded to the potential suitor—smiling and nodding—made jealousy jump through Angus. Although compelled to stake his claim—an American expression he'd recently learned—he forced himself to keep his face expressionless.

Next to him, Fergus responded to the elderly woman, giving her some advice about the best liniment.

Angus quietly excused himself and slid through the crowd in Constance's direction. Several times, he was waylaid as people stopped him to talk, mostly introducing themselves or performing introductions for someone else.

Every new acquaintance welcomed him to Sweetwater Springs. Or, if they'd already met, they often mentioned the fine day—a comment that inevitably was followed by a warning the weather could change at any time.

Angus could hardly be ungracious and brush aside everyone's kindness. So he forced himself to take his time with each person before moving on a few steps.

Finally, he arrived at Constance's side, just in time to hear the man say, "Could I invite you two to my home for a picnic next Sunday after church?" The invitation was made to both women, but the suitor seemed to look more at Constance.

Miss Bailey clasped her hands together. "Your place sounds so beautiful!" She gazed at the man with wide eyes. "I'd love to see it. Please, Miss Taylor, may we go?"

Constance pursed her lips. "Well, there are a few challenges. The first is we wouldn't be able to leave right after the service because we do have to open the shop for an hour or so." She glanced up the street. "In fact, we should be going there in another minute. The second concern is how would we get to your home? Surely you don't expect us to walk there and back?"

The man's expression fell. From his sheepish grin, this fellow did expect exactly that. "I guess in my spontaneity I hadn't thought through everything."

Angus stepped closer and inserted himself into the conversation. "If I may…I heard the word *picnic*, always a favorite activity of mine. Good food and nature. What could be better? I do believe my new horse and surrey—a four seater— will be here by next Sunday, Mr…?"

He thrust out his hand. "Canfield, Hank Canfield. But call me Hank."

"Well, Hank." He returned the man's strong handshake. "If I could include myself in yer invitation…. I could drive everyone there and bring the ladies back to town."

"Why, that sounds just dandy." Hank's grin was wide and guileless. "Aren't you the new doc?"

"Aye." He nodded. "Angus Cameron at yer service."

"If you don't mind, Doc, I'll hope *not* to have your service. Good thing I'm healthy." He winked at the ladies. "Clean living does that to a man."

"And what do ye do for that clean living?" Angus asked.

"A bit of this and that. Some gardening, hunting, and breeding horses."

Miss Bailey touched Hank's shoulder. "How many horses do you have?"

"Just a stud and two mares, so far, both with foals."

While the man's attention was on the young woman, Angus decided to ease Constance out of the conversation—if she'd go with him. "May I walk with ye to the shop?" He didn't offer his arm, not wanting to risk a public rejection.

"Please." Constance took his arm. To Elsie, she said, "We're going ahead. See you in a few minutes." As she strolled with him down the street, she gave Angus a bold glance, as if challenging him. "Thank you for the love letter."

He jerked. Her unexpected response couldn't have shocked him more. "Love letter?" The collar of his shirt suddenly felt too tight.

Constance raised her eyebrows and flashed a look of obvious amusement. "Was it not?" she asked, her tone innocent. The breeze riffled the peacock feather on her hat.

Her rose perfume wafted his way. Angus tried to swallow. "I...." He nodded at an elderly couple passing by and then reached up to tug on his collar. "Yer not angry?" His gaze dropped to her waist.

Her brow furrowed, and her smile fell away. "*If* I choose to wear a loose corset, I'll need to let out the seams of *all* my clothing, not just the top layers." Her tone sounded tart. "*Quite* a time-consuming job, and one that will have to go at the bottom of a long list of other tasks."

Not sure how to take her response, Angus repeated the question. "Are ye angry with me?"

She sighed. "A little. However, perhaps a little with myself, too. I knew the information you referred to. But I'd never really stopped to *think through* the consequences. I still haven't." She glanced up and met his gaze, her expression serious. "But I will ponder your suggestions."

Relief made him lightheaded. "That's all I could ask for." Angus smiled and briefly placed his hand over her fingers curled around his arm. Yet, as they walked toward the Gordon Building, he couldn't help but wonder what conclusions Constance would come to once she was done mulling over everything.

Chapter Fifteen

All week, a sudden rash of summer colds, injuries, the birth of a baby girl, and a dying elderly man kept Angus and Fergus busy, deprived of sleep, and often spending long hours on the road. Angus was coming to know his brother as a man. The two of them talked of their childhoods, their brothers and parents, their time at the university, unusual medical cases, and the inhabitants of Sweetwater Springs.

Angus was also learning his way around the territory. At this rate, he soon could go off on his own calls.

A few days earlier, Nick Sanders had brought Zeus to town. The rancher left word with Noem Krutsky, the stableman, that he'd given the horse some extra training on pulling a surrey, and Zeus had done well.

Aside from a quick visit to the stable to check to make sure the horse's injury was, indeed, healed, Angus barely even saw the gelding, which was a source of growing frustration. Noem had exercised Zeus and assured Angus the Morgan was settling in just fine.

Then on Friday, the train delivered his surrey. With Fergus and Angus miles from town treating a family very ill from the grippe, Noam took Zeus to fetch the vehicle home.

Angus suffered a pang at not being the first one to drive the horse and new equipage. But their patients came first before his own indulgences.

Unfortunately, that included a certain lovely dressmaker. Although he'd meant to call upon Constance and take her to Sugarplum Dreams, Angus had neglected her, also out of necessity. All week, he hadn't so much as caught a glimpse of Constance, and, to his surprise, discovered he missed her presence. *That lack doesn't bode well for my future peace of mind.*

By Saturday evening, the crises seemed to have died down. Fergus agreed if no emergencies came during the night and Angus managed to get a good night's sleep, he could take the day off and drive the women to visit Hank Canfield's place for the picnic.

After church this morning, Angus briefly chatted with Constance, Elsie—as the girl insisted he call her—and Hank. The four made preparations to meet in front of the Gordon Building in two hours.

When he arrived home, Angus asked Noem to hitch Zeus to the surrey, resolving to go for a short drive alone to get in some practice before he had passengers to witness his novice efforts.

He walked into the house to eat a snack, don driving gloves, and fetch his doctor's bag. When he came back outside, Noem stood next to the harnessed horse, waiting. The stableman had brushed the horse until his dark hide gleamed like satin in the sun.

"Zeus looks good, Noem. Thank you."

"Don't he, though? Fine animal, that he is. Responsive and easy-tempered. Real pleasure to work with."

The surrey was all black, from the canopy overhead to the big, spoked wheels. The tufted leather seats looked comfortable, and a glass lamp on either side of the driver's seat would provide illumination during nighttime drives.

Angus's chest swelled with pride. *I can't wait to try out my brand spanking new surrey.* Being the youngest of seven sons, almost all he owned and wore growing up were hand-me-downs from his brothers. As an adult, aside from clothes and items necessary for his medical practice, Angus hadn't purchased many new things for himself. Thus, this horse and surrey seemed like years of presents all rolled into one.

He imagined driving down a country road with Constance sitting next to him, admiring his skill with the reins. He'd take her hand.... *Well, maybe not on this trip. I'd better keep both hands on the reins until I'm confident.*

Noem rubbed Zeus's nose. "I polished the seats, Dr. Angus, and oiled all the wood. A preventative act to keep them looking nice longer. If I'd had charge of Dr. Cameron's surrey from the beginning, it would be in much better shape now."

"I appreciate your care, Noem." Angus ran a hand over the gelding's arched neck and finally moved toward the back of the surrey to stow the bag on the floor of the second seat. Then he climbed into the front seat, inhaling the smell of new leather, and took the reins. The brake released, and with a deep breath to steady his nerves, he made a clicking noise and flicked the reins.

Zeus tucked his head and started forward.

Angus gave Noem a huge grin and drove away. Once on the main street, he moderated his expression somewhat so he wouldn't look vain and foolish. *Professional demeanor*, he reminded himself. Nevertheless, the grin kept breaking out.

Luckily, the worse of the Sunday traffic had already cleared away, as families anxious to get home for dinner headed out of town. Still, plenty of people walked the streets, along with a few riders, and a vehicle or two.

Uncertain how Zeus would react to the bustle, Angus gripped the reins tightly, holding the horse to a steady walk. From the corner of his eye, he could see plenty of curious glances coming his way, but he kept his attention on the gelding. Except when the wheels hit a rut, the well-sprung surrey kept the jostling to a minimum.

Aside from some flicks of the ears and a couple of head tosses, Zeus behaved perfectly. After they reached the edge of town, Angus was able to relax. Although he still remained vigilant, he enjoyed the feeling of driving his very own horse and carriage—

the air moving against his face, breathing in the scent of pines and grass.

Angus wished he could increase the gelding's speed, but he didn't want to tire the Morgan. The horse would have to travel almost a third of the way up and down a mountain today.

Not too far past the town, Angus stopped in a wide area where the road branched off in several directions. He took out his pocket watch and checked the time. Still an hour remained before needing to meet the others. Carefully, he guided Zeus to turn around and headed home.

Driving back through town was easier. Angus was less tense, and the main street wasn't as crowded. As he reached his brother's house, he saw Hank out in front, pacing back and forth along the white picket fence, the climbing rose bushes bursting with red flowers.

He reined in Zeus next to the man. The breeze blew the smell of roses his way. The scent reminded him of Constance and that this man was a potential suitor.

"Mighty fine rig you've got there." Hank cast an admiring eye over the horse and surrey. "I'm early, so I thought I'd catch you here before we pick up the ladies."

"Climb on up," Angus surprised himself by offering.

Hank flashed a grin and did just that, settling on the seat next to Angus. He ran his hand over the leather upholstery. "Mighty fine, indeed. I planned to ride my mare home, but maybe I'll tie her to the back and travel with you all instead."

"Might as well. Hard to converse otherwise." Angus gave the man a quick glance.

Hank looked struck by the wisdom of that suggestion. "Alrighty, then." He glanced around the vehicle. "You all kitted out?"

"I haven't purchased a rifle yet. Meant to do that this past week, but I was too busy."

Hank shrugged. "I have my gun belt and Colt in a saddlebag at the livery. But the mercantile is still open. You could buy one now. After all, I won't be with you on the drive home."

The idea of owning a rifle made Angus smile, feeling as excited as a boy. *Maybe the Winchester Model 1895 Flatside that Fergus showed me in a catalogue.* "No time like the present."

Hank grinned back. "Sounds good to me."

As they drove down the street, Angus reflected on how much his life had changed in ways he hadn't expected.

A horse, a surrey, a rifle.... He thought of Constance. *A wife?*

As soon as the last customer left, clutching a parcel of black lace, Constance grabbed a fan from the desk drawer and wafted it through the air. "Goodness, her perfume was strong. We might smell like her now, Elsie." She kept the door open to air out the place.

Her assistant sniffed. "I have no way to tell because all I can smell is her." She reached into the glass case, pulled out a fan painted with a Chinese scene, and waved it around. "I thought she'd never leave! She took *fifteen minutes* to compare two kinds of lace inch by inch."

"But she purchased the more expensive one." Constance set down her fan, moved toward the cabinet with the bolts of cloth, and, one by one, pulled out any messy ones. Then she unrolled and neatly rewrapped them, tamping down excitement about spending the afternoon with Angus.

"Wasn't it strange that woman wouldn't introduce herself even when you asked?" Elsie straightened the scraps of hanging fabric. "She just brushed off your question."

Constance shrugged. "When you have a business, you deal with all types. I've never seen her before, though. Not that I've met every woman who lives around here."

"She's pretty—in an older, faded way, that is. I think she dyes her hair. Otherwise, she'd probably have some threads of gray in amongst the black." Elsie's eyes gleamed. "Perhaps, she's secretly in Sweetwater Springs to visit a lover."

With a chuckle, Constance shook her head. "Stop letting your imagination run away with you. We have a picnic to attend, remember?"

"Hank will be here soon." Elsie slid a glance toward Constance. "Doctor Angus as well." She put away the fan and then rushed around the room to get things in order.

"I see which man's important," Constance teased, smoothing out the length of gray-and-black twill.

Elsie wrinkled her nose. "Doctor Angus is sweet on *you*," she retorted. "No sense tossing a hook in his direction." She grimaced. "Hank's probably sweet on you, too. After the service, he made a beeline for you."

I hope not. That situation would make today's outing very awkward. "At seventeen, you're too young to be thinking about marriage, anyway."

"Not according to my ma."

"Selfishly, I hope to keep you with me for quite a while longer. Living on that mountain would mean you couldn't work here." After only knowing the girl for two weeks, Constance would miss Elsie dreadfully if her assistant left to wed. She slid a bolt of rumpled indigo cashmere from the shelf and unwound several yards of crooked fabric.

"I'm not going anywhere. I'll wait to marry until I'm *twenty*."

"Such a vast old age." She thought ruefully of her own twenty-three years. She deftly rewound the cashmere. "You'll be an old maid by then, although not as bad as me." Wishing she didn't feel a pang at her words, Constance re-shelved the bolt.

"You're not old," Elsie said loyally. "An old maid is a woman no man wants to marry. Any bachelor in this town would snap you up in a minute."

"Where do you get these ideas?" Constance was half-amused, half-horrified and thinking of only one redhead who charmed her. "I'm sure there are plenty of old maids who've refused suitors. It's far better to be a spinster than marry the wrong man." She glanced around taking in the tidy shelves and neat counter. "We're all set."

"Do you want me to straighten out the back room?" Elsie waved a hand in that direction.

"No, leave it. I've finished cutting out the pattern for my divided riding skirt, as well as the one Mrs. Thompson ordered. The fabric is too similar in color. I don't want the pieces to jumble together and to have to sort through them again." As she spoke, Constance gathered her hat, gloves, and reticule. She turned off the lights and locked the door. They headed upstairs to their rooms.

As an experiment, Constance had let out a few seams of her gowns and loosened her corset. She discovered that climbing up the stairs was certainly easier. She'd always taken for granted the need to pause on the landings of staircases to catch her breath. All the ladies she knew did.

Now, Constance possessed more stamina than ever before. She wondered how much stronger and sounder of wind she could possibly become.

Wanting to contribute to the picnic, they'd prepared food to bring to the feast. Elsie made sandwiches, slathered with butter, sliced beef, cheese, and pickles. She'd wrapped each one in waxed paper and stashed them in the icebox.

Yesterday, Constance purchased several kinds of cookies from the sweetshop. Before church this morning, she'd set two Mason jars of water outside, each with a ball of leaves inside to make sun tea.

While Elsie was charged with fetching the tea and packing everything into a basket, Constance went into her bedroom to change. After removing the outfit she'd worn to church, she donned a shirtwaist of ruffled pink cotton, paired with a rose-colored skirt. She'd let out the side seams of both to accommodate her twenty-inch waist. She debated about bringing a parasol to shield her skin from the sun but thought that accessory might be too ridiculous for where they were going. *I'll tilt my hat forward to shade my face.*

She opened the enamel box on her dressing table that held her hatpins and tossed in the ones she'd worn to anchor the toque with peacock feather that she'd worn to church. The rings of blue crystal on those hatpins wouldn't match the boater she intended to wear. She fished around for the two studded with pearl beads. They'd look better amid the garden of pink peonies surrounding the brim.

Once Constance was ready, she and Elsie took turns using the bathroom before gathering shawls, reticules, and the picnic basket, and going downstairs and into the sunshine. They didn't have long to wait on the steps before a beautiful black equipage pulled by a gleaming dark horse stopped in front. A gray horse, Hank's apparently, was tied to the back of the surrey. Angus flashed them a grin.

"Oh my!" Elsie breathed.

Oh my, indeed.

Elsie bounced on her toes. "I can't believe we're going for a drive in *that*. I'll have to pinch myself to make sure I'm not asleep and dreaming."

"Let me oblige you." Smiling, Constance gently pinched the girl's arm. "There. You need to be awake so you can enjoy the company of those two handsome gentlemen."

Exhaling a happy sigh, Elsie stood. She held the handle of the basket with both hands.

With athletic grace, Hank jumped down from the passenger side of the front seat. "Howdy, ladies. Good day for a drive in the park, eh?" He laughed and held out a hand for the basket. "What's this? I have plenty of food. But I won't say no to more victuals."

Elsie gave him the basket.

He hefted it, raising his eyebrows. "What's in this thing? Rocks?"

The girl giggled. "Just you wait and see, Hank Canfield."

"I'll stow this in the back and switch the doctor's bag to the front."

Constance moved to the horse and ran a hand over Zeus's glossy neck, glad she'd chosen not to wear gloves. She rubbed his head, admiring the intelligence in the gelding's dark eyes. "Hello, sweet boy. I should have thought to bring you a treat. Next time," she promised.

Hopefully, there will be a next time.

Constance leaned sideways to glance at the horse's chest, perusing the long scar that appeared nicely healed. Straightening, she called to Angus, "You do good work."

He smiled and gave her a thumbs-up.

I wouldn't have thought he'd use such a lighthearted gesture. Constance wondered if he intended to climb out to greet her. Then she realized, even with the brake set and reins tied off, Angus probably would be more comfortable remaining where he could easily gain control of the horse, if needed.

She made a stay-there motion and moved around to the front seat. The iron step was high and would be difficult to reach without assistance. She eyed the stretch from the ground and raised her skirt to clear her boot.

"Hank." Angus gestured with his chin.

Hank moved around her to set the doctor's bag in the front footwell and then extended a hand. "Up you go, Miss Taylor."

"It's Constance, thank you." Grateful for his assistance, she climbed into the seat next to Angus, careful not to kick the leather bag on the floor between them.

Angus had changed out of his frock coat and was dressed much like Hank, wearing a Stetson, a blue cotton shirt tied at the collar with a string tie, and a leather vest that looked unworn.

She raised an eyebrow and nodded at the vest. "A new look?"

"Just purchased everything from the mercantile." He flicked the reins, and the horse started up. "Along with a few other items such as a rifle. Made Mrs. Cobb quite happy."

"I don't believe that's possible," she retorted pleasantly.

"Aye, the woman oozed charm." His eyes twinkled.

"Now who's oozing charm?" she teased.

"Me, lass?" he asked in an innocent tone. "Na' possible."

Constance rolled her eyes. Settling back against the comfortable leather cushions, she ran a hand over the wood in front of them, glanced up at the overhead covering, and then shifted to look into the second seat.

She nearly laughed aloud. Her assistant sat with her arms tight against her sides, her legs pressed together, looking prim and proper, and not at all Elsie-like. The girl carefully refrained from glancing at Hank. No doubt she was experiencing her first taste of the difference between *imagining* driving with an attractive man and actually being jostled against his body when the wheels of the surrey struck ruts and bumps.

Turning back, Constance said, "This is a *beautiful* surrey, Angus."

In the different clothing, he looked relaxed and approachable. The color of his shirt made his eyes look even bluer, and a grin lightened his normally serious expression. "I admit to some pride in it. Are ye comfortable?"

"Aye. How could I not be in this fine equipage of yours?"

He chuckled.

How could I ever have thought him dour?

Constance made herself look away from the man and enjoy the ride through the outskirts of town that she hadn't yet seen, responding with a polite nod to curious glances.

Angus increased their speed to a trot, and they headed into a cool, green forest. As the trees closed around the surrey, she shivered, picturing wolves and bears and maybe even Indians lurking behind the thick trunks, watching.

Angus must have caught the movement, for he glanced her way with a cocked eyebrow. "Ye all right?"

She flushed. "Just my imagination running wild."

"That happens out here."

When they reached the foot of the mountain, Hank proved to

be quite the tour guide, pointing out the flora and fauna and telling humorous stories of his various adventures.

"I've never heard a man talk as much as you, Hank," Elsie said in an admiring tone, evidently relaxing about the circumstances of driving with a man. "You say as much in one day as my pa does in an entire season."

Constance exchanged an amused glance with Angus.

"Well," Hank drawled. "I don't have much of a chance to converse. When I speak with my livestock, the horses, chickens, and pig don't talk back."

Elsie giggled.

Hank leaned forward, grabbing the seat in front of him and pointing over Constance's shoulder. "Turn-off coming up 'round the bend. Go right at the bur oak. Don't worry, Doc." He had a grin in his voice. "The trail is just wide enough for your pretty surrey. This week I took an axe and cut back any brush and overhanging branches. Wouldn't want to scratch up your beauty here." He patted the seat back.

Angus tossed a quick glance over his shoulder. "Appreciate that," he said fervently. "I know the surrey will become battered in time. But I'd like to enjoy the shiny newness for a few more days." He slowed Zeus to carefully navigate the bend.

Constance leaned forward, peering through the trees to see ahead. But no house was in sight. "You sure live in an isolated area, Hank." She twisted around in the seat to look back at him.

"Na. Two other men live close by. We call ourselves the bachelors of Three Bend Lake. We're not in sight of each other because of the way the lake curves. But as the canoe glides, we're only about fifteen, twenty minutes apart. Maybe double that on foot."

"Why, that's not bad at all," Elsie exclaimed. "Where my family lives, the walk's an hour to the nearest neighbor."

The distance sounded plenty *bad* to Constance. She gazed at the forest around them and gripped the edge of the seat. *I'll have to learn how to be less of a city girl.*

Hank pointed up the mountain. "If you keep going up the road, 'bout half an hour's climb, you'll hit the Swensen place."

"Swensen," Constance echoed. "Do they have beautiful, little blonde girls?"

"Got that right. Nicest family you ever met."

She shifted so she could see all three of them. "I saw five of the girls in the sweetshop once. They were so adorable, I wanted to adopt them all."

With a raised eyebrow, Angus gave her a curious glance. "Planning to steal away the girls from their parents, eh?"

She slanted him a Cheshire cat smile. "The thought might have flitted through my mind."

"They are little sweethearts," Hank agreed. "I see Swensen more than his wife and girls, though. We sometimes cross paths when we're both out hunting. He's got a baby boy now. Pleased as Punch, he is."

Constance regaled them with the story of the girls using their pennies to pay off their parents' debt at the mercantile. Just as she finished, the trees opened up.

They drove into an alpine meadow, where a few horses and foals grazed. Grassland dotted with flowers sloped to a small blue lake that reflected the puffy clouds in the sky. Beyond was a spectacular view of the snow-covered peaks.

"Oh," she sighed. "How lovely."

As the surrey drew closer, Constance could see the lake didn't end but took a bend to the right. Two swans floated on the placid water. A canoe lay upside down on the shore. She released a pleased breath. *How beautiful and peaceful.*

Angus guided Zeus toward the front of a log house and reined in. The home was unexpectedly charming, with blue-painted shutters and front door. A square table and chairs, already decked out with four place settings and a Mason jar of wildflowers, occupied one side of the wide porch. On the other side, two rockers invited guests to sit and rest a spell. Behind the house, a barn made of logs rose up.

Hank waved toward the right side of the house. "Ladies, while we see to Zeus, you'll find a privy and pump in back."

"My ma always said she liked a man who knows a woman's needs," Elsie exclaimed with a smile in his direction. Then, obviously embarrassed to speak so freely, she covered her mouth with both hands.

"I believe I'd like your ma." Hank climbed down and hefted out the picnic basket.

Constance held back an eye roll. Unless in case of severest necessity, in a social situation, a lady didn't comment to a man about bodily needs. Nor did she cover her mouth and bring attention to her lack of tact. For now, she held back a reprimand, not wanting to spoil the girl's enjoyment of the day.

The men helped Constance and Elsie down from the surrey, and the two strolled behind the house to find the privy. A pump in a half-barrel set into the ground was situated between the barn and the cabin. This side of the house also had a narrow back porch—convenient for access to the pump water.

Once they'd used the privy and washed their hands and faces, Constance and Elsie returned to the front, where the surrey remained parked. Zeus and Hank's mare were turned loose in the meadow. The picnic basket rested on the table, and the men were not in sight.

Elsie placed her hand on the porch railing, angling her face toward the closest window. "This is a pretty house. I wonder what the inside's like. Do you think we can go look?"

"Let's wait for our host to invite us in."

Luckily for the girl's obvious impatience, they didn't have long before the men came around the side of the house, talking with gestures that indicated the topic was their surroundings. They stopped before Constance and Elsie.

Hank cocked an eyebrow and waved toward the table. "You ladies hungry yet?"

"If you gentlemen don't mind, I'd like to walk around some," Constance said. "We've been sitting too much today."

Childlike, Elsie clasped her hands together, reminding Constance that she had just turned seventeen and had been raised in an isolated area in which ladylike refinements were not stressed.

"Can we please feed the swans, Hank?" Elsie's brown eyes pleaded.

He nodded. "I have some bread in the house."

Constance let out a happy breath. "You are so lucky living on the water with such a beautiful view." She pointed to a narrow path winding beside the shore. "I'd like to explore along the lake."

Angus offered his arm. "How 'bout if we take a look around—enjoy the sights—while Hank and Elsie feed the swans. Say twenty minutes or so? Then we can all join up and have that picnic."

"That sounds just right." She liked the idea of being alone with Angus and glanced to see if Hank and Elsie were fine with that decision.

A frustrated look crossed the man's face before he pulled on the accommodating expression of a host.

Perhaps Elsie's right that he's interested in me. Although uncomfortable with that thought, Constance kept a smile on her face. She took Angus's arm and tugged him along the path. "We'll be back soon," she said over her shoulder.

Before long, they reached the end of the meadow and entered the wooded area. The trees grew more sparsely here, or perhaps Hank had thinned them out. Dappled sunlight played on wildflowers nestled among the trunks. *I'll have to purchase a guidebook to learn about the trees and flowers.* An unseen bird chirped. *As well as the birds and animals.*

The path ran alongside a sandy beach, which would be a perfect spot for bathing—*if* she had privacy and a bathing costume.

Constance paused to admire the view. "The lake is like a giant mirror. I can't believe how perfectly the surface reflects the sky and the mountains. Just those slight shimmers on the water show the illusion. If merfolk lived in the lake, do you think they'd see a double sky? Or would the surface of the water be their sky?" She wondered if he'd scoff at her fanciful musing.

Angus winked. "I do na' know. But I'll make sure to enquire when next I meet up with a selkie."

"Selkie?"

"Our version of merfolk. Seals and otters and such who can come ashore, shed their pelts, and become human." Angus removed his Stetson and hung it on the broken-off spike of a nearby branch. "There're plenty of stories I could tell ye about them. But at another time." He held her gaze, the line of his jaw taut. His lashes were thick, the same auburn as his hair. The blue of his eyes matched the sky overhead. Bright sunlight glinted on his hair like a nimbus of fire.

He touched her cheek. "Ye look verra fine, lass."

She pressed her hands to her waist and swayed her hips. "Twenty inches. I'm trying your advice."

"Aye. I'm verra glad of it, too."

She lowered her arms.

He placed a hand on her side above her hip and tugged.

She yielded to the pressure until she was only an inch away and very aware of the rise and fall of his chest. Her breath hitched. "Angus." His name was just a whisper.

"Aye, lass." His eyes darkened. "My heart may stop with wanting ye."

Her chest ached, growing heavy with longing. The looser stays made taking a deep breath possible. She'd never felt this way with any man. Something stronger existed between her and Angus. *Dare I trust the feeling?*

"Constance, I do na' think I can go on without kissing ye. Will ye allow it?"

Her heartbeat kicked up. "You didn't ask before."

"I'm trying to be a gentleman here. But yer making it verra difficult."

"Aye," she said, her voice husky.

Deliberately, his gaze capturing hers, Angus reached up to pull out her hatpins, lift the boater from her head, and hang the hat next to his, jabbing the pins into the straw.

Her heart stuttered.

He brought one of her hands to his lips. His mouth was soft, sending a pulse up her arm. Her fingers relaxed.

With one more kiss, he lowered her hand, and then released her, only to trail his fingertips softly down her cheek, brushing along her neck over her pulse points and then lingering on her collarbone.

The light touch drew a shiver from deep within her. Constance wanted...she didn't know what she wanted. *To push him away? To cling closer? For him to never let go?*

She curled her fingers around his, her nails digging into his skin in response to a growing need. Then, as if making the choice without her will, her lips parted. She peeped through lowered eyelashes and, with a teasing smile, invited him closer.

Angus slid a hand around the nape of her neck, drawing her to him. He bent and his mouth covered hers, the pressure persuasive rather than demanding, coaxing apart her lips.

His tongue glided into her mouth, softly at first, then bolder, going deeper, tempting her.

Flutters filled her belly. Her knees shaky, she clutched his shoulder. Reality fell away, leaving only the magic of their connection.

He coaxed her to follow his lead, to mate her tongue with his. A wild rush of hunger made her squirm in response. Wanting more closeness, she rose on her tiptoes, her fingers kneading the strong muscles of his shoulder.

A man's shout jarred her. Then came another, loud and desperate, from the direction of the house.

They broke apart, both breathing hard.

Constance gasped. *Elsie! Has something happened to Elsie? Please, Dear Lord, may she be all right!*

Chapter Sixteen

Hearing the fear in the man's yell doused Angus's ardor. Energy shot through him, making all of his protective instincts come alive. "Let's go," he urged Constance as he set her away from his body.

She pulled down her hat from the branch, yanking out the hatpins. "Weapons." She brandished them before placing her hat on her head and stabbing the hatpins through the crown and into her hair.

Under other circumstances, he would have laughed at the idea the pins anchoring that flowery concoction had any lethal purpose. But he didn't know what they might be heading into. His thoughts went to bears and panthers, Indians and outlaws. *Not that hatpins can protect her from those. Thank God, I bought the rifle.* He grabbed her hand.

Constance caught up the front of her skirt with her other hand.

They hurried up the path, not moving as fast as Angus wanted, but probably faster than they could have if she hadn't worn a looser corset. He didn't dare release her and race ahead. He couldn't risk any danger befalling her. Yet, if no danger threatened and someone needed his medical skills, time might be of the essence. Still, he kept his pace to hers.

It seemed to take forever before they burst through the trees into the meadow and rushed toward the house. With relief,

Angus saw Elsie and Hank hurrying to meet a man running toward them from the other direction, rifle in one hand.

The stranger skidded to a stop in front of Hank. He was tall and lanky, dark hair swept back from a clean-shaven face. His chest heaved as if he'd run a mile.

Angus and Constance hurried to join them.

"Torin, what's wrong?" Hank grabbed the man's shoulder.

The stranger looked at Angus and Constance, and then at Elsie, panic in his dark blue eyes. He shook his head, obviously holding back from saying more.

"Is it Jewel?" Hank asked. "Torin, we can't help if you don't tell us."

Again, Torin swept a reluctant glance at the three of them.

Hank jerked a finger at Angus. "He's a doctor. If something's wrong with Jewel, now's not the time for secrecy."

"She's gone, and I can't find her," Torin blurted.

"Brian Bly, do you think?" Hank released the man and glanced at Angus. "Brian's our neighbor," he explained, pointing in the direction of the lake. "Lives the farthest away."

Torin shook his head, an expression of despair on his face. "I checked with him first. Brian hasn't seen her, but he's searching his area."

Angus needed more information. "If you'd tell us who's missing."

"His daughter," Hank explained. "She's—"

"She's not right," Torin said in a defiant tone, jutting his chin. His eyes held guilt. "My sweet girl. She's eleven, but really maybe three. Jewel wanted to go for a walk by the lake. I told her we would later because I was busy weeding the garden. She wasn't long out of my sight." Frowning, he shook his head. "I didn't think Jewel would go off on her own. She never has before."

Fear clutched at Angus. So much could happen to a child in these parts, especially one who wasn't *right*, who functioned on the level of a three-year-old.

Hank glanced around, obviously searching. "Jewel can't be far. She walks too slow."

"I called and called." Torin's voice was ragged. "I'd hoped she'd come here. You know how she loves watching the swans."

"She might have," Hank said. "But I was in town."

"We'll help you look," Constance offered. "What is she wearing?"

Good question, and one I wouldn't have thought to ask.

Torin glanced at her, and then his gaze sidled away. He appeared torn, as if afraid to trust them. "Red. She likes red," he mumbled.

Angus touched the man's arm. "What do ye mean by 'not right'?"

Torin narrowed his eyes and shot Angus a defiant glare, as if expecting judgment.

"It's all right, Torin," Hank said. "Go ahead and tell them."

He nodded. "When Jewel was a few months old the doctor said she was an *idiot*." He spat out the word, and then crossed his arms as if shielding himself from their judgment. "But she's not! She may not be like other children, but she's mine."

"I understand." Angus kept his expression sympathetic and his tone compassionate, knowing a calm response was important when dealing with a panic-stricken parent. "Is Jewel afraid of strangers?"

"I have no idea!" Torin said, desperation on his face. He uncrossed his arms. "She only knows Hank and Brian, and they keep our secret."

"Well, it's best we first find her," Angus said matter-of-factly. "If yer daughter's afraid when she sees us, we won't approach her until ye're there."

"That would be best." Torin glanced toward the lake. "What if she's drowned?"

"We came from along the shore, and she wasn't ana'where there." Angus didn't mention they would have noticed a body in red floating in the water. He patted the man's shoulder. "Ye head back in the direction of yer home in case Jewel returns. Ye can search more carefully in her familiar areas. Ye might have missed her earlier in yer haste."

"I can do that."

Angus continued to snap out orders. "Elsie, if ye'd stay within eyeshot of Hank's house in case Jewel comes here. Hank, first search yer barn and other places nearby, then move farther afield." He pointed toward the forest. "I suggest that way for ye know the place and won't get lost like we might. No sense making a bad situation worse." He glanced at Constance. "We'll take the opposite direction across the meadow. Set up a shout if ye find her."

Hank shook his head. "Better to fire three shots. Can hear them farther."

"Shots, then," Angus agreed.

Just having a plan seemed to calm Torin somewhat. "Thank you. All of you." He turned and trotted back the way he'd come, carrying the rifle and yelling Jewel's name.

Angus looked toward the surrey. "Let me get my bag." He hastened to the vehicle, grateful to be wearing less restrictive clothes that allowed for freedom of movement, and snatched up his bag from the footwell and the Winchester from under the seat before hurrying back to Constance. "Ready?"

She nodded before casting a glance around them.

"The temptation is to move fast and cover as much ground as possible," he explained. "But we might overlook an important clue, especially if the lass is asleep or hiding."

"Where would I go if I were a small girl?" Constance glanced around and pointed toward a clump of flowering bushes near the woods. "That way. The flowers might appeal to her."

"Good choice."

They searched for fifteen minutes, peering behind trees and under bushes, his fear rising as time passed without a sign of the girl. Then, to his great relief, Angus heard a mewing sound. He stopped and held up a hand.

Constance froze, looked about, and then pointed. "Behind the bush! She's crying, poor girl."

"If Jewel's crying, at least she's alive," he said tersely.

She lifted her skirts, obviously preparing to run in the girl's direction.

"Wait." Angus grabbed her arm. "Let's approach slowly. We don't know if there's danger. Nor do we want to frighten her."

They rounded the bushes to see a dark-haired girl in a red sack-like garment sitting on the ground and crying. The hem of her dress was bunched up to her knees, and pink blossoms spilled from her lap. Her bare legs stretched in front of her. The left shin had a long scratch that looked bloody, but not serious.

A crumpled bunch of wildflowers lay on the ground nearby.

Jewel had her father's hair color. Her almond-shaped eyes, now drenched with tears, were the same blue as his. "Hel-lo."

She's responsive and not afraid of us. Good.

"Oh, sweetheart!" Constance crooned. "Have you hurt yourself?"

"Ye-s."

Angus set down his bag and motioned for Constance to go closer.

Constance took careful steps around the girl until she could kneel on her other side. "Hello, Jewel. My name is Constance."

The girl's brow wrinkled. "Con. Con-stan."

Constance smiled. "How about you call me Connie? Can you do that?"

"Con-nee." The word was guttural but audible.

"Cover her ears," Angus warned. He moved off some distance and fired three rounds high and in the direction of the lake so the bullets would land in the water. He hurried back to Jewel and set down his rifle a safe distance away.

"Your papa's been looking for you," Constance said. "Are you hurt?"

"Ow." Jewel pointed to her foot. One ankle was swollen. "Hurts."

"I can see it does. But Doctor Angus here—" smiling, she gestured toward him "—will fix you right up."

Jewel briefly glanced at him before returning her attention to Constance. She fastened her gaze on the pink peony hat. "Pretty."

"Here, darling." Constance pulled out the hatpins, driving them into the ground well out of Jewel's reach. "I'll provide distraction, Angus, so you can examine her." Removing her hat, she held it out to Jewel.

As gently as he could, Angus ran his hands over the girl's legs.

The child began to cry again, but she grabbed for the hat.

Constance helped guide the hat to Jewel's lap. "Aren't the flowers pretty?"

"Pretty," the girl agreed between sobs. She fingered one of the blooms.

"That's a peony. Can you say peony?"

"Pe-ne."

"Very good, Jewel," Constance praised. "Would you like to wear the hat?"

The girl's eyes brightened. She gave Constance a big smile around her pink tongue.

Angus prodded Jewel's swollen right ankle.

"Hurt," she said with a sob and tried to pull away.

With his other hand, he held her firm, even as she cried out in pain, until he'd finished his examination and gently lowered her leg to the grass. "Nothing broken, thank the good Lord. Aside from the laceration, she's probably bruised all over, puir lass. Hopefully, there's an icehouse around here. Ice will help the swelling go down and ease the pain."

"Surely there must be, when they can take ice from the lake."

Angus reached for his bag, opened the closure, rummaged through the contents, and pulled out a cloth and the bottle of iodine. "Let me clean up the cut. I doubt she'll need stitches. Then we'll return this wee lassie to her da." He doused the cloth. "This is going to sting, Jewel, but it will be over quick." He dabbed at the laceration.

Jewel's crying increased.

"What a relief that she's not badly hurt." Constance placed the hat on Jewel's head, tilting it back so it didn't overshadow the child's face. She smiled and touched the girl's cheek. "You're a pretty girl."

Jewel stopped crying and reached to touch the hat, wonder on her face. She grasped Constance's hand. "Thann' you."

Tears welled in Constance's eyes.

Happy tears. Angus could tell, and the sight moved him deeply. He had to blink away the moisture blurring his gaze. As he looked into Constance's smiling face, saw the handclasp with a child many people wouldn't even acknowledge, much less touch, and his heart filled with love and a powerful need to make his kind, loving woman his own.

The question is, does she have love in her heart for me? The answer was vital to his happiness.

Jewel drooped against Constance's shoulder, obviously exhausted by her adventures, the hat threatening to fall off.

Maternal instincts welling, Constance straightened it. "I do believe my wardrobe will be minus one peony hat."

"She can't walk." Angus frowned, his brow creasing. "I can carry her piggyback." He rose to his feet and then crouched, holding out his arms.

"No." Jewel shrank against Constance. "Mean man."

Constance chuckled. "Oh dear."

"Hopefully, I have a solution." Angus fished in his bag. "My brother warned me to always carry candy for the children. Luckily, I purchased some at the mercantile today." He held up a peppermint stick. "Here ye go, Jewel." He gave it to her.

The girl must have been familiar with candy for she sat up and reached for the stick. "Thann' you." She placed the end in her mouth and giggled.

The treat apparently changed Angus from a tormentor to a friend, for Jewel allowed him to carry her piggyback to Hank's house as she yelled "horsie" and pulled his hair with her plump, sticky hands.

Constance carried the rifle and the bag. Watching Angus and Jewel together made her laugh. The happy feeling bore down deep into her heart, where it swirled and ached. She'd fallen hopelessly in love with this man and didn't mind the feeling one bit. Time enough in the future to know if he returned her feelings. This moment was too special to mar with worries.

When they saw Jewel with them, Hank and Elsie came running.

"Watch her right leg," Constance called as soon as they came close. "Jewel sprained her ankle."

Hank took the child from Angus and gave her a big smacking kiss on the cheek. "Jewel baby, you worried us so."

"Hank, hurt." Frowning, she pointed to her leg.

"I know, baby. We'll get you home, and you'll feel better."

"Con-nee pretty hat." Jewel placed a hand on the crown.

"Jewel's pretty hat," Constance corrected.

Angus gestured toward the surrey. "If you ladies would climb inside, we'll give Jewel to you while we hitch up Zeus."

Constance and Elsie obeyed.

Hank gave Jewel to Constance, who settled the girl on her lap, careful not to jar her ankle, and he went to help Angus.

Soon, Zeus was hitched to the surrey. The picnic basket and Hank's food were loaded, for they were all famished. Then they were on their way to reunite Jewel with her frantic father. The swaying of the surrey made the girl's eyes droop.

Moments later, they met Torin on the trail. He came at them at a run. "I heard your shots," he yelled, puffing. "Is she…?"

"The lass is well," Angus called.

Torin's face lit with joy. He loped to the surrey, handing Hank the rifle and reaching for his daughter before Angus even reined Zeus to a halt.

"Her right ankle is sprained," Constance cautioned, releasing the child to her father's arms.

Torin grabbed Jewel in a fierce embrace. He wept with joy and relief, making the rest of them, even Angus and Hank, tear up and exchange happy glances.

Constance shifted closer to Angus, and Torin squeezed onto the front seat with Jewel.

After a few minutes drive, they arrived at Torin's home—a surprisingly big house made of logs—with a beautiful view of the lake. Behind the house stood a shed, open to a small pasture where a dairy cow and calf grazed.

Everyone alighted. They trooped into the house after Torin, who refused to release his daughter. Inside, the pleasant furnishings and décor contrasted with the rough log walls. They strode through the entry and into a parlor, furnished almost as nicely as the Nortons's, with a leather settee, several round-backed chairs with embroidered cushions, shelves overflowing with books, and a grandfather clock.

Torin carried Jewel to the leather settee and sat with her on his lap, pressing kisses to her head and murmuring endearments.

"Pa-pa," she murmured, pointing to her scrape. "Ow."

"Yes, sweetheart. Ow."

"Ow." This time Jewel pointed to her ankle.

"Have ye ice?" Angus asked. "I want some for her sprain."

"In the kitchen in the icebox. There's more in the icehouse if needed."

"I'll see to it." Hank went to the kitchen to chip ice from the block in the icebox.

Elsie followed him.

Hank returned with chunks of ice in a towel and handed the wad to Angus.

Elsie entered the room, carefully carrying a glass of milk.

Angus wrapped the makeshift ice bandage around Jewel's ankle.

The tired girl didn't seem to mind the cold.

The peony hat slipped charmingly to the side of Jewel's face. Constance took the glass of milk from Elsie, coaxing Jewel to drink.

Even with all the fussing, the girl was asleep in ten minutes. Her head drooped, and the hat fell to the floor.

"Someone needs a nap," Constance suggested, stooping to pick up the hat.

Torin glanced down at his daughter and smiled. "I almost don't want to let her go." He removed the icepack and handed it to Constance. He stood with effort and carried her to the bedroom.

Through the doorway, Constance saw him lay her on top of the red-quilted coverlet on her bed.

Jewel stirred just enough to clutch a faded pillow in the vague shape of an animal to her chest and then was out again.

Constance walked into the room and placed the hat on the dresser next to the bed.

One by one, each of the party entered the tidy room and stooped to press a kiss to sleeping Jewel's brow, as if needing the contact to express their relief and gratitude for her recovery, and then filed out.

Torin led them into a small dining room with a table that sat six. He eased into a chair at the foot of the table, his shoulders slumping, his lip quivering, looking about to cry again.

Constance selected the chair to his left, and Angus sat beside her.

Hank ambled to the other side to pull out a chair for Elsie, then took a seat at the head of the table.

With a long sigh, Torin looked around at all of them. "I haven't dared let anyone see Jewel but Hank and Brian. She's happy and loving and *vulnerable*. I didn't want people to hurt her."

"Why would they, Torin?" Elsie asked. "Jewel is so sweet."

Hank shot Elsie a pleased glance, as if really seeing the young woman for the first time.

Dear Elsie, kind, innocent, and big-hearted, Constance mused. *A young woman who in the company of older adults, naïvely perhaps, speaks her mind—a refreshing contrast to many girls her age.*

"Surely, no one would hurt her?" Elsie asked again.

"Her mother did…." Torin swallowed. "We married young because we had to. My wife was convinced the baby was a curse because of our sin. Mary wouldn't look at Jewel, couldn't see her sweetness. She deserted me and returned to live with her parents. Left practically everything behind." He made a vague hand motion to indicate the contents of the room. "She refused to speak to me ever again."

Elsie's eyes widened, and her mouth gaped.

"The doctor insisted Jewel would never be more than a vegetable." Torin drew in a ragged breath. "That was his word—*vegetable*. He informed us she wouldn't live long—thirteen or so years, if we were lucky or unucky from his point of view. Most likely that she'd die within five years. My parents and my in-laws, all insisted I institutionalize her. My father was quite harsh about the decision. He owns a successful manufacturing business, which I used to work for, and he informed me that I could no longer work there if I refused to follow his advice."

Constance gasped. "You mean his *orders*?"

Torin smirked in obvious agreement. "I refused. I fell in love with my daughter, perhaps desperately so, because everyone saw her as something shameful."

Angus sighed. "*They're* the ones who did something shameful."

"My father was not entirely hard-hearted. I know he thought he was doing the best for me." Torin blew out a breath. "He was just wrong."

His story fascinated Constance. "You've all paid the price."

Hank tapped the table with his knuckles. "Torin, why did you never tell me?"

Torin shrugged. "Out here, life is in the *present*, not the pa Jewel's eleven now. I don't know how much longer I'll have n daughter, but every day is precious. That's why today…." H turned his face away, and his shoulders shook. He reached in his pocket and pulled out a handkerchief, mopping his eyes and blowing his nose.

Tears came to Constance's eyes. She drew out her handkerchief from her sleeve to wipe them away, and saw Elsie doing likewise. *Are we all watering pots today, or what?*

Angus stood and walked around the table to lay a hand on Torin's shoulder. "Do na' fash yerself, laddie. Yer doing the best ye can. And a mighty fine job of it from what I can tell. Jewel's a good girl."

Torin looked up. "But she's hurt."

"Well, then, she's a bairn." Angus patted Torin's shoulder. "Bairns have adventures and sometimes get hurt. 'Tis not what we want for them. But unless we keep them on leading strings until they're adults, then accidents will happen. Seems most of my brothers, including me, broke a bone or sprained a limb. Cuts, scrapes, bruises." He shrugged and moved back to his seat.

Constance looked over at the sideboard, laden with Blue Willow china, and then back to Torin. "How did you come to live in Sweetwater Springs?"

"I knew Joshua Norton. My family is friends with his wife's family. They're neighbors."

"You know the Bellaires?" Constance asked in confusion. Torin didn't sound southern.

Torin's brow crinkled. "Bellaires? No." He shook his head. "The Maynards. Joshua's married to Esther Maynard. Those two are missionaries in Africa. When I needed to leave Cambridge, I remembered some of his stories about Sweetwater Springs. Montana sounded isolated enough. So I moved here with Jewel."

Hank rubbed his forehead. "We really are insulated living up on this mountain. I just learned last Sunday that Joshua Norton—*Reverend* Joshua Norton—has returned to town. He has a wife and a son. I didn't know him before, so I didn't realize his arrival was significant enough to tell you, especially since you don't attend church."

"But..." Constance glanced at Angus in puzzlement. "Reverend Joshua's wife is named Delia, and they've only recently married. I don't really know the details because I'm newly arrived too."

Angus shrugged. "As am I."

"I'm not new here," Elsie piped up. "But I grew up on a prairie homestead, and we rarely got to town and know very few people."

"Joshua's back?" Torin shook his head, as if doubting what he'd heard.

All four of them nodded.

Torin ran a hand through his hair. "When I first moved away, my mother would write and tell me the local gossip. But she's been gone for the past several years. My father, too. My brother doesn't write. That's why I hadn't heard any news about Joshua and Esther. She must have passed away."

He's had to deal with so much loss. Constance leaned forward. "Were you close with Esther?"

Torin shook his head. "They were an odd family. Strict and religious. Abner Maynard is a minister and professor at a seminary. They only spoke Hebrew, Greek, or Latin at meals. Made for uncomfortable dinners, I can tell you." A smile flickered. Then he looked down and absently ran a fingertip along the wood grain of the table. "I'm divorced. My wife claimed I deserted her."

Elsie scowled. "How mean of her when she was the one who left *you*."

"I don't care. She remarried. Has several healthy children. I hope she's happy. I'm grateful," Torin said fiercely. "If Mary had stayed, I've no doubt she'd have made our lives miserable."

Constance touched Torin's hand. "I'm sure Reverend Joshua would love to meet you again," she said gently. "I believe you'll like Delia, his wife. They are both very kind. I can't see them criticizing you for raising your daughter."

"What if Joshua thinks she's a curse? Abner Maynard did."

Constance sucked in a breath. "He won't. I promise."

Angus leaned forward. "I've seen other bairns who look like Jewel. A British doctor, John Langdon Down, has done considerable studies of Mongolism, which is the condition Jewel has. Mongoloids, he named them, from the shape of their eyes. They share certain characteristics."

Torin's shoulders relaxed, and his gaze stayed fixed on Angus's face. "Like what?"

Angus leaned forward. "The facial features, round faces, a weak tongue, which makes it difficult to articulate, their eyes. Most die young. The ones who live will have the mind of a child, even in adulthood. At eleven, yer daughter's already a miracle. They have fragmented, guttural speech, difficulty with hand skills, and an unsteady gait, so they fall easily."

Torin straightened. "That's probably what happened to Jewel today, for the ground is uneven."

Angus turned over his hand. "They have a simian crease across their palm." With his forefinger, he drew a line on his palm.

Torin looked at his own hand. "I noticed that with Jewel but didn't think anything of it."

"Jewel's condition is not inherited. We don't know why it happens." Angus's voice hardened. "But I'll tell ye true. What makes her different is *not* a curse. My cousin had a Mongoloid son who died at age three. Rory was the third of four children. He has his father's eyes. So no anticipating or breaking of the marriage vows occurred. The family is loving, kind, generous, and devout. No reason whatsoever for God to curse them. Although I know people can be cruel, I'd be offended on Rory's behalf if anyone were to suggest such an outrageous thing."

"Of course you would," Constance commiserated, appreciating his fierce defense of his relatives.

With a long, slow sigh, Torin covered his eyes with a hand. After a moment, he lowered his arm. "Why didn't the doctor tell me this?"

"Not all doctors have the same knowledge or skills." He made an impatient gesture. "Some are downright quacks. I was interested in the condition, so I read Dr. Down's paper on the subject. When I worked in London, I visited his hospital, toured the facility, and spoke with one of his sons, a doctor who's also researching the subject."

"I wish I could write a scathing letter to my father with this information."

"You have the information now," Constance smiled. "And that's what's important. You said so yourself—to live in the present."

Torin's defensive rigidity seeped away. His smile banished the lines of care around his eyes, making him look years younger.

Constance could see the handsome man he must have been. *Oh, my. We must coax Torin back into civilization.*

She started mentally matchmaking, scrolling through a list of her unmarried acquaintances back in Chicago, wondering if one would suit. *She'd need to be tolerant, patient, and kind, and also be willing to live far from town—a stringent list.* She set aside the task to ponder another day.

Now, for the next order of business. "I've already become attached to Jewel. May I make her a dress? My gift."

In obvious embarrassment, his gaze slid away. "I sew her clothes myself—a tube with sleeves. She doesn't know how bad they look."

"The fabric is pretty," Constance assured him. "That's probably all she cares about. Her clothing is crafted with love, which means more than the most expensive dresses."

"I brought you that soft fabric from the mercantile 'bout a month back, remember?" Hank asked. "You cut into it yet?"

"Nope." Torin smiled. "I'd like Jewel to have a new wardrobe. One that fits her, but I'm more than able to pay for what she needs." He made a wry twist of his mouth. "An inheritance from my grandfather who died when I was a child."

"Not the first dress," Constance said firmly. "That's a present from me. But I'll allow you to pay for the rest," she said in a teasing tone. "And please call me Constance. After the events of today, we've all become fast friends."

"You have a deal." Torin's smile charmed.

"Perhaps Jewel will wake up before we leave, and I can take her measurements. I have my tape measure in my reticule. If not, we can return another time."

"Regardless, I'd like another visit and so would my daughter."

Pleased with her success, Constance decided to push a bit more. "When we leave here today, I'd like to pay a visit to the Swensens and tell them about Jewel."

Eyes wide, Torin shook his head. "Oh, no."

"Those girls are sweet and thoughtful, and I think they'd have empathy for your daughter. They'll pet and indulge her."

Torin just looked at her, his eyes sad and vulnerable.

"Please, let me try?" Constance begged, wanting friends for Jewel. "Wouldn't you like her to have playmates?"

"Very well." Torin let out a long slow sigh. "Let's start with the Swensens. If all goes well, I'll think about contacting Reverend Joshua."

Angus grinned. "That's a good first step."

Constance glanced around the table at the others, feeling the bond that had sprung up between them. "We haven't yet had our picnic. No sense letting the food go to waste."

Elsie clapped her hands together. "Why don't we bring the picnic inside?"

"Good idea," Constance agreed. She glanced at their impromptu host, whose home they were about to invade. "If you'd like, that is?"

With wonder in his eyes, Torin looked from her to Elsie and then at the men.

She could almost see him assimilating the fact his life had just changed.

"My friends." Torin paused, obviously struggling to contain his emotions. He took a deep breath. "My new friends," he repeated. "You have changed my life. I can't thank you enough for what you've done for Jewel and me today. For the first time in many years, I feel hope for the future."

Beneath the table, Angus's warm hand clasped hers. He glanced at her, a hint of vulnerability in his eyes.

As their gazes connected, she smiled and her heart swelled, filling with the certainty of her love for this man. She *knew* Angus cared for her. She could feel that. However, Marcus had cared, too.

Caring isn't enough. I want more. I want to know he really loves me. Forever.

Chapter Seventeen

During their meal—not really a picnic because they ate at Torin's table—the group was filled with merriment despite the more formal setting.

As they finished up dessert—the cookies from Sugarplum Dreams brought by the women and Hank's contribution of a sour cherry pie—Angus plotted to steal Constance away for some private moments, although he couldn't quite come up with how he'd manage that.

Jewel awoke. After she'd eaten, the girl demanded a game of patty cake. Her father, Hank, and Elsie were all too happy to take turns obliging the child.

Constance, though, pleaded tiredness and the desire for some quiet by the lake.

The sideways glance she gave him proved all the impetus Angus needed to offer to escort her.

With her hand resting on his arm, Angus guided Constance down the path by the lake. Some gauzy clouds drifted across the blue sky. Faint mist blurred the reflection on the water. The shoreline arched, forming a small cove. A narrow strip of sand bordered by tall grass and sheltered by trees provided privacy.

The serenity of their surroundings made him relax, and he decided this was the perfect spot to ascertain Constance's feelings for him.

Constance let out a sigh of obvious pleasure. "I wish I could live here." She fluttered a hand. "Well, not really make my home here. I'd miss the activity in town, and there's my business. This area is too isolated and far away. But the beauty fills my soul, and the peace and calm feels so restful."

"I couldn't live here, either, much as I'd like to. A doctor needs to be accessible." Still, he started thinking about a lakeside cottage—mulling over possible ways and means. "What about a summer house? A cottage to escape to from time to time?" The idea took hold. "Fergus and I could buy it together and take turns visiting. Sometimes, I'd use the place, and other times, he and Alice would."

Her eyebrow rose. "And you'd come here alone, would you?"

"Absolutely not." With a tender smile, Angus reached to take Constance's hand and drew her toward him. "I've a companion in mind."

"You do?"

"Aye, she's a fair lassie, with eyes like emeralds." He stopped and pulled a face. "How unoriginal," he said in a tone of self-mockery. "Ye've probably heard that compliment plenty of times."

She grabbed his arm and shook it. "*Don't* do that to yourself, Angus. Don't speak so harshly. I *loved* hearing your compliment. How dare you ruin it?"

"But ye have heard that before?"

"Not from *you*, Angus. From you, the words are *special*—meaningful." Her expression turned playful, and she lightly smacked his arm. "In fact, since you ruined your first attempt, you should try again." She made a little *go on* hand wave and assumed a waiting posture.

"Compliments are a tad difficult fer me," he admitted, his brogue thick. He rubbed his neck.

Constance rolled her eyes. "I *might* have noticed. I *might* have fallen in love with you in spite of your dismal way with words." She raised her chin in an obvious challenge, but her eyes showed vulnerability.

"Yer in love with me?" *Did I hear right?* His heart pounded as he awaited her answer, needing to hear the words again.

"So I said," she said tartly, crossing her arms and tapping her foot.

He groaned in mock dismay. "Yer a hard taskmaster, lass, that ye are."

She raised her eyebrows, waiting.

"Constance." He placed his hands on her crossed arms to tug them open.

For a few seconds, she resisted and then relaxed.

Angus slid his palms down her arms to her hands and held tight. He took a deep breath. *No more teasing.* He needed to convince her of his earnestness. "Constance," he repeated. "Yer eyes are beautiful, like emeralds. I look into them, and I'm mesmerized," he said with all the sincerity in his heart. Regardless of whether she'd heard the compliment before, Angus *knew* no man had ever said the words to her with the depth of feeling he gave them.

Her lips parted.

"My plan for coming to America, practicing medicine with my brother, didn't include falling in love and marrying. But the verra first day I saw ye, I was bowled over by ye. I have na' been the same since."

"You scowled at me." She mimicked the expression.

With one fingertip, he smoothed the crease between her eyebrows. "Aye, and bad of me 'twas to do so." He trailed his fingers down the side of her face and brushed his palm along her neck. His hand lingered on her shoulder. "Will ye forgive me, lass, my beautiful Constance? Will ye marry me?"

With a playful look in her eyes, she tapped her lips with one slender finger.

He couldn't breathe. What she'd say next were the most important words of his life.

She lowered her finger to touch his chest. "I'm not giving up my business."

The statement hurt. With an exhale of pain, Angus lowered his arm. "Do ye think I'd be such an arse to ask that of ye? Do ye ken me so little, then?"

She flattened her palm against his chest—obviously to soothe, not push him away. "Most men would, and I had to state my position. We must have no misunderstandings between us. Surely, you can see that?"

"Aye."

"You've already made objections about some of my practices, although—" Constance touched her waist "—as you know, I'm already implementing some of your suggestions and intend to do more."

Angus appreciated her honesty and commitment. "Doctor and dressmaker," he said with a sudden lightness of spirit. "We'll have a verra full life, that's for sure." He grinned. "We'll make our careers work, *hen*. I promise."

Her sudden smile took his breath away.

Constance reached up to cup his face with her hands. "Well then, my love. *Aye*—" she slipped into a brogue. "I'll marry ye."

Angus wanted to shout with laughter, to fall to his knees and weep. Instead, he lovingly gathered her tightly to him, right next to his heart where she belonged, and sealed their pledge with a tender kiss.

THE END

Sign up for Debra Holland's newsletter at
http://debraholland.com.

Dear Reader,

I hope you enjoyed *Bright Montana Sky*. The story of Constance and Angus first came to me in 2011, while I was at my family's cabin in Big Bear Lake, California, writing *Stormy Montana Sky*. I quickly jotted down the first scene and then returned to *Stormy*, inserting hints in the story that Constance and Angus would soon be arriving in Sweetwater Springs.

At that time, I couldn't foresee how popular the Montana Sky series would become. I'd only indie published *Wild Montana Sky* and *Starry Montana Sky*. A traditional publisher for my "big" Montana Sky books and USA Today and New York Times bestselling status were still in my future. I knew I intended to write *Mystic Montana Sky*. But I had no idea that I'd write twenty-five Montana Sky stories (including *Mystic*) before I got around to *Bright Montana Sky*. In the meantime, several years had passed in Sweetwater Springs, without Constance and Angus appearing. So, to cover that time, I sent Constance to Europe and Angus to London before they could finally arrive in Sweetwater Springs, where they belonged.

If *Bright Montana Sky* is your first Montana Sky series story, and you want to learn more about some of the characters you met here, you'll find Felicity Woodbury and Lars Aagaard in *My Girl*; Julia Bosworth and Sam Ritter in *Sugarplum Dreams* in *Sweetwater Springs Christmas*; and Ant Gordon and Harriet Stanton in *Stormy Montana Sky*; Nick Sanders and Elizabeth Hamilton in *Wild Montana Sky*; Reverend Joshua Norton and Delia Bellaire in *Glorious Montana Sky*; and Caleb Livingston and Maggie Baxter in *Mystic Montana Sky*.

Torin and Jewel Rees were relatively late additions to the story as I was writing the ending of the book and figuring out which of Hank's neighbors would need Angus's doctoring skills. One morning, I woke up with the idea of a protective father of a child with Down syndrome and *knew* I'd found the right characters. (I think they might have their own story someday.) I did some historical research as well as contacted Christi Caldwell, an author friend whose sweet son Rory has Down Syndrome, in order to pick her brain.

I know using the terminology of the time, labels such as idiot and Mongoloid, as well as the common practice of secrecy, rejection, and/or institutionalization of children with Down Syndrome, might offend modern readers. However, I strive for historical correctness and hope my readers know I'd never deliberately want to hurt or offend anyone.

I have a wonderful team to thank for the production of this book—my three editors, Louella Nelson, Linda Carroll-Bradd, and Adeli Brito; four of my family members who also help with editing, Larry and Hedy Codner, Honey Holland, and Christine Holland; cover designers Delle Jacobs and John Mitchell; my audiobook narrator, Lara Asmundson; my formatters Amy and Kirby Atwell; and some friends for their support and contributions, Katharine West, Mike Samples, Alexis Montgomery, and Matt Orso. I'm very blessed to have you all in my life.

What's next for the Montana Sky series?

The novella, *My Girl*, Felicity Woodbury and Lars Aagaard's story, which was published in the anthology *Romance Ever After*, will come out as a standalone novella in April 2018. If you're not already subscribed to my newsletter for announcements, please go to my website: debraholland.com and join my list.

Montana Sky Justice will release in August 2018 with Sheriff K.C. Granger's story and is available on preorder. http://debraholland.com/book-montana-sky-justice.html Keep reading for an excerpt of *Montana Sky Justice*.

My Montana Sky Kindle World continues to grow with over seventy stories by other authors set in Sweetwater Springs and Morgan's Crossing and more books to come. You can find the books listed on my website: http://debraholland.com/kindle-worlds.html

Happy reading!
Debra Holland

Excerpt from

Montana Sky Justice

Sweetwater Springs, Montana
Labor Day, 1896

All her senses alert for any potential trouble, Sheriff K.C., Granger strolled down Main Street, which was decorated in red, white, and blue bunting. Almost everyone wore their Sunday best and smelled of soap, and in some cases, horse. She dipped her chin to those she knew.

Those who didn't know her wouldn't recognize a woman inside the man's clothing—trousers, starched gray cotton shirt, leather vest, and string tie. She'd pinned up her braid under her black Stetson. But they would notice the metal star pinned to her vest and the two Colts in the gun belt at her hips.

For this event, the population of Sweetwater Springs had swelled from some five hundred people to about three times that amount, which stretched her ability to keep everyone safe and law-abiding.

While she was glad for the church building fund and the businesses that would prosper from today's visitors, she had a lot of strangers to keep her eye on, in addition to the known town troublemakers.

Her sleep had suffered the last few nights, as she ran through various scenarios—the most likely being overflowing jail cells due to too many drunk and disorderly men and small time pickpockets creeping into Sweetwater Springs from other locations. Many of her trusting townsfolk would be easy pickings. Then there was that elusive gang—if, indeed, as her instincts told her, one existed—and the random crimes over the last few years weren't isolated incidents.

This time, the culprits weren't Indians. From her trips to the reservation, bringing food and other supplies, she was sure of that much at least. Hopefully, she and the three men she'd deputized for this occasion would be enough.

Next to Cobb's Mercantile, a man wearing a suit and standing behind a small table caught her attention. Dark hair flowed to his shoulders, framing a face with nondescript features dominated by a thick handlebar mustache. He used wide hand gestures and a cajoling voice to sell rectangular packets wrapped in white paper and neatly stacked in front of him.

"Step right up, folks," he called in a silky baritone.

K.C. didn't recognize the salesman and strolled closer. *Good thing the Cobbs are probably too busy with all the customers to know the man is in their territory and taking away the sales that they'd consider rightfully theirs.*

The gent held out his arms in a benevolent gesture of welcome to the gathering crowd.

K.C. could see he wasn't wearing a gun at his hip, probably to appear more innocuous. Then again, most of the men living in Sweetwater Springs didn't go around armed—the town being a peaceable place, and all—unless they traveled beyond the outskirts.

The salesman's compelling gaze swept the crowd. "I'm Hieronymus Orloff, and do I have a product for you." He held up one of the packets. "Soap. But not ordinary soap."

What kind of snake oil salesman is he? K.C. edged closer to the edge of the crowd made up of about half Sweetwater Springs residents and half strangers.

"Yes, folks, I tell you, this soap will do more than get you clean from head to toe." Hieronymus's words flowed from him with practiced ease. "Why, this soap contains medicinal herbs known to the ancient Egyptians and imported at *great* expense from the Orient. These magical ingredients will protect you from illness. Regular usage will smooth the wrinkles from your skin and turn any gray hairs back to their original color, giving you a more youthful appearance. My good people, the scent may seem mildly pleasant, but a special secret ingredient will both calm your nerves, enhance your vigor, and make you *most* attractive to the opposite sex."

K.C. rolled her eyes and hoped no one would be foolish enough to believe him.

"You might think the sum of five dollars a bar is a bit steep, but really it's a small price to pay for the fountain of youth I hold here in my hand."

I'll say. Five dollars is highway robbery. K.C. made a quick count of the bars stacked on the table. *Thirty. Times five would be a hundred and fifty. A princely sum.*

Hieronymus waved his arm down the street in the direction of the lot where the new church would go up. "*Half* of all my proceeds will be given to the building fund."

That's a good enticement. Throwing in philanthropy only made her more suspicious.

"And now folks—" Hieronymus rested a hand on a stack of soap bricks "—as a bonus to encourage you to try my amazing product, fully one third of these packets have money inside— dollar bills, five- and ten-dollar bills, and even, for *two* lucky customers, a *twenty*-dollar bill." He laughed. "You might end up *making* money from me."

That's a new angle. K.C. frowned and glanced around, relieved to see no one move toward the table to buy.

Hieronymus waved the packet. "Who will be the first to test their luck?"

"I will," shouted a stocky man wearing a parchment-colored shirt and red suspenders. He pulled off a battered gray Stetson and waved the hat, displaying thinning dirty-blond hair. He pushed through the crowd to slap what must be a five-dollar bill on the table.

"I like a man of decision." Hieronymus deftly swapped the bar he held for the man's money. "Go ahead and open it, my friend, so we can see if you have bonus money, in addition to the usage of this excellent product."

The buyer made to tear off the paper.

"Carefully now," Hieronymus warned in a carrying voice. "You don't want to ruin the money."

The crowd quieted, as if collectively holding a breath, and leaned forward to see better.

The man finished unwrapping and yelled in triumph. He waved a bill into the air. "Five dollars!"

People gasped, and some cheered. Conversations buzzed through the crowd.

"I'll have me some of that there miracle soap," shouted an older man. He was on the tall side, with hunched shoulders. The crowd parted to allow him through.

K.C. didn't know him.

"I could use me some vigor." The tall man pulled some coins from his pocket and counted them out in his palm before handing them over.

While he made quick work of pulling off the wrapping, K.C. studied his features. A white beard obscured the lower part of his face, but she noted the wide brow, pale eyes, and long nose. "Hee haw!" He held up a bill. "I got me a greenback. A dollar on top of this soap for vigor. I'm a lucky man."

"I want one," a woman called from the back of the group. From the look of her faded black clothing, she was a widow. A black sunbonnet shielded her face from sight.

K.C. sidestepped to get a better look at the woman but didn't recognize her.

People shifted to let the widow through.

When she reached the table, Hieronymus gallantly bowed

and waved a hand across the top of the table, inviting her to choose.

"This is all the money I have left in the world." Her voice trembled, and she fluttered a hand to her bosom. "I'm taking a big risk here. But perhaps your soap will bring back my looks and help me find another husband...."

Something about the way the woman turned to address the crowd and projected her low voice so most could hear, almost as if she were on stage, made K.C.'s neck prickle. She narrowed her eyes, memorizing what she could see of the widow. *Mid-thirties*, she guessed. *Curvy body. Pretty, lined face. Dark eyes.* She squinted to spot any hair under the bonnet, and thought she might have caught a glimpse of black tresses but couldn't be sure if she saw only shadow.

The widow selected a package and carefully tore open the paper around the middle of the bar to expose the part of a greenback. She cried out in gladness and clasped the soap to her breast. "Twenty dollars! Thank the Good Lord, my prayers have been answered!"

Hieronymus beamed at the widow. "Even better than a new husband." He preened and twisted one side of his mustache. "Well, my dear lady, I'm honored to be an instrument of the Almighty."

"Bless you, sir!" Holding tight to her winnings, the widow scurried away, stopping here and there to show curious people the money still wrapped around the soap.

As if in a feeding frenzy, the crowd descended on the table, money extended.

As she debated her next action, K.C.'s lips tightened. Selling "magical" soap wasn't against the law. *Should I shut down what I'm sure is a snake oil scam?*

This quandary was the fine line she walked concerning the ethics of being the sheriff. Her job was to *uphold* the law, not *become* the law. She knew plenty of locales where the sheriff ran the town and did what he pleased. Right or wrong, people jumped when he said jump. But Montana was a state now, and she'd sworn to uphold both the state and federal laws. She didn't always agree with those laws. In some instances, they were too strict and unfair. In other circumstances—as with this snake oil salesman—they didn't cover enough areas.

But I need to protect my people. She decided to mosey over and stand next to the table, crossing her arms and scowling at anyone who approached. She figured her presence would be enough of a deterrent to the gullible.

Mr. Swensen, a father of seven children, made a beeline for the table, his blue eyes blazing. The man and his family lived in a one-room cabin in the mountains. They got by on hunting, trapping, and what grew in their garden. Five dollars was probably the total sum of his savings. He and his wife were young and healthy enough to not need the soap for any of the so-called benefits. So, he must caught up in gambling fever.

K.C. moved to block his path, frowned, and shook her head.

He pulled off his straw hat, newly woven probably for this occasion, and nodded respectfully. His blondish, scraggly beard was neatly trimmed. His gaze slid around her to the table. "I have a chance to make real money here, Sheriff Granger," he said in a heavy Swedish accent. "I could buy my wife a pretty dress. Ja, and new ones for all six of my girls."

"You'll only be buying yourself a heap of trouble, Swensen." K.C. jerked a head toward the table, where the soap was almost gone. "You hear anyone else yelling about winning big money? *Two* people, only *two*, have won a *dollar*. No more big bills are wrapped around that soap." She patted the gun in the holster at her hip. "And I'll bet my Colt those three who originally won money were all friends of Hieronymus."

The blazing light died out of his eyes, and his shoulders drooped. He gave her a sheepish look and tugged on his straggly beard.

K.C. glanced over his shoulder at Mrs. Swensen, holding her baby son and looking worried.

Six blonde daughters clustered around their mother, their dresses—hand-me downs from the Carter daughters—clean and pressed.

At least, I can relieve Mrs. Swensen's worry. "Return to your family. This is a special day. Go and enjoy yourselves."

Smiling, Mr. Swensen grabbed for her hand and shook it. "Thank you, Sheriff. I will." He spun on his heel and hurried over to his family, picking up his littlest girl and swinging her into his arms.

With a shake of her head, K.C. turned back to the salesman just in time to see the last bar of soap disappear.

In an obvious rush, Hieronymus stopped talking to the people around him and bent to snap shut the legs of the folding table.

He's about to make his escape. K.C. pushed through the people eagerly opening their soap packets.

Hieronymus tucked the table under his arm and took several steps in the direction of the livery.

With a long stride, K.C. positioned herself in front of the man.

Hieronymus glanced over his shoulder and didn't see K.C. until he almost ran into her. Muttering an "excuse me," he tried to move around her side.

No, you don't. She slid to block him.

He shuffled in the opposite direction.

She shadowed his moves.

Hieronymus's gaze dropped to her badge and then back up, his eyes showing awareness of who she was.

K.C. pointed a finger down the street. "I do believe you're heading the wrong way, Mr. Hieronymus Orloff. *If* that's even your real name, which I doubt."

With a pained glance, he placed a hand on his chest. "Sheriff, you wound me with your accusation. I haven't done anything wrong. I've merely been doing my bit to see that the great unwashed have a chance to bathe."

"You haven't been doing anything *illegal*," she corrected. "But definitely, you've been doing *wrong*. You are a cheater and a crook, scamming people out of their hard-earned money. Nevertheless—" she lifted her chin, pointing in the opposite direction "—the church is that way. I do believe you promised a donation of *half* your proceeds. But you'll need to head toward the bank. That's where the donations are being collected."

"Yes, ma'am," he assured her and nodded. "I was just going to put away my table and then return."

How does he know I'm a woman? While her gender wasn't a secret, outsiders wouldn't know that fact. K.C. gave Hieronymus a feral grin, noting his unusual gold eye color, as well as the shape of his cheekbones and chin. She was tall for a woman, and he was just about her height. With or without the handlebar mustache, she'd know him again. "Of course you were," she said, her tone ironic. She raised her hand and whirled a finger in a *turn around* motion. "But *now* is a better time."

He scowled. "Really, sheriff. Don't you have better things to do? Criminals to hunt? Kittens to rescue from trees?" In his annoyance, his voice changed, becoming thinner and lighter.

His true voice, she figured, making a mental note of how he sounded. She kept her gaze cold but widened her smile. "Your donation, Mr. Orloff. The good people of Sweetwater Springs will be most appreciative." Her hand drifted downward to brush her Colt.

His gaze followed the movement, and he made an instinctive reach for his own non-existent gun.

A tiny give-away, but she caught the gesture.

With an abrupt jerk, he propped the table against the corner of the mercantile, turned, and marched down the street.

K.C. caught up and dropped a tight hand on his shoulder. She kept pace with him, ready for a more secure grab if he tried to run. She wouldn't shoot him for fear of hitting someone else.

Curious gazes followed them.

At first, Hieronymus hunched his shoulders. Then he tossed his head and straightened, obviously portraying a proud man unjustly detained by the sheriff.

They headed for the bank, a whitewashed brick building in the middle of town, owned by Caleb Livingston. K.C. knew either Reverend Norton or his son, Reverend Joshua Norton, would be inside accepting the money people brought in to donate. Then Horace Wittig, the bank clerk, would lock the funds in the safe. In addition, as money hopefully accrued from other events, the funds would be brought to the bank for safekeeping.

When they reached the bank, K.C. escorted Hieronymus past a planter of daisies, up the steps, across the short porch, and through the door.

Horace, the elderly, balding clerk, stood behind a high counter chatting with the senior Reverend Norton, who stood in front of the counter. At their entrance, both men turned and smiled in welcome.

She released her charge, who slowly moved toward the men.

Reverend Norton had the severe appearance of an old-testament prophet, but kindness shone in his vivid blue eyes. "Good morning, Sheriff Granger." He glanced at Hieronymus, his white eyebrows raising in obvious inquiry. "You'll have to forgive me, sir. You look familiar, but I cannot place you. I'm Reverend Norton."

Interesting. Has he seen Hieronymus before?

Reverend Norton has lived in Sweetwater Springs since he was a young preacher. He knows everyone and, unlike me, has a long history with these people.

"We've never met," Hieronymus said hastily, averting his face from the minister's scrutiny. "My name is Orloff, and this visit is my first to your town." He snuck glances around the room, his gaze lingering on the big, black safe.

Not liking the man's curiosity about the bank, K.C. gestured at a wicker basket on the counter. "For your donation."

His movements stiff with apparent reluctance, Hieronymus pulled out several bills in one- and five-dollar denominations and dropped them into the basket.

The elder Reverend Norton beamed. "We are grateful, Mr. Orloff."

K.C. leaned closer to the crook's ear. "*Thirty* bars of soap," she said in a low voice so the minister wouldn't hear. He'd worked hard for this special day, and she didn't want to spoil it.

"I'm feeling benevolent today, Reverend," Hieronymus said, using his snake oil tone. With a big gesture, he pulled out more money, tossing each bill into the basket.

K.C. silently counted each one and watched closely in case he'd try a sleight of hand to trick her.

Reverend Norton's eyes widened. "For that amount, Mr. Orloff, you can commemorate a pew. We'll set a small plaque on the side with your name engraved. Or the name of your family or a loved one whom you wish to honor or commemorate."

"I'm not one to parade my generosity, Reverend Norton," Hieronymus said in an unctuous tone. "Please consider my small donation as merely a gift."

"I hope you'll be staying in our fair town and can attend Sunday service tomorrow."

He shook his head. "I'm afraid that won't be possible. My family expects me home tonight."

"Another time, perhaps. When your family can worship with you."

"Perhaps," Hieronymus said noncommittally. Once more, he twisted his head to glance in the direction of the safe.

Only because K.C. shifted when Hieronymus moved did she catch the smirk. She narrowed her eyes, wondering what he was up to.

He turned back and offered the minister a two-fingered salute. "Good day, Reverend Norton. I *sincerely* hope you have a windfall here."

Something about his tone sent goose bumps feathering across K.C.'s arms. She stiffened.

With his back to the other men, Hieronymus shot K.C. a

malicious glance. Then straight-backed, he stalked out of the bank.

She stared after him, her neck prickling. Instinctively, she lowered a hand to her gun. *The man's trouble.* Somehow, K.C. knew she hadn't seen the last of Hieronymus Orloff.

To order Montana Sky Justice go to:
http://www.debraholland.com/book-montana-sky-justice.html

Montana Sky Series

In chronological order:
Sweet historical Western/Prairie Romance

1882
Beneath Montana's Sky

1886
Mail-Order Brides of the West: Trudy
Mail-Order Brides of the West: Lina
Mail-Order Brides of the West: Darcy
Mail-Order Brides of the West: Prudence
Mail-Order Brides of the West: Bertha

1890s
Grace: Bride of Montana
Wild Montana Sky
Starry Montana Sky
Stormy Montana Sky
Montana Sky Christmas
A Valentine's Choice
Irish Blessing
Painted Montana Sky
Glorious Montana Sky
A Rolling Stone
Healing Montana Sky
Sweetwater Springs Scrooge
Sweetwater Springs Christmas
Mystic Montana Sky
Singing Montana Sky
My Girl
Bright Montana Sky
Montana Sky Justice (August 2018)

2015
Angel in Paradise

About the Author

DEBRA HOLLAND is the New York Times and USA Today Bestselling author of the award-winning *Montana Sky Series* (sweet, historical Western romance) and *The Gods' Dream Trilogy* (fantasy romance.)

Debra is a three-time Romance Writers of America Golden Heart finalist and one-time winner. In 2013, Amazon selected *Starry Montana Sky* as one of the Top 50 Greatest Love Stories.

When she's not writing, Dr. Debra works as a psychotherapist and corporate crisis/grief counselor. She's the author of *The Essential Guide to Grief and Grieving*, a book about helping people cope with all kinds of loss, *and Cultivating an Attitude about Gratitude, a Ten Minute Ebook*. She's also a contributing author to *The Naked Truth About Self-Publishing*.

To learn more and join her newsletter list go to:
http://debraholland.com

Made in United States
Orlando, FL
05 December 2022